HAUNTED
LIGHTHOUSES

HAUNTED LIGHTHOUSES

Phantom Keepers, Ghostly Shipwrecks,
and Sinister Calls from the Deep

Ray Jones

Guilford, Connecticut

To buy books in quantity for corporate use
or incentives, call **(800) 962-0973**
or e-mail **premiums@GlobePequot.com.**

Copyright © 2010 by Ray Jones

ALL RIGHTS RESERVED. No part of this book may be reproduced or transmitted in any form by any means, electronic or mechanical, including photocopying and recording, or by any information storage and retrieval system, except as may be expressly permitted in writing from the publisher. Requests for permission should be addressed to Globe Pequot Press, Attn: Rights and Permissions Department, P.O. Box 480, Guilford, CT 06437.

Design: Sheryl P. Kober
Layout: Kevin Mak
Project manager: Kristen Mellitt

Library of Congress Cataloging-in-Publication Data

Jones, Ray, 1948-
   Haunted lighthouses : phantom keepers, ghostly shipwrecks, and sinister calls from the deep / by Ray Jones.
      p. cm.
   ISBN 978-0-7627-5660-5
   1. Haunted lighthouses—United States. 2. Haunted lighthouses—United States—Guidebooks. 3. United States—Guidebooks. I. Title.
   BF1476.J66 2010
   133.1'22—dc22

                                                                                    2010020110

Printed in the United States of America

10 9 8 7 6 5 4 3

CONTENTS

Contents

INTRODUCTION

At the New London Ledge Lighthouse in Connecticut, a ghost named Ernie stares back at anyone brave enough to look into a mirror. At Owls Head in Maine, a phantom spaniel warns ships away from deadly rocks with its incessant barking. Near Delaware's Cape Henlopen an enigmatic Corpse Light lures unwary mariners to destruction on the shoals of Delaware Bay. On North Carolina's Outer Banks, the ghost of Aaron Burr's demented daughter, Theodosia, walks the beach beside a mysterious stone circle marking the original location of the historic Cape Hatteras Lighthouse. Not far from the Point Lookout Lighthouse in Maryland, invisible Confederate prisoners cry out in pain or sing Civil War songs to help them forget that they are imprisoned not just by their Union captors, but now by death as well. When Gulf breezes blow harder than usual, the Bolivar Point Lighthouse near Galveston, Texas, wails, perhaps to lament the thousands who died there in a mighty hurricane more than a century ago. When a cold wind whips past the Presque Isle Lighthouse in Michigan, the stormy Witch of November screeches to let sailors on Lake Huron know she is coming. In Oregon, Terrible Tilly screams to let others know that he and a host of other monsters now possess the offshore Tillamook Rock Lighthouse. And in California a murdered widow searches the tower of the Pigeon Point Lighthouse looking for her missing stomach.

When speaking of such weird, eerie, spooky, or seemingly unnatural phenomena, people who are interested in ghosts—and that includes just about everybody—sometimes employ the term "paranormal." This often used and almost as often abused word means "beyond normal experience" and generally is applied when referring to something that cannot be explained by scientific or rational means. However, the word "paranormal" is of very little use when talking about lighthouses. That's because there is so little about lighthouses that could rightly be described as "normal."

Lighthouses and the keepers who lived in them and faithfully maintained their beacons have always existed outside the realm of normal day-to-day human experience. The grand light towers and the keeper's residences that accompanied them were often located on remote cliffs or islands far from the nearest town or village. There they were exposed to the worst imaginable storms, to earthquakes and flood, and during times of war, to the enemy.

The men and women who lived in lighthouses and lit their lamps each night were a breed apart. They had to be, because otherwise they never could have survived the hard work, terrible weather, danger, and loneliness. Sometimes the conditions at lighthouses drove keepers or members of their families out of their minds—or to put it differently, into another, utterly separate reality.

However, except when they were climbing the steps of their light towers, most keepers kept their feet firmly planted on the ground. They held onto their sanity by throwing themselves into their work with a hard-minded devotion that is difficult to comprehend, especially given that they were usually paid only a few dollars a month. Despite the low pay and the often harsh climates they were often forced to endure, they kept at their task day and night, displaying their beacons and saving the lives of sailors they would never meet and who would never know the keepers' names.

Some keepers served so long and so faithfully that they could barely be distinguished from the lighthouses in which they worked and lived. It was as if their very spirits had been absorbed by the wood of the floors, the brick and stone of the walls, the cast iron of the tower steps, and the polished glass prisms of the lenses in the lantern room. Is it any wonder that when their physical bodies were finally worn out and buried, their spirits were sometimes thought to have remained behind in the form of ghosts?

AMERICA'S FIRST LIGHTHOUSE GHOST

It doesn't take a heightened sensitivity or any special sort of vision to notice the ghosts at the Boston Lighthouse on Massachusetts's Little Brewster Island. The ghosts here don't hide under the floorboards. They walk right through the walls or they knock on the door.

Maybe that's because the Boston Lighthouse is the oldest navigational beacon in North America. It has had three centuries to become haunted.

The first keeper of the Boston Lighthouse was a man named George Worthylake. A shepherd and harbor pilot by day, Worthylake thought he could earn a little extra money by keeping the Boston Light burning at night. His first evening on the job was September 14, 1716, and with the sun descending in the west and a blanket of gloom racing across the ocean from the east, he hurried up the tower steps and put a match to the station's tallow candles for the very first time. On that night and the many thousands of nights since, the masters of ships headed for Boston have seen the light and known that safe water lay ahead. Mariners still see it today, almost three hundred years after it first shined out over the harbor.

With the light on Little Brewster to give it a commercial boost, Boston became a magnet for shipping, and merchants and warehousemen along the city's waterfront prospered. The new lighthouse proved far less profitable for Worthylake, however. Fate had no fortune in store for him. His salary of 50 pounds a year was supposed to be supplemented by the fees he earned for serving as a harbor pilot. But Worthylake's responsibilities as keeper proved much more arduous and time-consuming than he had expected, and there was little time left for steering ships.

To help feed and clothe his family, the keeper ran herds of sheep on Little Brewster and other nearby islands, but Worthylake had no more luck as a shepherd than he did as a pilot. During a terrible winter gale in 1717, several dozen of his sheep wandered out onto a spit where they were soon stranded by the tide. Since he could not in good conscience abandon his post in the midst of a storm, Worthylake could do nothing to assist these hapless animals. From the high lantern of the lighthouse, he watched in despair as one after another of his sheep washed off the spit and into the sea.

Worthylake lost fifty-nine sheep to the storm. To help ease the financial burden of this loss, the town of Boston agreed to increase the keeper's salary to 70 pounds. Unfortunately, Worthylake never got to spend the money. As he was returning from Boston, where he had gone to collect his pay, his boat capsized only a few hundred yards from the safety of the dock on Little Brewster Island. The shepherd turned lighthouse keeper drowned, and his body washed ashore on the same spit where his sheep had recently perished. By the time his remains were discovered, the money he had received in Boston had mysteriously vanished.

During the centuries since Worthylake drowned, the Boston Lighthouse has had at least sixty keepers—that's more than the United States has had presidents. Few of them remained on the job for more than a few years, but likely most were far happier on Little Brewster than was its first keeper. On nearly 100,000 evenings, they climbed the tower steps, lit the light, and kept it burning, and this way of life and work continued for Boston keepers right on up until the eve of the twenty-first century, when their job was finally taken over by computerized timers. During all this time, whether they lived on the island by themselves or with their families, Boston Lighthouse keepers never felt alone on Little Brewster. They always felt that someone was with them. Many of them believed that someone was George Worthylake.

Lighthouse keepers didn't just keep lights. They kept logbooks, much the way sea captains would in their ship cabins. The logbooks at the Boston Lighthouse were mostly filled with mundane information detailing the weather, the condition of the tower and lighthouse apparatus, the quantity of food and other supplies on hand, and routine day-to-day events. Occasionally, however, keepers on Little Brewster took note of some very strange happenings: doors and windows that opened and closed all by themselves, eerie lights out in the water or down along the shore, strange footsteps on the tower staircase, loud banging noises on the walls and ceilings of the residence, and voices that seemed to come from nowhere.

Since their island was located a considerable distance from the mainland, keepers here rarely received visitors. Even so, they often heard knocks at the door. When the keepers answered the knock, there was almost never anyone outside. On a couple of occasions, however, the keepers opened the door and found standing before them a middle-aged man dressed in what appeared to be eighteenth-century shepherd's clothing. Then, before they could speak, the man was gone. He didn't turn and walk away, he just vanished. Sometimes the man didn't wait for the keeper to answer his knock. He walked right through the closed door, across the floor, and then out through the wall on the opposite side of the room.

When keepers reported these bizarre occurrences, their superiors on the mainland likely thought they had gone stir crazy out there on the lonely island, but this was not true. Like most keepers, they were sound of mind and body. They had to be in order to do their work and keep the light burning each and every night. And anyway, they had their own explanation for the strange phenomena they sometimes encountered on Little Brewster. "It's just old George up to his tricks," they said.

REALM OF LIGHT AND SHADOW

A lighthouse makes a perfect home for ghosts. The interiors of lighthouse towers are dark and shadowy and they nearly always feature spiral staircases likely to resound under the heavy tread of a weary old phantom. The bedrooms of light-house residences sometimes feature cloudy antique mirrors that may reflect the faces of people who are not necessarily standing in front of them. The kitchens have dishes, pots, and pans to rattle, and windows that can be opened and closed without the help of flesh-and-blood hands. And lighthouses have expansive grounds that can be walked by sailors drowned in early-nineteenth-century shipwrecks, mothers searching for children lost in tragic accidents more than a century ago, or keepers fatally wounded by Civil War shot and shell.

Life, death, and drama have always swirled in and around lighthouses, and these things make a lasting impression on places and structures. They leave behind a spiritual residue that causes some people to call them historic and others to call them haunted. It is probably safe to say that every lighthouse in America is now considered historic and that every last one of them is also haunted.

Does this mean that every lighthouse has its own resident ghost? Who can answer that? Certainly there are lighthouses—though perhaps not as many as you may think—that have never been directly linked to any ghost story or unexplained phenomena. That may not continue to be the case, however. Sometimes ghosts hide under the steps or in the closets of buildings waiting for the right person to come along, someone who knows where to look for them and has the sensitivity to see or hear them. The plain fact is that some people have an eye and an ear for ghosts, and others do not.

If you possess the sort of vision it takes to recognize a ghost when you see one, then you are going to love this book. It's filled with stories that will take you to the edge of reality and beyond. It will help you reach out into the night, like the beacon of a lighthouse, and shine a light on a place we all know exists but we just can't see.

Haunted Lighthouses contains twenty-eight of the scariest and most fascinating ghost stories you are ever likely to encounter. Since lighthouses and the ghosts that haunt them vary from region to region, the book is divided into four sections: East, South, Great Lakes, and West. There are also three highly informative appendixes. The first offers a quick look at a couple dozen other haunted lighthouses that may interest you. The second introduces you to some of the key terms and important people associated with lighthouses, and it explains how they may be linked to the haunting of these historic structures. The third provides some brief travel information to help you find the lighthouses, if not the ghosts that inhabit them.

Part One

EAST

Chapter 1
Ernie's Domain

New London Ledge Light
New London, Connecticut

Offshore lighthouses are cold, damp, and drafty, and life there was terribly hard for keepers and their wives. One of these lonely outposts was hardly the ideal place for a man to bring his bride, especially not a lovely and romantically inclined young lady like the one who plays so prominent a role in the following story. Apparently the isolation of her new home, surrounded on all sides by tossing ocean waves, proved too much for her. She soon cast her eyes toward the twinkling lights of nearby New London and its ferry terminal with tragic—and haunting—results.

It can be seen from several points along Pequot Avenue in the old colonial port city of New London, Connecticut, or from Ocean Beach Park just south of town. Look toward the east and, if the weather is not too stormy, you'll behold one of the most mysterious sights in all of New England. Out there in the distance near the mouth of the Thames River is a house that appears to be floating on air just above the shimmering surface of Long Island Sound.

Anyone unfamiliar with this spectral building will probably have great difficulty identifying it. So incongruous is its appearance and location, those who see it from shore will likely be seized by one or another wild surmise. Has someone built a mansion out there in the middle of the sound? Or has one of the grand old estate houses along the

Connecticut shore somehow slid down into the water and floated out to sea?

The structure is indeed an impressive one. Its brick-red walls are lined with rows of tall windows framed by sashes trimmed in white, its gray mansard roof broken by dormers. It has a distinctly Old World look and feeling suggestive of earlier times, far-off places, and perhaps of mysteries yet unsolved. In short, it is just the sort of place one might expect to be inhabited by a ghost, all the more so because this is not a house in the ordinary sense of the word. It is a lighthouse—the New London Ledge Lighthouse, to be exact—and it does have a resident ghost. His name is Ernie.

According to most accounts, Ernie has haunted the light since one fateful—and heartbreaking—day sometime during the Roaring 1920s. As is the case with nearly all well-known ghosts, there are many versions of Ernie's story. This is one of them.

HOW IT ALL BEGAN

Ernie's story and that of his lighthouse are, in many ways, one and the same. Although established more than a century ago, the New London Ledge Lighthouse is by no means an old-timer when compared to other New England beacons. For example, just upriver from New London Ledge stands one of the oldest lighthouses in North America. Established in 1760, the New London Harbor Light has guided mariners for more than 250 years. Given its extraordinary age, this venerable, octagonal stone structure is no doubt haunted by ghosts of its own, but their names are not known—at least not as well as Ernie's.

Shortly after the turn of the twentieth century, officials of the U.S. Lighthouse Service decided that New London merited something more substantial than a harbor beacon. Although the 1760 lighthouse had served New London faithfully during the days of the old wooden windjammer fleets, times had changed. The steel-hulled, steam-driven freighters and ferries that now visited the wharves in New London and in nearby Groton needed a first-rate coast light to guide them. It took a few years to wrangle sufficient funding from Congress for the project, but construction began about 1907, and the lighthouse was finally completed in 1909.

To make the new beacon as useful as possible to mariners, Lighthouse Service engineers decided to place it offshore. The combination tower, utility building, and keeper's dwelling were built in a shallow area atop a craggy shelf of submerged rock that had damaged and sunk more than a few vessels over the years. From here the light could not only point the way to New London but also warn ships away from the shoal. Of course, these purposes might have been served just as well by a more traditional-looking lighthouse. The one the Lighthouse Service decided to build served its function well enough, but it also caused passing sailors and observers onshore to shake their heads in disbelief.

No one knows for certain why government architects chose such an extraordinary design for the structure. Perhaps they felt that the Second French Empire facade was in keeping with the appearance of the grand homes that could be seen in the distance along the shore. Or perhaps they wanted to make the point that lighthouses need not have a cold, utilitarian appearance.

Whatever their reasons, they were likely lost on the keepers who lived at the lighthouse and tended the beacon. Their day-to-day existence had little in common with the leisurely lives of the wealthy Connecticut aristocrats who built mansions along the water. The keepers, as often as not with the assistance of their wives, bent their backs every day and every night maintaining the light, cleaning the station's imported crystal lens, polishing brass work, and repairing broken equipment. All this they did for modest pay—in many cases no more than a few hundred dollars a year. To these hardworking men and women, the design of the building must have seemed supremely incongruous.

ERNIE ARRIVES AT NEW LONDON LEDGE

One of the first keepers to serve at New London Ledge was a man named George Hansen, who lived and worked here from 1913 to 1915. The next keeper about whom much is known was Howard Beebe, who arrived in 1926 and tended the light for more than a dozen years—in fact, right up until 1939, when the Lighthouse Service was absorbed into the U.S. Coast Guard. It is not clear who was keeper of the New London Ledge Lighthouse during the eleven years between the time Hansen left, a couple of years before the United States entered World War I, and the mid-1920s, when Beebe took over. Probably several keepers served here during this period. Likely one of them was a man remembered today only as "Ernie." No trace of Ernie can be found on the station's official list of keepers, and it may be that his name was changed or left off the list to, as they used to say in old-time mystery stories, "protect the innocent."

It is believed that Ernie joined the U.S. Lighthouse Service—at that time a civilian government agency—at some point during the early 1920s. Soon afterward he was assigned to the New London Ledge Lighthouse, which for the next few months or years would be his home. In those days, keepers usually lived either alone or with their families at their lighthouses. In most cases, the vital beacons were not automated. This meant that the keepers had to stay near the tower so they could be on hand to turn the beacon on in the evening and turn it off again each morning. Since it might prove impossible to reach offshore lights from the mainland during storms and heavy weather—just when the beacons were most needed—it was especially important for the keepers of lighthouses like the one at New London Ledge to live where they worked.

Apparently Ernie was recently married, and he brought his young wife with him to New London Ledge. It is hard to say how she had lived when she was single, but she may have found her life at New London Ledge to be lonely and depressing. Like the wives of so many other lighthouse keepers, she worked hard cooking and cleaning while her husband spent long days and nights repairing machinery and tending the light. There would have been little to break the tedium of her existence at this isolated outpost surrounded by water and miles from the nearest shopping or entertainment. There was, of course, no television in those days, commercial radio was in its infancy, and there were no neighbors with whom she could chat or gossip.

To lift her spirits, Ernie's wife often took time away from her husband and his lighthouse to visit friends and family. Ernie rowed her in the station boat to New London, where she would catch ferries to Block Island, Long Island, New Haven, or other such destinations. These places must have seemed bright, cheery, and utterly delightful compared to her rather bleak home on New London Ledge. Over time, her trips became more frequent, and they lasted longer, but it may be that Ernie barely noticed. He was preoccupied by his duties, and anyway, he encouraged her to take the occasional trip, since naturally enough, he wanted his wife to be happy.

Likely he thought she was happy—or wanted to believe it. She had been home for a while and life had seemed normal until the morning that Ernie clambered downstairs after a long night's vigil and encountered an eerie silence. The kitchen and bedroom were empty. Instead of the hot breakfast that usually awaited him on the table, he found a note. It read something like this: *I cannot stand it here any longer. I took the boat and left during the night, and I'm never coming back. I'm in love with*—she gave a name—*and I'm going away with him. Farewell.*

Ernie knew the man his wife had mentioned. He was the captain of the Block Island Ferry, and as it turned out, that very vessel was just then slipping out of the harbor and heading out into Long Island Sound. Ernie ran up into the lantern room at the top of the tower. From there he could see the ferry steaming past the lighthouse and off into the distance. It is easy to imagine that he could also see his wife waving goodbye to him from the deck.

Ernie had been caught completely unaware by this turn of events. Before this moment, he'd had no inkling that his wife was dissatisfied or that she planned to leave him. Brokenhearted and unable to bear the thought of life without her, the devastated keeper decided to put himself out of his misery as quickly and efficiently as possible. Ernie climbed through the windows of the enclosed lantern room out onto the roof of the lighthouse and jumped. His body was never found.

THE HAUNTING

That part of Ernie's story is composed mostly of legend and conjecture. The part of the story that is much better known and well documented is the haunting. Howard Beebe, the keeper who took over here in 1926, was probably the first to notice that certain rooms in the lighthouse were unexplainably cold, even though the weather was warm and there were no open windows. Lights came on and went off again even when no one stood anywhere near a switch. Footfalls could be heard on the steps leading up to the lantern room when supposedly there was no one in the tower. Beebe is said to have reached the conclusion that a ghost was responsible for all these strange happenings. It may have been Beebe who gave the New London Ledge Lighthouse ghost the name Ernie.

Later keepers, who unlike Beebe were members of the U.S. Coast Guard, might have been expected, as military men, to take a skeptical view of all this. As it turned out, they did not. Over the years, Coast Guard keepers reported dozens, if not hundreds, of unusual or bizarre occurrences at the lighthouse. Doors and windows opened and closed all by themselves. There were mysterious knocks on bedroom doors in the middle of the night. The station radio and later its television—modern appliances did eventually reach New London Ledge—came on while everyone in the building was asleep. Furniture moved around by itself, too, especially in the room where Ernie and his wife were said to have slept.

One keeper reported seeing the face of a second person in the mirror while he was shaving. When the startled keeper turned to see who it might be, there was no one in sight. The same keeper's wife awoke to see a tall bearded man standing silently at the foot of her bed. When she screamed, the man simply vanished like smoke caught in a draft.

It is said that one day a fisherman stopped by for coffee with the keeper, who was a longtime acquaintance. The two men got into a friendly debate over whether Ernie was real. The fisherman argued that the ghost was merely a hoax. Later when the fisherman returned to his boat, which he had tied securely to the station dock, he found that it had been set adrift.

Nowadays, the lighthouse itself has been set more or less adrift on the tides of maritime history. Lighthouses are no longer an absolute necessity for safe navigation since mariners can rely on computerized global positioning equipment and a wide assortment of other sophisticated electronic gear. The old beacon remains in operation, but it has been more than twenty years since a keeper actually lived at the lighthouse. The light was automated in 1987, and afterward the lighthouse no longer required the steady hand and daily care of a keeper.

Few of the keepers assigned over the years to this remote outpost—so near and yet so far from civilization—would have complained about the change in the station's circumstances. They were more than happy to take up new assignments in more comfortable and companionable surroundings ashore. Just before he stepped into the station boat and headed for land, the last official U.S. Coast Guard keeper left the following entry in the lighthouse logbook: *Rock of slow torture. Ernie's domain. Hell on earth—may New London Ledge's light shine on forever because I'm through. I will watch it from afar while drinking a brew.*

Chapter 2

A Sea Captain and Two Frozen Lovers

Owls Head Lighthouse
Rockland, Maine

Few lighthouses are as thoroughly haunted as the one that marks the harbor entrance of the old stone-shipping port of Rockland, Maine. Among the ghosts that occupy the buildings and walk the grounds of the Owls Head Lighthouse are those of a dog said to have once saved a ship with his incessant barking, a young couple said to have been found encased in ice on the deck of a ship that had run aground on the rocks below the tower, an aging sea captain assumed to be a former keeper, a smiling lady who may have been the faithful wife of a former keeper, and two scalped Indians.

Indeed, Owls Head is a haunted place, and looks it. Even on bright sunny days—and there are not many of those along this stretch of the Maine coast—dark shadows reach down to the water's edge from the forested cliff tops across a jumble of strangely shaped rocks. Likely, the shadow-draped boulders that abound here were responsible for the eerie name given to this distinctive promontory. Sailors headed for Rockland sometimes swore that in the rocks they could see the face of a giant bird. They would gesture toward a pair of caves forming the eye sockets and a series of pointed rocky outcroppings that gave the great bird a nose and beak as well as a pair of owlish ears.

"There it is," they would say. "There's the owl. Can't you see it?" Then their less imaginative friends would laugh and say they saw nothing on Owls Head but rocks—and a lighthouse.

Built in 1825 during the presidency of John Quincy Adams to guide lime freighters into Rockland Harbor, this lighthouse is one of the oldest navigational stations in New England. Unlike those of most other old light stations, its tower has never been pulled down and rebuilt. The tower is only about twenty feet tall, but because it rises from high ground, its fixed white light shines from about a hundred feet above the water. A fourth-order Fresnel lens focuses the light, which can be seen from about sixteen miles at sea.

The mysterious owl on Owls Head has seen many strange happenings. For instance, in 1745, long before the light-house was built, an Indian war party swooped down on Owls Head, overwhelming Thomas Sanders, a young English soldier who had apparently been stationed here to single-handedly defend this strategic headland. The warriors took Sanders prisoner and might very well have executed him, but as it turned out, the Englishman proved a bit too quick for his captors. A flight of ducks landed in the waters near the spot where Sanders was being held, and he asked the Indians to loan him a musket so he could shoot a few of the birds. In a truly extraordinary display of gullibility, his captors obliged, and Sanders, brandishing the borrowed musket, escaped into the woods.

Later on, the English would return in force and establish a military outpost here. In the early summer of 1757, a fleet of thirty canoes brought a large Penobscot Indian war party to attack the little fort. Although outnumbered, the English soldiers fought off the attack and, turning the tables on the Indians, scalped two of them.

As they sailed out of Rockland Harbor on November 9, 1844, sailors on the fine new brig *Maine* may have looked back at Owls Head and argued over whether, indeed, it resembled the head of an owl. None of them would ever get another chance to resolve the question. This was the *Maine*'s maiden voyage—and also its last. The *Maine* never arrived in New Orleans, where it was scheduled to deliver a load of Rockland lime. As if plucked from the seas by a giant predatory bird, the brig disappeared, along with its crew of nine local sailors. Then, three years later, a ship dropped anchor in Rockland Harbor. Onboard were a mahogany chest, a ship's atlas, and a navigation book, which Rockland residents swore belonged to members of the *Maine*'s crew. According to the captain of the visiting vessel, three Portuguese sailors had left these items behind when they jumped ship in Vera Cruz. No further traces were ever found of the *Maine* or her crew.

During the 1930s Owls Head Light had, believe it or not, a dog as an assistant keeper. The dog, a sharp-eared spaniel named Spot, barked loudly whenever he heard a ship. He would also ring the fog bell by pulling on the rope with his teeth. It is said that Spot once saved the Matinicus Island mail boat from smashing into the Owls Head rocks. A blizzard had cut visibility to near zero and frozen up the fog bell so that it could not be rung. But Captain Stuart Ames, master of the mail boat, heard the alert dog's persistent barking and managed to bear off from the rocks just in time to avert disaster. Spot is said to have been buried in the thin, rocky soil not far from the former location of the fog bell.

THE FROZEN LOVERS

Certainly the strangest of all the stories associated with Owls Head and its lighthouse is that of the frozen lovers. A few days before Christmas 1850, a small coasting schooner dropped anchor off Jameson's Point near Rockland. The vessel was without its captain, who had gone ashore to get himself a hot meal and a pint or two of ale. He never returned. Some say the owners of the schooner fired their hard-drinking captain, but others claim he had a premonition and decided to flee from fate. However, the schooner's mate, who knew nothing of any dark premonition, saw his skipper's absence as an opportunity. He had recently proposed to a lovely young woman, and with no one to order him otherwise, he invited her to his cabin.

Only the mate, his bride-to-be, and a deckhand were aboard on the evening of December 22, when a vicious winter gale blew in off the ocean and snapped the schooner's anchor cables. Although the sailors fought hard to save their vessel, the storm drove it relentlessly forward, finally crushing its hull on the cruel ledges near Owls Head. Held in a viselike grip by the rocks, the schooner filled with seawater but did not sink. Instead, it became a target for giant waves, which threw spouts of freezing spray over the three frightened people huddled on its deck. Their clothes and even their skin quickly became rough and crusty with ice.

The mate knew that he and his fellow shipwreck victims would soon freeze to death unless something was done. Faced with the horror of having coaxed his beloved into an apparent death trap, he came up with a desperate plan. To save themselves, he and his companions would roll up in a blanket and lie down together beside the stern rail. The mate hoped the freezing spray would form a protective shell of ice on the outside of the blanket. This it did, but the layer of ice grew much faster than he had anticipated. All night the sea continued to douse the three until they were entombed in a layer of ice several inches thick.

Under the suffocating weight of the ice, the mate and his girl lost consciousness, and by morning the deckhand believed that he was the only one left alive. Slashing at the ice with a small knife and using his bleeding hands as hammers, he managed to free himself. When he was strong enough to stand, the sailor saw that the tide had gone out and a narrow bridge of exposed rock now connected the schooner with the shore. So, bloodied and nearly frozen, he dropped down off the deck and stumbled off toward the Owls Head Light, which he could see shining through the storm. Overwhelmed by cold and exhaustion, he made the last part of the journey crawling on his hands and knees. But he eventually reached his destination, and in the warm kitchen of the keeper's dwelling, he told his incredible story.

The keeper had little hope of finding anyone alive aboard the schooner, but nevertheless he organized a rescue party and headed for the wreck. There the rescuers found a man and a woman locked in a lover's embrace and frozen in a solid block of ice. It took picks, chisels, knives, and several strong men to free the pair. Everyone was sure they were dead, but even so, an attempt was made to revive them. Hurried ashore to a home near the lighthouse, their seemingly lifeless bodies were treated with cold-water baths and constant massage. In two hours the woman regained consciousness. An hour after that the mate also showed signs of life. It took the two several months to recover from their ordeal, but by June they were strong enough to stand together in front of a preacher and pronounce their vows.

Ironically, the sailor whose grueling trek through the storm had brought help and saved the lovers from certain death never fully recovered from his adventure. He did not go to sea again and lived out his life on the waterfronts of towns near Owls Head. He never tired of telling strangers about his struggle in the blizzard of 1850 and about the frozen lovers of Owls Head.

THE OWL'S GHOSTLY COMPANIONS

Each day during the summer, ferries leave Rockland Harbor en route to Vinalhaven and several of Maine's other populated islands. Tourists on the vessel may strain their eyes looking for the famed owl on Owls Head, but any longtime Rockland residents or islanders who happen to be onboard aren't likely to bother. If anyone asks them about the owl, they're likely to say: "I don't like twisting my head around and putting a crick in my neck, and anyway, what's up there to see but a bunch of rocks?"

Some locals claim that the owl is gone and the rocks that once formed its visage have worn away. Others say there never was any owl and that people have always seen what they wanted to see when they gazed out toward the headland. And what about the lighthouse? Is it haunted?

"Sure, she's haunted," they'll say and then, likely as not, launch into one of the many ghost stories that are regularly told concerning the Owls Head Lighthouse. The stories they tell may depend on whether they are speaking to another native Mainer or to somebody "from away"—that is, a tourist or some other person whose family has not lived in Maine for more than half a dozen generations. For instance, they may tell the story of the frozen lovers and forget to mention that, on occasion, passing fishermen have seen the figures of an ice-encrusted man and woman standing at the base of the Owls Head cliffs—the couple are always holding hands. They may describe a personal encounter with the old man dressed in a sea captain's uniform who sometimes walks the lighthouse grounds on foggy evenings. The old salt will not respond if spoken to and if approached he vanishes. Is he a former keeper or, perhaps, the long-vanished master of the nineteenth-century brig *Maine*? Nope, they just can't say.

They may talk a bit about the "Little Lady" who sometimes haunts the kitchen of the Owls Head keeper's residence. Is she the wife of a former keeper? Nope, they can't say much about that either, one way or another. Whoever she is, she has white hair and a kindly appearance, and those who have encountered her say she fills everyone who approaches her with a sense of peace and of well-being. So what if she sometimes slams doors and rattles the cups, dishes, and silverware?

Of course, no one has any trouble identifying the dog who still barks wildly when Owls Head is blanketed in an especially thick layer of fog. Surely that has to be Spot. Or maybe it's just some neighbor's dog that has gotten loose on the lighthouse grounds.

All of the above are stories that Rockland locals or Maine islanders may tell to anybody, but there is one story they are unlikely to share with anyone other than a native Mainer. And who would want to hear it anyway unless the lights are up and there are plenty of people around. If travelers from away listen closely and don't make their presence too obvious, they may hear a Mainer mention that a pair of young Indians are sometimes seen standing along the shore below the Owls Head cliffs. Their heads are bloody because they have been scalped.

Chapter 3

Hanged Patriot
Walks the Hook

Sandy Hook Lighthouse
Highlands, New Jersey

The grounds of America's oldest standing lighthouse are said to be haunted by the spirit of Joshua Huddy, a patriot hanged by the redcoats during the Revolutionary War. More than a century after Huddy's execution, a Sandy Hook keeper found a mysterious skeleton in a secret room beneath the floors of the lighthouse residence. Are these grisly events related? It is a question that may never be answered, at least not by the living.

During much of the Revolutionary War, British forces made New York City their primary base of operations. British armies were housed on or near Manhattan Island and British fleets were anchored in the lower Hudson River. For all of these reasons the British were very protective of the Sandy Hook Lighthouse, which guarded the seaward approaches to the strategic Hudson.

Several times Continental forces attempted to destroy the lighthouse, hoping that without its guidance, British warships and supply freighters would get lost, run aground, and be smashed to splinters by the surf. Patriot raids were beaten back, however, and the Sandy Hook beacon continued to shine. Unable to put the lighthouse out of commission, the Continentals could do little to prevent the British from landing large numbers of troops and vast quantities of supplies in New York.

Even so, it greatly benefited the Continental cause to learn exactly when the troop ships and supply freighters arrived, since this gave George Washington and his army time to prepare for British attacks. For this information, the Continentals relied on spies to keep an eye on British ships moving in and out of the Hudson. One such watchful patriot was Joshua Huddy.

Huddy's house near Highlands had an excellent view of Sandy Hook, its lighthouse, and most important, of the Hudson's Lower Bay. Huddy observed the comings and goings of the British and reported what he had seen to Continental officers farther inland. Huddy also took part in several of the raids aimed at disabling the Sandy Hook Lighthouse. Unfortunately, during the last of these attacks in 1782, Huddy was captured and imprisoned by the redcoats. The British hoped to prove that Huddy was a spy so they could hang him as an example to other patriots along the New Jersey coast. However, they were unable to gather enough evidence to make the charge stick.

While Huddy was behind bars, a British soldier named Philip White was shot and killed, perhaps by a Continental sympathizer or a fellow redcoat who harbored a grudge against him. Making a mockery of both common sense and justice, British authorities accused Huddy of the crime. The charge was preposterous since Huddy had been in jail at the time White was murdered. Even so, the British led Huddy to a hastily erected gallows and, with drums beating, hanged him. Meanwhile, local patriots kidnapped a British officer, intending to hang him as a reprisal for Huddy's execution. It has never been entirely clear whether the officer was hanged or what actually became of him. Little more than a year after these dark and disturbing events, the United States officially secured its independence from Great Britain.

In 1783, the British hauled down the Union Jack from flagpoles at Sandy Hook, New York City, and elsewhere throughout their former colonies. It may be, however, that some very old soldiers are still fighting the Revolutionary War. During the past two centuries, Sandy Hook and Highlands residents have frequently encountered a ghostly figure dressed in what appears to be a Continental Army uniform. The specter is usually seen at twilight walking the beaches of Sandy Hook or the grounds of the Sandy Hook Lighthouse. It is said this is the restless spirit of Joshua Huddy, who unbeknownst to his British captors held the rank of captain in the Continental Army. It is also said that Huddy continues his walks to keep an eye out for British warships lest they someday return to these shores.

TOWER THAT LIT A REVOLUTION

Interestingly enough, if the redcoats should return, they would find the Sandy Hook Lighthouse as sound and sturdy as it was during Revolutionary times. As a matter of fact, its lamps were first lit in 1764, more than twelve years before the signing of the Declaration of Independence. Today, nearly two and a half centuries later, the light at the very top of the old tower still burns each night. This is not America's first lighthouse—that honor goes to the Boston Light, established in 1716 and destroyed by British troops in 1779—but it is the nation's oldest still standing and operating navigational aid.

Although located in New Jersey, the Sandy Hook Light was known for many years as the New York Lighthouse.

Indeed, it was built and paid for by New Yorkers. Weary of losing commerce to better-marked harbors at Boston and elsewhere, a group of New York merchants petitioned their colonial council for a lighthouse. The New York Assembly then held a lottery to raise money and hired Isaac Conro to build a tower near the mouth of the Hudson. To defray the costs of maintenance and pay the keeper's salary, the assembly levied a tax of 22 pence per ton on ships arriving at the Port of New York.

When completed, Conro's handiwork was described as follows: *This House is of an Octogan Figure, having eight equal sides; the Diameter of the Base 29 feet; and at the Top of the Wall 15 feet. The Lanthorn is seven feet high; the Circumference 15 feet. The whole Construction of the Lanthorn is Iron; the Top covered with Copper. There are 48 Oil Blazes. The Building from the Surface is Nine Stories; the whole from Bottom to Top 103 feet.* The dimensions of the tower remain roughly the same today.

After the Revolution the Sandy Hook Light precipitated a different sort of war. Since the lighthouse was located in New Jersey but owned by New York, the two states fell into a heated dispute over control of the station. The verbal and legal squabbling continued for years, until the U.S. government finally put an end to this almost-comical conflict in 1790 by making the Sandy Hook station and other lighthouses a federal responsibility.

When the Lighthouse Service began its massive effort during the 1850s to rebuild and modernize America's outdated light stations, inspectors were sent to see whether the Sandy Hook tower needed to be replaced. Their report on the board is a compliment to the work Conro did almost a century earlier: "The tower at Sandy Hook main light was constructed in 1764 under royal charter, of rubblestone, and is now in a good state of preservation. Neither leaks nor cracks were observed in it. The mortar appeared to be good, and it was stated that the annual repairs upon this tower amount to a smaller sum than in towers of any of the minor lights in the New York District."

The Lighthouse Service did decide to replace the reflectors in the lantern with a third-order Fresnel lens. The old lens still guides ships into the Hudson with a fixed white light visible from about nineteen miles away.

TWO GHOSTS AT SANDY HOOK?

When the Sandy Hook beacon comes on in the evening, it sometimes illuminates low-lying patches of fog or lights up the spray thrown up by waves crashing onto local beaches. It is at times like these that the ghost of Joshua Huddy is most often seen. As with all such specters, Huddy's ghost is, at least in part, in the eye of the beholder. It is very interesting to note, however, that people sometimes see not one but two ghosts dressed in Revolutionary War style down near the Sandy Hook Lighthouse. One is dressed in Continental Army attire and is thought to be Joshua Huddy. The other wears a British uniform. The two seem to be talking, but no one can guess the topic of their discussion. Politics, perhaps? The justice or injustice meted out by military tribunals? Or maybe just the weather?

Those who have seen both ghosts have surmised that the second figure is that of the British soldier who was supposed to have been executed as revenge for Huddy's hanging. According to Revolutionary War historians, British Captain John Asgill was being held prisoner by the Continentals at the time of Huddy's execution and was to have been hung as a reprisal. Instead, Asgill was spared, partly in response to a request made by Marie Antoinette, the queen of France, through the French ambassador in Philadelphia. In the end, the British apologized for the Huddy incident, Asgill was released, and in this way, additional bitterness between Britain and her soon-to-be-independent colonial subjects was avoided.

Although some believe the spectral figures seen at Sandy Hook are the ghosts of Huddy and Asgill, for others the identity of the second ghost remains in question. They conjecture that the pardon and release of Asgill was actually an official cover story for a much darker turn of events. They think it likely that infuriated New Jersey patriots, some of them close friends of Joshua Huddy, had already taken revenge by kidnapping and killing a British officer. No proof of this can be found in historical records, but such a thing could certainly have happened. If it did, then the specters on Sandy Hook may be representative of not one but two unjustly condemned men.

At some point during the late nineteenth century, the story of the Sandy Hook ghosts became even more mysterious and gruesome. In about 1890, a Sandy Hook Lighthouse keeper discovered a hollow space beneath some floorboards in the station residence. The hollow space turned out to be a narrow passage leading to a subterranean room. In the cramped, nearly airless room was the skeleton of a man who had apparently been walled in and left to die. Was he a British officer subjected to the most terrible punishment imaginable in an act of revenge? Likely no one will ever know, because the skeleton was removed and buried, the room and passage were filled in, and the entire bizarre episode all but forgotten.

Chapter 4
Victims of the Man-Eating Hobomock

Minot's Ledge Lighthouse
Scituate, Massachusetts

It may be that Minot's Ledge was already haunted long before a lighthouse was built here. Massachusetts Indians said a monster lived on the ledge and they offered gifts to keep it from getting angry. The monster must have been very angry indeed in 1850 when a storm destroyed the year-old Minot's Ledge Lighthouse and claimed the lives of two young assistant keepers. Some believe their spirits have returned to keep the light of the replacement tower, which was completed shortly before the Civil War.

Minot's Ledge is a long, knifelike blade of rock that, at low tide, rises just above the waves about a mile east of Scituate, Massachusetts. Native Americans who lived along the bluffs overlooking the ledge were terrified of it. They believed that a man-eating monster they called Hobomock lived there. They also believed that when Hobomock grew angry, he unleashed storms capable of destroying their villages, dashing their canoes, and drowning their warriors. To put Hobomock in a good mood, they made offerings to him, paddling out to the ledge at low tide to leave food, ornaments, and flowers on the rock. In periods of good weather, at least, the offerings seemed to help by causing Hobomock to slumber peacefully in his watery lair. Unfortunately, when the weather was not so good, Hobomock often rejected their gifts and tore into the shore with a terrifying ferocity that forced the Indians to run and hide in the hills and forests far from the sea.

Apparently European settlers and seamen were even less talented than the Indians had been at keeping the peace with Hobomock. Time and again during the seventeenth, eighteenth, and nineteenth centuries the monster rose up to shatter the hulls of ships and snuff out the lives of mariners. The problem was that most of the time pilots and navigators approaching the harbors along this stretch of the Massachusetts coast could not see the ledge. Since it rose above the waves only at low tide, they often slammed into it without ever having realized it was there, nearly always with tragic results.

The fact is, few navigational obstacles anywhere along the American coast have destroyed as many ships and lives as Minot's Ledge. A survey compiled in 1847 by lighthouse inspector I. W. P. Lewis listed dozens of barks, brigs, coasters, ketches, schooners, and large ships torn apart by this vicious subsurface obstacle. At least four hundred lives had been snuffed out in these wrecks, and Lewis estimated property damage of more than $360,000.

Although government officials had long recognized the dangers of the ledge, none had ever seriously suggested building a lighthouse there. The feat was thought to be impossible. Any lighthouse on Minot's Ledge would be exposed to the full force of the ocean. How long would it stand in a winter gale?

But Lewis was convinced that something had to be done, and armed with his survey, he forced the hand of Treasury Department Fifth Auditor Stephen Pleasonton, the country's top lighthouse official. A tightfisted conservative, Pleasonton was highly suspicious of new ideas, especially if they cost money. In this case, however, Pleasonton decided to take a chance and approved plans for a radical new lighthouse design, one that showed promise of surviving the punishments the sea heaped upon the Massachusetts coast.

Instead of the usual solid cylinder, the tower would consist of eight iron pilings, each of them sunk five feet into the rock and cemented in place. The keeper's dwelling and lantern would perch atop the legs, supposedly out of harm's way, some seventy-five feet above the ocean. In theory, the tower's reinforced legs would offer little resistance to the wind and water, and even the most formidable ocean waves would pass right through the open superstructure.

The U.S. Topographical Department itself designed and built the skeleton lighthouse, for this was no small feat of engineering and construction. Crews worked from a schooner anchored beside the ledge, and more than once the ocean swept drill rigs and other equipment off the rocks. The work took three years and a great deal of money to complete, with a grimacing Pleasonton signing the checks. Finally, on New Year's Day in 1850, the lamps at the top of the lighthouse were lit.

Captain William Swift, who designed and supervised construction of the lighthouse, proclaimed that it could weather "any storm without danger." But Isaac Dunham, the station's first keeper, did not share his confidence. Dunham, who could feel the new lighthouse swaying in the wind and hear its legs groaning under the stress of constant pounding by waves, had grave doubts about the safety of the structure. So, apparently, did the lighthouse cat. Dunham had brought a feline friend from shore to help keep rats at bay and provide him with some warm and fuzzy company. Unfortunately, the cat did not approve of its new surroundings. During a late summer gale, the tower lurched suddenly, terrifying the poor creature and causing it to dive over the side into the sea.

The loss of his cat discouraged Dunham and so did the increasing instability of the iron tower. Following a series of particularly violent autumn storms that he said "would have frightened Daniel Webster," the keeper quit the post. As it turned out, Dunham's resignation, after just nine months on duty, may well have saved his life.

FOR WHOM THE BELL TOLLS

Dunham was not the only one who had doubts about the skeletal lighthouse. Author and philosopher Henry David Thoreau frequented the Massachusetts coast and in 1849 he paused to gaze in wonder at the offshore structure, which at that time had only just been completed.

Thoreau later described it in his journal: *Here was the new iron lighthouse then unfinished and in the shape of an eggshell painted red, and placed high on iron pillars, like the ovum of a sea monster floating on the waves. When I passed it the next summer, it was finished and men lived in it, and a lighthouse keeper said that in a recent gale it had rocked so as to shake the plates off the table. Think of making your bed thus in the crest of a breaker.*

Obviously Thoreau recognized that the lighthouse, which stood on eight spidery legs with their feet in the ocean, was experimental and a very dangerous experiment at that. What he could not have known was that in a raging storm in the early morning darkness of March 17, 1851, the experiment would fail.

A man named John Bennett had replaced Dunham as keeper, and two assistants were appointed to help him tend the light. When the gale had set in the previous night, Bennett was on the mainland purchasing supplies. The weather was so severe that no boat could safely take to the water, and this left the keeper stranded ashore. Unable to return to his post, he was forced to leave the light in the hands of assistant keepers Joseph Antoine and Joseph Wilson. As the storm grew worse and titanic waves began to roll in from the east, Bennett and other spectators onshore began to wonder whether the lighthouse could possibly stand up to the pounding. Their fears proved well founded.

Shortly after one o'clock, the skeleton began to sag toward land. The tearful Bennett, who realized now that he would never again speak to Antoine or Wilson, noted with bitter pride that somehow his assistants kept the light burning right down to the last instant. As the lantern room neared the water, just before the lighthouse collapsed and fell into the sea, the waves began to hit the station fog bell, causing it to ring wildly.

The tragedy had an additional casualty. It may very well have focused the attention of Congress on Stephen Pleasonton's spotty thirty-year record as administrator of the Lighthouse Service. A congressional panel, convened during the spring of 1851, at about the time of the Minot's Ledge disaster, found the nation's navigational aids in terrible shape. Pleasonton had allowed so little money to trickle through to the service that lighthouse walls were cracking and towers were literally toppling into the sea. Pleasonton was summarily dismissed and authority over U.S. lighthouses was passed along to a Lighthouse Board composed of engineers and military officers.

As one of its first tasks, the Lighthouse Board undertook construction of a new Minot's Ledge Lighthouse. The effort consumed eight years and more than $330,000, but by August 1860, a second tower was complete. This time the tower was built with granite blocks laid in parallel courses atop foundation stones weighing two tons each. In this case, at least, stone has proven stronger than iron. The lighthouse still stands, more than 150 years after its construction. Giant waves have actually swept over the top of the ninety-seven-foot tower, breaking windows but causing no serious structural damage.

The lantern still delivers its distinctive warning to mariners: one white flash, followed by four flashes, followed by three more. The one-four-three rhythm reminds lovers of the words "I love you," and as a result, Minot's Ledge is known to the more romantically inclined as the I Love You Light. However, while young lovers may take a bright view of the beacon, a shadow falls over the dull gray tower when it appears off the port or starboard bows of passing ships. Seamen are so sure the old lighthouse is haunted, they steer well away from the tower when moving along the coast.

GHOST WHO SPEAKS PORTUGUESE

For eighty-seven years, keepers lived in the cramped confines of the Minot's Ledge stone tower. They faithfully kept the beacon, and by doing so no doubt saved the lives of countless mariners. Unlike the assistant keepers of the previous lighthouse, they managed this without sacrificing their own lives. However, some of them may have sacrificed their sanity when they were driven stir crazy by the hollow loneliness of the place.

Surrounded by constantly churning waters that much of the time could not be safely navigated by small boats, keepers and their assistants could be stuck at the lighthouse for long periods of time. During storms and heavy weather they were cut off from the mainland and left completely on their own. Understandably, Minot's Ledge was a very unpopular posting for professional government lighthouse keepers. It is also easy to understand why some keepers came to believe the old stone tower was haunted.

More than one keeper noted strange occurrences in the official logbooks. Keepers often noticed a tap, tap, tapping on the granite walls of the tower. They heard pounding on the heavy tower doors even during storms when no one could possibly have been out there knocking. And they heard voices that seemed to come from every direction at once. What was the explanation for these mysterious happenings? No one could say for sure, but some suspected that the tragic events of 1851 may have played a role.

In 1947 the U.S. Coast Guard automated the light at Minot's Ledge. Keepers were no longer needed to maintain the light and the station's resident staff was removed. No one was unhappy to say goodbye to this dark, dank, drafty, and definitely haunted place.

Now that no one lives at the Minot's Ledge Lighthouse, the tall gray tower may be even more ghostly. Fishermen passing the lighthouse on their way into Scituate Harbor occasionally see the dark figure of a man trying to climb the iron ladder leading to the outer door. They say the small, swarthy man calls out to them in a foreign language, possibly Portuguese. Joseph Antoine, one of the young assistant keepers killed when the first Minot's Ledge tower collapsed in 1851, was born in Portugal. And boaters passing the tower sometimes say they've seen—and heard—a very wet and anxious cat standing on the station's boat landing and squalling at the top of its lungs.

Chapter 5

Seguin Island
Piano Plays On

Seguin Island Lighthouse
Popham Beach, Maine

Hotel lobbies sometimes feature grand pianos that play all by themselves. No pianist, whether visible or invisible, is required. The keyboard is automated and driven by an electronic version of the mechanism found in old-fashioned player pianos. The music can be entertaining, of course, but watching the piano keys dance without the assistance of living human fingers is spooky. It is almost as if a ghost were sitting there on the stool hammering out popular tunes. Imagine, then, how strange it is to hear piano music in a place lacking both the pianist and the piano. Travelers adventurous enough to visit the lighthouse on Maine's rugged Seguin Island may very well have just such an experience.

Seguin Island rises from the tossing Atlantic waves about a mile off the end of one of those long scraggly fingers of land that make the coast of Maine look as if it has been raked by the claws of a giant beast. Located near the mouth of the navigable Kennebec River, the island is both strategic and historic. Two small ships, the *Gift of God* and the *Mary and John,* dropped anchor near the island in 1607. They had brought settlers who hoped to establish the first English colony in North America. The settlers planted a flag and built a small town on the banks of the Kennebec, but they had not counted on the terrible weather and hardships they would face. Hunger, illness, and a harsh Maine winter killed many and caused the survivors to abandon the colony and sail back home to England. No doubt the would-be colonists wished they had never set eyes on this stretch of coast or the rock that guards the approaches to it.

Even the Indians, who gave Seguin its name, were wary of the island. "Seguin" is an English corruption of an Indian word loosely translated as "place where the sea vomits." Considering that Indian fishermen had to fight choppy seas in flimsy canoes to reach the island, they may have intended to describe it as a place where they themselves vomited.

For the better part of two centuries, a fine old lighthouse has warned mariners to keep a safe distance from the island. Fitted with a powerful first-order Fresnel lens, the Seguin Island Light ranks as one of America's foremost navigational stations, and it has quite a history. George Washington himself gave the order to build the first tower here in 1795, and Congress appropriated $6,300 to see the job done right. But despite the money allocated, which was considerable for the time, the tower was constructed of wood, which cannot long survive the sort of weather that regularly slams into Seguin Island like the blade of an ax. By 1819 the sea had all but demolished the lighthouse, and it had to be rebuilt. This time the builders used stone and billed the government less than $2,500.

The original wooden tower lasted less than twenty-five years, but it stood up to Seguin's harsh weather a lot longer than did Count John Polersky, the station's first keeper. Born to a noble family in the European principality of Alsace, Polersky immigrated to America, where he served as a major in Washington's Continental Army. Polersky's salary was set at $200 per year, an income that was barely sufficient to keep him alive, let alone allow him to live in a style befitting a European nobleman. Polersky pleaded for a raise but was repeatedly turned down. Meanwhile, the station's cruel weather turned his home into a shack, smashed and sank his three boats, tore apart his barns, beat down his gardens, and left his health in ruins. After five years on the island, during which time he faithfully tended the light, Polersky died.

DAY OF THE AX

An even more tragic chapter in the Seguin Island story opened during the mid-nineteenth century when the keeper here married a young city woman and brought her to his isolated lighthouse home, where the couple's only friends and neighbors were seals and seabirds. However, the bride was a lively and romantic soul who loved music and longed for happy times and stimulating company. The keeper was a quiet, work-minded man who could not provide much in the way of interesting conversation or entertainment, but he loved his wife. To lift her spirits he bought a piano in nearby Brunswick and floated it across from the mainland on a raft. With considerable effort, the heavy piano was hoisted up the steep slopes of the rocky island and installed in the parlor of the lighthouse residence.

The keeper's wife seemed genuinely delighted by the gift and duly appreciative of the trouble her husband had taken to bring it to the island, but alas, the lady was not much of a musician. With a great deal of practice, she learned to play only a single tune, but having little else with which to occupy her time, she played it over and over again. The keeper praised her—she was obviously talented, he said—and subtly hinted that she should play other tunes.

Unfortunately, she was either unable or unwilling to comply and kept pounding out the same song day and night.

Soon the keeper became less subtle. "Play something else," he demanded, but to no avail.

Apparently his wife was obsessed, and the keeper became increasingly concerned for her sanity. As it turned out, he should have been worried about his own. Wherever he went in the lighthouse he could hear the notes of that one maddening song repeated again and again as his wife's fingers raced over the keys. He could hear them in the kitchen when he was pouring himself a cup of coffee. He could hear them when he was working with the supplies and equipment in the tower and supply rooms. He even began to hear them late at night after his wife had gotten up from the piano keyboard and gone to bed. Soon he could not sleep at all. He could only hear the music.

Finally the day came when the keeper could stand it no longer. He had to put an end to that terrible, never-ending refrain. He went to the tool shed, pulled out the ax he used for chopping firewood, and walked determinedly into the parlor where his wife sat on a stool playing her favorite tune. Then he lifted the heavy ax above his head and with all his strength brought it down onto the piano. The keeper's wife screamed and the instrument itself cried out as the ax blade splintered polished wood, smashed the soundboard, severed steel strings, and shattered keys. Whatever had snapped inside of him had unleashed a terrible violence, for, having destroyed the piano, the keeper then turned the ax on his wife, who was too paralyzed with fear to run away.

The keeper had always been a good and decent man, and of course he could not live with what he had done, perhaps in a temporary flash of madness. Some say he took his own life by jumping into the ocean. Others say he shot himself, and still others maintain that he used the ax on himself, splitting his own head wide open with the blade.

According to members of the local historical society, this horrific story is only a legend. Lighthouse Service records, now part of the U.S. Coast Guard archives in Washington, DC, would seem to support this point of view. Government files contain no reports of an ax murder on Seguin Island; at least, no such reports can be located. However, tourists and lighthouse buffs who visit the island during the summer often say they hear piano music here. Generations of lighthouse keepers who lived on Seguin Island along with their wives and children also reported hearing a piano. When a hard wind blew or a heavy rain fell, it was as if the lighthouse itself was a piano soundboard, always vibrating with the same song.

Some people say they've heard not only strange music on Seguin Island but also disembodied voices. The walls of the Seguin Island residence whisper, and shadows inside the tower fall at odd angles. Usually there is no one on the island at twilight, but if there were, what might they encounter? Perhaps if they looked out along the rocky cliffs they might see the figures of a man and a woman walking hand-in-hand. Would this be the keeper and his wife, now reconciled in death? Perhaps, but it is more pleasant to imagine that it would be the murdered keeper's wife and another romantic spirit, that of Count Polersky, who having been a European nobleman, no doubt loved piano music.

Chapter 6
Beware All Men

Southeast Lighthouse
Block Island, Rhode Island

Tourists should bring their cameras when they visit Block Island's Southeast Lighthouse. For their troubles they'll get a photograph of one of the most remarkable structures in America, and they may even get a picture of a real live—or real dead—ghost. Probably there is more than one ghost hereabouts, lots of them, in fact, but women and children need not fear them. Men, on the other hand, should beware.

If someone was going to make a movie about a haunted lighthouse, one might think it would be set on Block Island. Located more than half an hour by ferry from the mainland coast of Rhode Island, this great pile of sand, clay, and rock juts unexpectedly from the ocean's surface not far from the entrance to Long Island Sound. Crowning its two hundred–foot-high bluffs is the Southeast Lighthouse, built in 1875. The architecture of the redbrick tower and attached two-story dwelling is so decidedly Victorian—as if its image were torn from the pages of *Wuthering Heights*—that the place looks as if it must be haunted, and sure enough, it is.

Not far from the lighthouse, cliffs drop sharply into the ocean more than 160 feet below. These cliffs must have seemed even loftier to the war party of fifty Mohegan Indians who were trapped here in 1590. The Mohegans, who were from Long Island, New York, appeared suddenly in their swift battle canoes and launched a raid against the local Indians. But the Block Island warriors quickly defeated the invaders, drove them back to the bluffs, and threw them over the cliffs. Having died in so sudden and dramatic a manner, the Mohegans may have remained behind in spiritual form to keep Block Island under siege, and indeed, the island has seen its share of trouble over the years.

Block Island has been especially troubling to mariners who have difficulty seeing it as they approach Long Island Sound from the east. For this reason and others, helmsmen give Block Island a wide berth. Ringed by submerged boulders and sandy shoals, the six-mile-long island has ended the careers of countless ships and no few sailors. In a single twenty-year stretch during the early 1800s, thirty-four schooners, fifteen sloops, eight brigs, and two larger ships were wrecked on the island's shores.

To cut these losses, the Lighthouse Service built the Southeast Lighthouse along with a second light tower on the opposite side of the island. The Southeast tower was fitted with a huge first-order Fresnel lens fashioned by the Henry-LePaute Company of Paris. The lens cost the U.S. Treasury $10,000 and the entire facility cost more than $75,000. Both these sums were thought outlandish during the nineteenth century. To put this into perspective, consider that Henry Clark, the station's first keeper, was paid only $600 a year to maintain the beacon.

Despite the unimpressive salary, Clark was happy with his work and his life. The same could not be said, however, of some of those who followed Clark as keeper. For instance, among them was a man who brought with him to the lighthouse an angry wife who nagged him incessantly. He could not keep his clothes clean. He could not keep his hat on straight. He did not wear his uniform properly. He ate like a pig. He never kept promises. In fact, he never did anything right at all. He wasn't even a good lighthouse keeper.

Over time the nagging grew so intense that the day came when he could no longer bear it. A terrible argument broke out between the keeper and his wife, and it ended with him throwing her down the steps of the residence. She was killed, and the keeper was charged and convicted of murdering her.

While the keeper was sent to prison, his wife apparently remained behind at the lighthouse, where she continued to harass keepers. This she did by banging pots and pans, hiding items of clothing, rearranging tools and furnishings, and locking or unlocking doors. The targets of her pranks were invariably male—women and children were spared her wrath—so the mischievous ghost that haunts the Southeast Lighthouse must have had an intense dislike of men.

On more than one occasion, the ghost made off with the lighthouse keys, locking the keeper into or out of the residence and tower. In one instance she howled at a sleeping keeper, frightening him so badly that he ran out into the snow dressed only in his underwear. When he recovered his nerve sufficiently to return to the residence, he found the door locked. The keys were inside.

It seems that nature played a mischievous prank on the lighthouse itself. When it was completed during the 1870s, the tower and residence stood several hundred feet from Block Island's high Mohegan Bluffs. However, the cliffs were composed not of stone, but rather of a chalky claylike material that washes away readily in the rain. A century of New England downpours tore away at the cliffs until they had almost reached the seaward walls of the lighthouse. By the 1990s the rampaging erosion threatened to undermine the building's foundation and send the historic lighthouse tumbling into the sea in much the way the Mohegan warriors did centuries ago.

To save the old building, preservationists raised more than $1 million to lift the lighthouse up and move it to a safer location a few hundred yards inland. The move was successfully carried out in 1993, and the venerable lighthouse seems likely to survive at least another century. So, too, does the Southeast Lighthouse lady poltergeist who apparently rode along with the building as it was being moved. It is difficult to say how much mass a ghost adds to a 2,000-ton building, but the men involved in the relocation project must have felt the extra weight. After all, weren't their hats on crooked, weren't they getting behind on their schedule, and couldn't they do anything right?

Chapter 7

Lady of
Matinicus Rock

Matinicus Rock Lighthouse
Atlantic Ocean, thirty miles off the coast of Maine

In most cases ghosts are manifestations, not so much of a super-natural presence as of our personal fears—especially the fear of death. For this reason, perhaps, ghosts are generally linked to melancholy people whose tragic endings mirror our anxieties, but this is not always the case. Sometimes a ghost story concerns an individual whose life force burns so brightly that it can be neither ignored nor forgotten. Such a story is that of Abbie Burgess, the youthful heroine of Matinicus Rock who defied one of the worst Atlantic storms in history to save her ailing mother, siblings, and even a pet chicken. No wonder she is sometimes seen waving to passing boaters from the door of the long-ago-abandoned Matin-icus Rock keeper's residence.

Located about twenty-five miles from Rockland, the nearest mainland port, Matinicus Rock is truly a remote outpost. Fog blankets the treeless island one out of every five days. When there is no fog, wind tears at the rock, and storms blast it with such fury that giant boulders are shifted by the surf. Exposed to the very worst the sea can throw at it, this would seem an unlikely place to build a lighthouse out of wood. But that is exactly what the Lighthouse Service did, throwing up two relatively flimsy wooden towers on the island in 1827.

John Shaw, the station's first keeper, must have shaken his head in dismay at the sight of the white wood-frame towers. They would surely fall in the first muscular nor'easter that passed this way. But surprisingly the towers stood up to the sea's anger a lot longer than did Shaw. Sixty-five years old when he took over the new station, Shaw fell desperately ill during his third year as keeper. By early the next year, the old man was dead, the life drummed out of him by the hard work, the sea, and Matinicus Rock.

Although most of them were much younger than Shaw, few of the keepers who followed him lasted very long on the rock. During its first decade of operation the Matinicus Rock station killed or drove off its keepers at an average of one every two years. The wooden towers themselves endured for just under twenty years, but by 1846 they, too, had succumbed to wind, weather, and waves, and had to be replaced.

This time the builders were sensible enough to use stone, but even the sturdy replacement towers, completed about 1847, did not last long. Lighthouse Service crews soon pulled them down and erected the taller granite towers that still stand on the island today. Only one of the towers remains in use, its white light flashing once every ten seconds.

However, another light burns on Matinicus Rock. It is the bright story of Abbie Burgess, the rock's most famous resident. Especially inspiring to young people, Abbie's story continues to be told and retold in children's books and lighthouse histories, but it is possible that her memory is kept alive in other ways as well. Fishermen and pleasure boaters in the Gulf of Maine have reported a young woman waving to them from the doorway of the abandoned Matinicus Rock keeper's residence. Is that Abbie waving to them? Who knows?

During the 1850s Abbie Burgess came with her mother, younger sisters, and brothers to live on the barren open ocean island where her father had been named keeper. Sometimes she went to school onshore with her siblings, but she spent most of her time on Matinicus Rock assisting her father with his work and helping her somewhat sickly mother raise the family. She must have dreamed of more populous places, of stores filled with colorful dresses and candy, or of the leisurely delights that more fortunate children took for granted. Perhaps she wished she could leave Matinicus Rock and join those children, but if Abbie did harbor such thoughts, she kept them to herself and remained her parents' dutiful helpmate.

Abbie had just turned seventeen when in the winter of 1856 a stubborn gale blew up out of the Atlantic and cut the station off from the mainland for nearly four weeks. When the storm hit, keeper Samuel Burgess was in Rockland buying supplies for his family and medicine for his bedridden wife. He had left his daughter Abbie to look after his wife and three younger daughters. Also, having taught Abbie to trim the wicks of the fourteen lamps in each of the two towers, he counted on her to keep the all-important Matinicus Rock lights burning.

The storm struck suddenly, packing winds so strong that boats could make no headway against them. Trapped in Rockland, Burgess could do nothing to help his family. As days stretched into weeks, with no break in the relentless gale, the keeper despaired. But sea captains who had fought their way out of the storm into the safety of Rockland's calm harbor brought hope. Those who had passed close to Matinicus Rock reported that they had seen lights in the towers there.

After nearly a month the winds finally let up, and Burgess was able to sail back home. What he found there astonished him. The storm had destroyed much of the light station. Only the foundation of the keeper's dwelling remained; the rest had been washed into the sea. But thanks to Abbie, the Burgess family had survived.

THE WORST SEA IS COMING

In a letter to a pen pal onshore, Abbie described how she and her family had survived the great storm. *You have often expressed a desire to view the sea out on the ocean when it was angry,* she said. *Had you been here on 19 January* [1856], *I surmise you would have been satisfied.*

> Father was away. Early in the day, as the tide rose, the sea made a complete breach over the rock, washing every movable thing away, and of the old dwelling not one stone was left upon another. The new dwelling was flooded, and the windows had to be secured to prevent the violence of the spray from breaking them in. As the tide came, the sea rose higher and higher, till the only endurable places were the light towers. If they stood, we were saved, otherwise our fate was only too certain. But for some reason, I know not why, I had no misgivings, and went on with my work as usual. For four weeks, owing to rough weather, no landing could be effected on the rock. During this time we were without assistance of any male member of our family. Though at times greatly exhausted with my labors, not once did the lights fail. I was able to perform all my accustomed duties as well as my father's.

You know the hens are our only companions. Becoming convinced, as the gale increased, that unless they were brought into the house they would be lost, I said to my mother, "I must try to save them." She advised me not to attempt it. The thought, however, of parting with them without an effort was not to be endured, so seizing a basket, I ran out a few yards after the rollers had passed and the sea fell off a little, with the water knee deep, to the coop, and rescued all but one. It was the work of a moment, and I was back in the house with the door fastened, but I was none too quick, for at that instant my little sister, standing at the window, exclaimed, "Oh look! look there! The worst sea is coming." That wave destroyed the old dwelling and swept the rock. I cannot think you would enjoy remaining here any great length of time for the sea is never still and when agitated, its roar shuts out every other sound, even drowning our voices.

A few years after the extraordinary month-long Atlantic storm described in her letter, Abbie married Isaac Grant, a young man who had worked as an assistant keeper at the Matinicus Rock Lighthouse. Later she and Isaac moved on to Spruce Island near Thomaston, Maine, where they shared keeping duties at Whitehead Lighthouse. Abbie is buried in a cemetery on Spruce Head, where she and her husband lived and worked for more than fifteen years. Her headstone features a lighthouse, an indication, perhaps, that Abbie's light still shines.

Chapter 8

Ship of Fog,
Faces of Stone

Cape Neddick Lighthouse
York, Maine

Ocean waves have etched mysterious faces into the boulders below the Cape Neddick Lighthouse. Some say they can see the faces of George Washington, Abraham Lincoln, and other famous people in these busts sculpted by nature. However, the faces may instead be those of ordinary seamen drowned near this stormy cape more than one and a half centuries ago. Their shattered vessel occasionally pays these coasts a return visit—or so it is said.

In a graveyard at Kennebunkport a headstone bears the name of Captain Leander Foss. The body of Captain Foss, however, does not rest anywhere nearby. It is assumed that Foss went to Davy Jones's locker along with his handsome ship, which disappeared under strange circumstances off Cape Neddick in 1842. Some say that Foss still sails the seas as captain of the ghost ship *Isidore*.

A seaman named Thomas King was supposed to ship out with the Yankee clipper *Isidore* when it set sail from Kennebunkport on the last day of November 1842. Two days before the scheduled departure, King woke up in a cold sweat from a terrible dream. He had a vision of a wrecked ship and drowned sailors floating in ocean waves. In King's dream the hull, masts, and rigging of the foundering ship turned to fog and were carried away by the wind. Meanwhile the faces of the ship's crewmen turned to stone and washed up on the shores of a barren island. King had no doubt that the vessel in his nightmare was the *Isidore* and that the drowned men with faces of stone were his fellow crewmen.

King told Foss about his ominous dream, but the old sea captain laughed at him. When Foss refused to delay the *Isidore*'s scheduled sailing, King begged to be let out of his contract and to stay behind. At this point Captain Foss put on a stern face, reminded King that he had already received a month's salary in advance, and told the frightened seaman in the plainest of language to be aboard the *Isidore* when she pulled away from the dock and set sail.

The following night another member of the *Isidore* crew had a disturbing dream. The sailor envisioned seven coffins and saw himself in one of them. Foss heard about this second nightmare, but having little respect for superstition and a tight schedule to keep, he made up his mind to sail first thing the next morning.

As November 30 dawned, the families and friends of the *Isidore*'s crew gathered at the Kennebunkport wharves to wish their loved ones well. But a cloud of dread and gloom hung heavy over the farewell, and there was little of the usual cheering and hat waving as the ship glided slowly out of the harbor. By this time the sky had added a few dark clouds of its own to the scene, and they quickly increased in size and number. It began to snow, and a bitterly cold wind came up out of the north to hurry the *Isidore* down toward the sea and into the realm of legend.

Among those who watched the *Isidore*'s masts disappear into the snowy distance was Thomas King. He had hidden in the woods until he was certain that the vessel was under way. King expected his acquaintances in town to scorch his ears for having jumped ship, and they did.

But his disgrace lasted only about one day.

On the following morning word came to Kennebunkport that pieces of a large ship were scattered all along the shore in the vicinity of Cape Neddick. It was the *Isidore*. There were no survivors of the wreck, and only seven bodies had washed ashore—one of them the sailor who had dreamed about the seven coffins. The body of Captain Foss was never located.

Imaginative residents and visitors to Maine's scenic coast have reported many sightings of the *Isidore* during the century and a half since the wreck. They describe a gray, close-reefed ship and shadowy figures that stand motionless on the deck and stare straight ahead. Maybe Thomas King later saw the phantom ship himself—in his dreams if not with his eyes. But if he ever again encountered the ghostly *Isidore*, he never said so.

STONE FACES OF CAPE NEDDICK

Just off Cape Neddick, near the old town of York, Maine, lies a small, utterly barren island long known to fishermen as the "Nubble." Here the rocks seem to have boiled up out of the sea, and nature has created a sculpture garden by carving fantastic shapes into the exposed stone. Below the century-old lighthouse is a rock formation called the Devil's Oven. As if to warn the devil against cooking up anything too evil in his oven, a stone preacher's pulpit stands nearby. But the most famous formation on The Nubble is Washington's Rock. Visitors often say they can see a striking likeness of the nation's first president in the rock—but most agree that this takes some imagination.

Probably no one has ever noticed a likeness of President Rutherford B. Hayes in the rocks of the island, but it was he who signed the order establishing a light station here in 1879. The government spent $15,000 building the lighthouse, keeper's dwelling, and support buildings. The tower, though only forty feet tall, still stands on the island's highest point, its light shining from an elevation of eighty-eight feet. The light flashes red every six seconds.

GHOST SHIP RETURNS

If the Cape Neddick Light had been flashing in 1842, perhaps it might have saved the *Isidore* and her crew from destruction. Of course, no one can say for sure, since it is impossible to know exactly what happened to the ship during her last terrible hours. Caught along with his ship in the grip of a mighty gale, Captain Foss may have tried to round Cape Neddick and make for safe harbor in Portsmouth a few miles to the south. Obviously he never made it, at least not as a living, breathing seaman.

However, the *Isidore* has been spotted off the cape many times since 1842. Instead of riding upon the waves, she floats on a bank of fog. Her captain and crew are gathered on deck, staring straight ahead, as if intent on sailing not toward a particular port, but into eternity. If anyone calls out to the ship from shore, it vanishes into the fog, which likely as not is the same stuff of which it is made.

Visitors to the Nubble and the Cape Neddick Lighthouse should keep an eye out for the *Isidore*, especially when the fog rolls in off the sea. They should also take a close look at The Nubble's red rocks. They may see in the tortured stone the faces of the *Isidore* crew, if not those of Washington or Lincoln. They may even see the face of Thomas King, who, it is easy enough to imagine, arrived here at last to share the fate of his shipmates.

Chapter 9
Vanished Delaware Light Still Shines

Cape Henlopen Lighthouse
Lewes, Delaware

One of America's oldest and most storied lighthouses fell into the surf at Cape Henlopen almost a century ago. Though the Cape Henlopen Lighthouse was never rebuilt, its light sometimes mysteriously reappears to guide storm-battered ships into the safe, calm waters of Delaware Bay. Another sort of ghost light once shined from the Delaware shores, but its purpose was not so benign. Mariners called it the Corpse Light because it lured them to destruction on the bay's deadly shoals.

Sometimes lighthouses themselves are ghosts. Much like the ships and sailors who depend on them, lighthouses are perishable. They may last much longer than the men and women they serve, but lighthouses do indeed grow old and die. Many of the nation's earliest lighthouses disappeared long ago. Storms bowled them over, or floods and beach erosion cut away their foundations, causing them to topple into the sea. A few were cut down by cannonballs, explosives, and other weapons of war. A surprising number have fallen victim to the same people who had them built in the first place—members of the Lighthouse Service or Coast Guard who pulled them down to make way for newer, supposedly better navigational facilities. Many others were abandoned, fell into ruin, and collapsed.

However, whenever lighthouses are destroyed, the lights they once displayed do not necessarily disappear along with them. Their lights seem to pop up again on the horizon just when they are needed most. Some old salts swear that when the weather is just right, they can see the faint ghost of a light emanating from a point where a demolished lighthouse once stood.

Seamen love to tell the story of an old schooner captain who followed the beacon of a lighthouse that no longer existed. One especially murky evening the captain's vessel was caught in a storm a few miles from its home port. Although blinded by the heavy weather and pitch darkness, the captain decided to make a run for the harbor. The approaches to the harbor were strewn with rocks and dangerous shoals, but the old seaman managed to avoid all of these obstacles, and before long, the schooner was riding safely at anchor in calm water.

Astonished by this display of skill, the schooner's young first mate asked his skipper how he had managed to navigate in such conditions.

"Nothing to it," replied the captain. "I just grabbed hold of the lighthouse beacon and followed her right in."

The first mate reminded the captain that the lighthouse guarding the harbor had collapsed and fallen into the sea many years earlier.

"Makes no difference at all," snapped the aging mariner. "I've been sailing these waters since before you were born, and I remember exactly where that light used to shine."

Perhaps this delightful story concerns the Cape Henlopen Lighthouse, which once marked the entrance to the Delaware Bay and the sheltered waters of the strategic harbor at Lewes. Or maybe it concerns some other beacon. This much is certain, however. The Cape Henlopen Lighthouse played too important a role in the nation's history ever to be forgotten. In the eyes of some, its light will shine on forever. Apparently the spirits of men and women long associated with the historic lighthouse or whose ships were guided by its beacon also continue to shine. On almost any evening, the sandy bluffs and beaches of Cape Henlopen are alive—if that is the appropriate term—with ghosts.

Cape Henlopen is now a Delaware state park, and visitors have reported all sorts of spectral sightings here. As with ghostly encounters nearly everywhere, these occur mostly at twilight or around midnight. Some park visitors say they've seen ghostly shipwreck victims or soldiers dressed in what appear to be eighteenth- or early nineteenth-century uniforms. Others say they've seen what they describe as sea captains pacing up and down near the bluffs where the old lighthouse once stood. Are these figures actually former keepers of the Cape Henlopen Lighthouse? It would be easy to mistake a Lighthouse Service uniform for that of a ship's officer. Some visitors have even seen the former lighthouse itself standing straight and tall above the cape with its beacon blazing. All of these sightings appear to have their roots in the extraordinary history of the Cape Henlopen Lighthouse.

GUIDING LIGHT THAT COULD NOT BE EXTINGUISHED

The Cape Henlopen Lighthouse was the seventh major light tower built in the original thirteen American colonies. Completed in 1765, it was financed and operated not by the people of Delaware but by those of Pennsylvania. The merchants of Philadelphia made handsome profits on goods brought by ships moving up the Delaware River. Naturally they wanted to make the trip to their bustling wharves as easy and safe as possible. In a manner that might seem familiar to citizens nowadays, Pennsylvania officials attempted to raise money for the project by means of a lottery. Proceeds of the game fell considerably short of the 7,674 pounds sterling needed for construction, however, so the provincial assembly issued a series of lighthouse bonds, at 6 percent interest, to make up the difference.

Built at considerably more expense than most other eighteenth-century American lighthouses, the Cape Henlopen tower was made to last. Construction crews used granite brought from quarries upriver near Wilmington, Delaware. Laying the granite down in courses, they gave the tower fortress-like walls, six feet thick at the base and sixty-nine feet tall. It had eight interior levels, each with its own window. On the eighth level was the lantern room, glassed in on all sides. A wooden stairway wound around the inner walls of the tower, providing access to the top. The original lamps were fueled by whale oil when it was available and by lard oil at other times. The tower stood on a sandy hill, which boosted the light to more than 115 feet above the water. Some captains claimed to have seen it from seventeen miles at sea.

Pointing the way to prosperous Philadelphia, the Cape Henlopen Lighthouse quickly became one of the most important landmarks in North America. Thousands of British and colonial ships followed its guidance and noted the light in their logbooks. It had shined for only a few years, however, when relations between the colonists and their mother country began to sour. By 1775 hostilities seemed inevitable, and the colonists placed a lookout in the Cape Henlopen tower to watch for approaching warships. Should he spot an invasion fleet, the lookout's duty was to ride for Philadelphia hell-for-leather, Paul Revere style, to give the warning.

Instead of an invading armada, the British sent individual warships to harass the colonists, who fought back with a tiny fleet of their own. The young John Paul Jones served aboard one of these small vessels, the *Alfred*. Nonetheless, the British were successful in bottling up the American ships in the Delaware River.

In 1777 the British warship *Roebuck* anchored off the cape. With his ship sorely in need of supplies, the captain sent a party of foragers ashore near the lighthouse to round up some cattle to feed his hungry crew. The Cape Henlopen keeper, a stout-hearted Patriot named Hedgecock, refused to sell his cows. To keep the British from commandeering—the military word for stealing—the beasts, he drove them into the woods. Hedgecock threatened to give the British "some bullets instead of beef." No match for the well-armed raiding party, however, Hedgecock had to take to the woods himself.

Having missed out on a steak dinner, the angry sailors set fire to the lighthouse. Feeding primarily on the wooden staircase, the fire gutted the tower. The light station would not be repaired and back on active duty again until 1784, just after the end of the war.

WHAT SO PROUDLY WE HAILED

A generation afterward, in 1812, Americans were once again at war with the British, and again the Cape Henlopen Lighthouse played an important role. During the early months of the war, the light guided U.S. naval vessels in and out of the Delaware. Privateers followed the light into the bay with British prizes they had captured at sea. But by the spring of

1813, the British had clamped a tight blockade on the Delaware, and American vessels could no longer get in or out.

To strike back at the British and make navigation as dangerous as possible for the blockading fleet, the Americans darkened the Cape Henlopen Light and removed all buoys and markers from the bay. This proved an especially damaging broadside, as time and again British ships slammed into obstacles or ran aground on shoals lurking just beneath the waters of the cape.

The British also had a very hard time obtaining provisions of meat and fresh water. More often than not, foraging parties were greeted with a fusillade of militia bullets. Facing critical shortages, the British sailed their fleet around Cape Henlopen, trained their guns on the town of Lewes, and demanded supplies. Its defenses bolstered by one thousand militiamen hurried to the cape from the north, the town flung the British demands back at them in the form of musket and cannon shot. In turn, the British replied with a mighty cannonade that lasted all day. In a Fort McHenry–style bombardment, they pounded the town with more than eight hundred thirty-two-pound explosive shots. But the marksmanship of the British gunners was poor, and they did very little telling damage. When evening fell, the American flag still fluttered over the town, and the British fleet was forced to withdraw. The proud militia commander reported to his superiors that the British attack had "killed one chicken and wounded a pig."

With the end of the war in 1814, the Cape Henlopen Lighthouse returned to its peacetime duties. The old lighthouse, however, was now locked in another battle, one that would last for more than a century and one it would eventually lose. This time the enemy was the Atlantic Ocean itself, which was constantly shaping and reshaping the cape. The beach was steadily eroding and the sandy cape retreating in a generally northwesterly direction. By 1884 high tides were approaching the tower's very foundation.

Alarmed lighthouse officials ordered a series of protective measures. Brush was piled up around the tower and dwelling to trap windblown soil, while piers and bulwarks were built along the beach in an attempt to dam the river of sand flowing to the north. These measures slowed the river but did not stop it.

The Cape Henlopen Light survived to serve in one more international conflict: World War I. Keepers kept an eye out for German submarines thought to be prowling just outside the Delaware Bay. But after the war the lighthouse began to lose its struggle with the sea, as tides cut farther and farther under the sand bank that served as its platform. After major storms sailors looked anxiously to the cape to see if the tower was still there. Its last day came on April 13, 1926, a sunny day with light winds. Shortly after noon the Cape Henlopen tower tumbled down into the sea.

Occasionally, at the last gleam of twilight, sailors on ships off Cape Henlopen report seeing a light emanating from a point near where the old lighthouse once stood. Some say these mariners have seen the Delaware Breakwater Light, which is often visible from beyond the cape. Others are not so sure, and when the night is especially dark, they scan the western horizon looking for the light that for more than 150 years so seldom failed them.

STONE DRUM LIGHT

Some stories shed a less positive light on the ghost beacon at Cape Henlopen. Locals tell of a cylinder of stone that rises from the evening mists and emits a bright light that navigators can easily mistake for a real lighthouse beacon. Anywhere near the mouth of the Delaware Bay such an error could be fatal, drawing ships out of the safe deepwater channel. The waters beyond the channel are strewn with shoals likely to crush the hull of a ship or hold it fast while storm-driven waves tear it to pieces. Consequently, any vessel that veers very far off course is likely doomed, along with its crew. For this reason mariners refer to the ghost beacon as the Corpse Light.

Native American tribes in Delaware had another name for the Corpse Light. They called it the Stone Drum Light. The evil magic of the Stone Drum Light supposedly resulted from a curse placed centuries ago upon ships bringing English-speaking settlers to North American shores. Supposedly the curse was intended as revenge for an attack by armed settlers on a peaceful Delaware Indian wedding celebration. It is said that in 1655, the Stone Drum Light lured the *Devonshireman*, a passenger vessel loaded with Quaker immigrants, to its destruction on the New Jersey shores of Delaware Bay. No one knows how many ships, crewmen, and passengers have been lost over the centuries because of the Corpse Light or Stone Drum Light, but mariners who navigate these waters today would do well to ignore any beacons that break mysteriously through the mist.

Chapter 10

Hunting Ghosts at Race Rock

Race Rock Lighthouse
Near Fishers Island, New York

Coast Guard maintenance personnel don't like to visit the isolated Race Rock Lighthouse, and it's not hard to understand why. Practically everyone agrees that this old Victorian stone structure is haunted. Shadowy figures are seen in the lantern room at night even though there has been no keeper here for decades. Chairs shift from place to place under their own power and water runs through pipes that were long ago disconnected from the station cistern. What's going on at Race Rock? Your guess is as good as that of TV's well-known Ghost Hunters.

Race Rock Lighthouse stands on an island that is not actually an island at all. It's a pile of broken stone put in place by construction contractors during the nineteenth century to provide a solid foundation for a much-needed maritime beacon. According to Native American chroniclers, however, there once was a real island here standing high and dry above the channel between Long Island and the shores of Connecticut. The Indians, who often plied these dangerous waters in their birchbark canoes during precolonial times, knew the island well, but they avoided it if at all possible. Its rugged shores could tear the bottom out of a canoe, and anyway, they believed the place to be haunted by the spirits of the dead.

Eventually the powerful currents rushing back and forth between Long Island Sound and the Atlantic Ocean wore away the island, leaving behind a subsurface shoal. These same currents made this area a nightmare for sailors and caused them to call it the "Horse Race." Shipwrecked seamen coined a name for the shoal as well. They called it "Devil Shoal" after it had thrust its stony pitchfork through the wooden hulls of their ships.

Later the mariners of New York and New England gave it the somewhat less dreadful moniker of Race Rock Reef, but this did not mean they considered it any less dangerous. They knew better, for during the 1700s and early 1800s, the reef sank ships at a rate of nearly one per year. In 1829 alone the reef claimed at least eight ships, and then in 1846 came the worst calamity of all. That year the passenger steamer *Atlantic* slammed into Race Rock Reef and sank, with the loss of fifty-seven lives.

Despite the threat it represented to shipping, the reef was not marked by a navigational light until long after many lesser obstacles along U.S. coasts were guarded by bright beacons. That is largely because government engineers believed it would be too expensive if not altogether impossible to build a lighthouse in the fast-moving waters of the Horse Race. They were finally forced to reconsider their opinions after the Civil War, when seagoing commerce increased dramatically and the reef began to claim ships and lives at an even more alarming rate. By the late 1860s, maritime officials felt they had no choice but to shoulder this extremely difficult project.

In 1869 Congress appropriated $90,000 to build a lighthouse atop Race Rock Reef. In this era when even well-paid workers earned only a few hundred dollars a year, this was a truly fantastic sum, but would it be enough? As things turned out, it wouldn't. Before the Race Rock light station was complete, its price tag would balloon to $278,716, placing it, comparatively speaking, among the most expensive federal construction projects ever undertaken. It was also one of the most remarkable engineering feats of its own or any era.

To attempt it federal officials employed F. Hopkinson Smith, a well-known and highly innovative construction engineer. In turn Smith hired as his foreman Thomas Scott, a sharp-tongued former ship's captain whom he described as a "bifurcated seadog." Smith and his sea dog started work in 1871, and before they had finished the job more than eight years later, Scott would employ every foul phrase he had learned as a sailor and, no doubt, would invent some more.

First a pier had to be constructed in thirteen feet of often turbulent water. To this purpose, Smith and Scott tried building an artificial island by dumping tons of stone onto Race Rock. Enormous loads of broken rocks and boulders—10,000 tons in all—were poured onto the site, but the strong currents swept away the fill almost as fast as boats could deliver it. Frustrated, Smith and Scott resorted to the much slower and more expensive technique of having divers lay cement on the sea bottom. This process took nearly two years but eventually produced a mass of concrete some nine feet thick and sixty-nine feet in diameter. Upon this pad they were able to construct a stone pier.

Even then the job was still far from finished, and it would proceed at a painstaking pace. Progress was impeded by storms, ice, sunken supply barges, exhausted funding, appropriation delays, and the death of two workmen in separate accidents. In all, it took almost a decade to complete the pier and lighthouse. It was not until February 21, 1879, that a keeper climbed the steps of the tower and lit the lamps for the first time. Nonetheless, mariners fighting the five-knot currents of the Horse Race were glad enough to see it.

Although it was a long time in coming, the Race Rock Lighthouse was meant to last. Built of large granite blocks, the two-story structure still stands on its massive stone pier, which rises almost thirty feet above high water. The attached square tower places the light approximately sixty-seven feet above the surface of Long Island Sound. The light alternates between red and white flashes and can be seen from fourteen miles away.

The isolated lighthouse was home to generations of keepers and their assistants. Of their lives, deeds, and misdeeds we know little. All we know for certain is that the last of them left the isolated, artificial island in 1979 when the light was automated and the residence was boarded up almost a century to the day after the lighthouse began operation. Were they happy to leave? Almost certainly, for the Race Rock Lighthouse was damp, drafty, and cold, and what was worse, some keepers and their assistants had come to believe that it was inhabited by a small army of ghosts. They heard strange noises, noticed that chairs and other furnishings seemed to move around on their own, and most disturbing of all, found footprints on the floor that they themselves had not made.

During the years since its light was automated, the Race Rock Lighthouse has built a reputation as one of the most haunted structures in America. Passing seamen say they've seen shadowy figures in the lantern room, and sometimes at night a light glows in the station residence even though

it has been closed up for decades. U.S. Coast Guard maintenance personnel don't like to visit Race Rock and refuse to
go there at night or anytime the sun is not brightly shining.
Even those who have spent time there during the day have
reported strange and eerie occurrences. They say they've
seen ghostly apparitions and watched as chairs were pulled
back by some invisible hand as if someone or something
were about to sit in them. They've heard footsteps on the
tower stairs as well as the sound of distant conversations
and laughter. Some even claim they've been touched on
the shoulder or poked in the ribs by some unseen presence.
Water pours through taps that are no longer connected
to the station cistern, and sometimes fresh footprints are
found in rooms and hallways the coastguardsmen have not
yet visited.

Over the years Coast Guard officials have grown tired
of hearing stories that suggest the Race Rock Lighthouse
is inhabited by ghosts or some other sort of supernatural
beings. To dispel what they regard as "wild and unsubstan-
tiated rumors," they allowed a television crew to visit the
facility in 2004. This resulted in a famous episode of the hit
cable TV serial *Ghost Hunters*. The intrepid hunters experienced many of the phenomena that others have reported in
the past—disembodied voices, water running through supposedly dry taps, and footprints they were certain that no
member of the film crew had made. They even managed to
film a chair moving across the floor in an otherwise empty
room.

No one, including the Ghost Hunters, has put forward
a satisfactory explanation for all these weird events. Those
with a penchant for the supernatural are certain the lighthouse is haunted by the ghosts of former keepers, of mariners

who drowned near Race Rock Reef, even of engineer Hopkin-son Smith and his "sea dog" construction foreman, Thomas Scott. Native Americans, if they were willing to talk about it at all, might say these sorts of things often happen in a place that belongs not to the living, but to the dead.

Part Two

SOUTH

Chapter 11

Theodosia and Virginia Visit a Circle of Stone

Cape Hatteras Lighthouse
Dare County, North Carolina

Two centuries ago somewhere along North Carolina's Outer Banks, pirates are said to have murdered Theodosia, daughter of the controversial American politician and duelist Aaron Burr. Today Theodosia haunts the beaches near the Cape Hatteras Lighthouse searching for the beacon that might have saved her. She is by no means the only ghost who walks these sands. There may very well be thousands, and many of them seem drawn to a mysterious stone circle not far from the old tower.

Dare County includes much of the Outer Banks, a 120-mile line of barrier islands that sweep from the North Carolina mainland almost 70 miles out into the Atlantic. Almost certainly it is the most haunted county in the entire United States. This is true in part because so many mariners have lost their lives on the ship-killing sands of the Banks, known to sailors as the "Graveyard of the Atlantic." It is true also because it was upon the Outer Banks that the English made their first attempt to plant a colony on the North American continent. The colony, established in 1587, failed and the would-be colonists—110 persons in all—disappeared under mysterious circumstances. After more than four hundred years, no one has yet discovered what became of them.

Among the colonists who vanished was one Virginia Dare, the first child born to English-speaking parents in North America. If Virginia's spirit does not haunt the Outer Banks, then no ghost haunts any place at all. She does haunt the Banks, however, and she has been seen in Manteo, Duck, Kill Devil Hills, Kitty Hawk, Nags Head, Rodanthe, Buxton, Hatteras, and many other places in her county. She also haunts the Cape Hatteras Lighthouse, and she is not the only famous female who does. Another is Theodosia Burr Alston, daughter of the notorious duelist, expatriate, and onetime vice president of the United States, Aaron Burr.

Countless other ghosts walk the sands of the Outer Banks. Among them perhaps are not just Virginia Dare, but the spirits of the other adventurous settlers who vanished along with North Carolina's "Lost Colony." Among them are thousands of mariners whose ships ran aground in the shallows of the Banks and were dashed to bits by the waves. Among them are the Lighthouse Service and U.S. Coast Guard keepers who saved countless lives by manning the maritime beacons at Bodie Island, Cape Hatteras, and elsewhere, and were so committed to their work that they refused to give it up even in death. Among them are even the Outer Banks themselves.

GHOST MOUNTAINS

Consisting largely of sand and loose gravel, the Outer Banks seem completely at the mercy of the Atlantic, a muscular and all too often unfriendly ocean. It is hard to understand how or why they exist at all, but the islands are definitely here and have been since at least the end of the last ice age. The materials that form the Banks are incredibly old. They are the pulverized remnants of solid rock that once composed a mountain range as extensive and lofty as today's Himalaya. Created 300 million years ago when the ever drifting continent of North America bumped into Africa, the great peaks—some more than 20,000 feet in elevation—were gradually worn down by erosion. They left behind today's Appalachians and Blue Ridge, referred to by some as "Grandfather Mountains."

Over the eons, crushed stone from the eroding summits of the original mighty ranges washed down rivers to be deposited at the edge of the continent, where they formed marshes and lowlands. In this way, the continental margin marched steadily eastward, encroaching on the Atlantic and forcing the ocean back hundreds of miles from the mountainous heartland. Then, about a million years ago, came the ice ages. When the last enormous glaciers melted between 10,000 and 12,000 years ago, the vast quantities of water they released raised ocean levels by as much as four hundred feet. As a result, the rising Atlantic halted its retreat in a counterattack that swept over beaches and flooded river valleys, forming the broad North Carolina Sounds and, well to the north, the Chesapeake Bay. Meanwhile, ocean waves bulldozed beach sands, piling them up into the lofty dunes that now form the Outer Banks.

So the beaches and dunes of the Outer Banks consist entirely of the crushed remains—the bones—of ancient mountains. It's hard to get one's head around such a notion when walking the warm Banks sands, but geologists know it to be true. However, an Outer Banks beachcomber whose mind and heart are attuned to spiritual things understands there is more to this story than geology. It's not just the bones of those incredibly old peaks that reside here. It is their very souls. The Outer Banks are the ghosts of dead mountains.

TWO MIGHTY RIVERS COLLIDE

The Outer Banks form an arrowhead-shaped point at Cape Hatteras. America's Mercury and Apollo astronauts were told to look for the cape when their orbits carried them over the East Coast of the United States. Although Hatteras is such a prominent feature that it can easily be distinguished from space, earthly mariners often have a difficult time seeing the cape. This is especially true at night or in foul weather, and there is plenty of that here.

Two mighty rivers in the ocean, the cold Labrador Current flowing down from the north and the warm Gulf Stream sweeping up from the Caribbean, pass close by Cape Hatteras. Somewhere off the cape they slam into each other, producing whirls, eddies, and blinding gales. What's worse, their strong currents push ships dangerously close to Hatteras and to Diamond Shoals, a broad system of shallows reaching up to eight miles into the ocean. As a result, Cape Hatteras and the barrier islands that extend northward and southwestward from it have claimed more than 2,300 large ships since the early 1500s. No one is sure how many passengers, ship's officers, and crewmen were killed in these wrecks, but the number must be very large indeed.

To make Cape Hatteras and the Outer Banks a little less dangerous, Congress authorized construction of a lighthouse here as early as 1794, but no brick was laid until late in 1799. The delay was caused, in part, by a political tiff. There were many in Congress who were adamantly opposed to spending money on such a project. However, Alexander Hamilton, who served as secretary of the Treasury under President George Washington, insisted that the government take action.

Hamilton's fervent support for the Cape Hatteras Lighthouse project had deep personal roots. In 1773, while still a young man, Hamilton had been a passenger on the bark *Thunderbolt* when it was caught in a gale near the Outer Banks. With no light on the horizon to guide him, the captain of the *Thunderbolt* tried to ride out the storm off Cape Hatteras, but his vessel took a fearful pounding from the high waves. The violent rocking caused coals to spill onto the wooden floors of the galley and started a fire that very nearly consumed the vessel. After the fire was put out and the crew nursed the badly damaged *Thunderbolt* back to port, Hamilton swore he would someday see to it that a lighthouse was built on Cape Hatteras.

That day came more than two decades after his brush with death off the Outer Banks, by which time Hamilton was serving as Treasury secretary. With a little help from his boss—Washington readily threw his support behind any project that might encourage maritime commerce—Hamilton was able to twist enough political arms to win a congressional appropriation for a Cape Hatteras beacon. Among the arms Hamilton twisted was that of New York Senator Aaron Burr, and the animosity this generated between the two men would eventually grow to tragic proportions. It would also lead to one of history's most bizarre coincidences.

Hamilton and Burr had been friends and comrades-in-arms during the Revolutionary War. Following the war, both men entered public life, and their political rivalry soon put an end to their friendship. Their differences went far beyond the question of appropriations for construction of lighthouses. Hamilton was a Federalist allied with Presidents George Washington and John Adams. Burr signed on with the emerging Democratic-Republican Party, led by Thomas Jefferson. The two men captained their respective parties in New York, one of the young nation's most populous and powerful states. Hamilton attempted unsuccessfully to prevent Burr from winning a seat in the U.S. Senate in 1791 and did manage to prevent Burr from becoming governor of New York, but the two were destined to play for even higher political stakes during the 1800 presidential election.

During that election, Burr had in essence campaigned as Thomas Jefferson's running mate. However, because of a quirk in the presidential election process at that time, Burr received exactly the same number of electoral votes as Jefferson, supposedly the top man on his party's ticket. This caused the election to be thrown into the House of Representatives, where Hamilton wielded a great deal of power. Although it took thirty-six separate votes in the House to finally sort out the confusion, Hamilton was able to secure the presidency for Jefferson. This left Burr with the vice presidency, but he took cold comfort in this secondary and largely ceremonial post. Privately, Burr was enraged by Hamilton's decision to side with Jefferson, and his anger festered as he and Hamilton began to trade vitriolic insults in the New York press.

Finally Burr challenged his rival to a duel, during which he shot Hamilton dead with a pistol. The incident utterly ruined Burr's once highly promising political career. Later Burr attempted to recoup his political fortunes in the West, where he still had many supporters. There he became entangled in an obscure plot that some said was aimed at carving out a new nation in the lower Mississippi region with Burr as its leader. The plot was uncovered, and Burr was put on trial for treason. Although acquitted, Burr went into voluntary exile in England, where he remained for several years. Then in 1812, just as the United States and Britain were about to go to war, Burr returned to New York.

LOVELY THEODOSIA

Among the most painful aspects of Burr's self-imposed exile was his separation from Theodosia, his much beloved only child. Following his wife's death from cancer in 1794, Burr had doted on his daughter, who blossomed into an elegant and highly attractive young woman. Burr often referred to her as the "Lovely Theodosia" and had made her head of his high-society household in Albany, New York. Eventually Theodosia married Joseph Alston, a politically prominent Southern aristocrat, and joined him in South Carolina. Theodosia had been deeply disturbed by the accusations made against her father and even more so by their long years of separation. News of his return to America greatly lifted her spirits. Not long after his arrival in New York, she decided to travel there from South Carolina for what was intended to be a joyous reunion.

Both Joseph Alston and Burr were afraid the journey might be too dangerous. The United States was now at war, the British had imposed a blockade on certain ports, and pirates had begun to prey on American freighters and passenger ships. Perhaps worse, winter was approaching and the coastal weather was often quite stormy at that time of year. Even so, Theodosia was determined to make the trip. During the early days of January 1813, she boarded the schooner *Patriot* in Charleston and set out for New York.

After a day or so at sea, the *Patriot* was stopped by a British warship. Armed British officers and marines boarded and searched the vessel, but having found nothing of military value, allowed the *Patriot* to continue on its way. The schooner then vanished into legend—along with Theodosia Burr Alston.

Normally it took about six days to reach New York from Charleston. When the *Patriot* failed to arrive as scheduled,

Burr was concerned, but in those days, ships were often late. Light winds could slow progress to a crawl, storms could damage sails and masts, or a ship might have to change course to avoid pirates or bad weather. There were countless reasons why a ship might be unexpectedly delayed, but after two weeks had passed, Burr began to fear the worst. In time he learned that a British warship had encountered the *Patriot* somewhere off the Outer Banks and that the vessel had been searched and released. He learned also that a powerful gale had swept over the Banks at about that time. All of this was said to have taken place just off Cape Hatteras, perhaps within sight of the Hatteras beacon. Weeks turned into months, and eventually both Burr and Alston gave up hope. Obviously Theodosia was dead. She had been lost at sea along with the *Patriot* and all onboard.

Burr would never recover from the loss of his daughter, and for the remainder of his days he would believe that she had been taken from him by a storm. Apparently this was not the case. During the 1830s, an aging seaman told a dark story of piracy and death off the Outer Banks. He said that many years earlier he had participated in the plunder of a schooner called the *Patriot* near Nags Head on the North Carolina Outer Banks. He said everyone onboard had been murdered.

During the late 1840s, a second former pirate confessed to the crime. His name was Frank Burdick, and on his deathbed he admitted to taking part in the brutal destruction of the *Patriot* and the murder of its passengers and crew. He said that a woman dressed in a fine white gown had been forced to walk the plank. Just before she plunged to her death in the Atlantic, the woman said her name was Alston and begged her killers to send word of her fate to her husband and father. Adding poignancy to his story, Burdick mentioned that he had noticed a fine portrait of the woman in one of the *Patriot* cabins.

After the Civil War a mysterious portrait of a lady dressed in white turned up in a North Carolina community not far from the Outer Banks. It had been owned by an old woman who said that members of her family had once made a living from looting vessels that had run aground on the Banks. She said that in 1813 they had found such a vessel, one that appeared to have been attacked by pirates. There was no one onboard, but there were still a few valuables scattered around, including the portrait. The old woman who told this story soon died, and the portrait made its way to descendants of Aaron Burr who confirmed that the likeness was probably that of Theodosia Burr Alston.

Ironically, Theodosia had met her gruesome fate not far at all from the lighthouse that owed its existence largely to her father's nemesis, Alexander Hamilton. Unfortunately for Theodosia, the navigational beacon some referred to as "Mr. Hamilton's Lighthouse" could have done little to save her. Or could it?

There are some who believe, and with good reason, that the *Patriot* was not attacked at sea. Instead it was lured to its destruction by pirates on land who confused the schooner's captain by displaying a false light at Nags Head. If the captain had seen the Cape Hatteras beacon instead, he might have saved his ship, and along with it, Theodosia. Some say that is why Theodosia's ghost is often seen in the vicinity of the Cape Hatteras Lighthouse, most often on foggy nights or in foul weather. The spectral lady is invariably dressed in white.

LIGHTHOUSE THAT ALMOST BECAME A GHOST

If in fact the captain of the *Patriot* did not see the Cape Hatteras beacon and that is what led to the demise of his ship, he was not alone in this respect. From the beginning the Hatteras Light had a spotty reputation as a coastal marker. The tower had been equipped with more than a dozen lamps designed to produce a light visible from eighteen miles out in the Atlantic. In reality the light was too dim and the tower was not tall enough for the beacon to be seen from that distance. Sea captains and navigators complained incessantly that they could not see the light, even when nearing the cape. In a report to the government maritime officials in 1851, U.S. Navy Lieutenant David Porter called Hatteras "the worst light in the world."

Describing his many journeys around the cape, Porter said: "The first nine trips I made I never saw the Hatteras Light at all, though frequently passing in sight of the breakers, and when I did see it, I could not tell it from a steamer's light, except that steamers' lights are much brighter." In response to Porter's report and to numerous other complaints, the Lighthouse Service had the tower raised to a height of 150 feet and placed in it a room-sized imported lens. Even this did not seem to help very much. The light remained dim if not invisible to ships far enough out at sea to avoid the Bank's deadly shoals and shallows.

Following the Civil War, the Lighthouse Service took radical action. The historic Cape Hatteras tower was blown up and replaced by one of the tallest brick towers ever built. Crowning the 193-foot tower was a $20,000 first-order Fresnel lens, the largest, best, and most expensive optical device available at the time. The result was a Cape Hatteras beacon that served mariners and the nation well.

Its bright light could be seen from twenty-four miles at sea, and consequently, the number of accidents along the Banks was reduced dramatically. Not only was the new lighthouse very effective, but because the stout tower was so well built and so sturdy, it has remained intact and in service to this day.

However, while human builders can erect long-lasting structures, they cannot halt large-scale changes caused by the forces of nature. For instance, they cannot hold back the ocean, and along the Outer Banks, the ocean has been on the march for many thousands of years. Originally the lighthouse stood almost a quarter mile from the nearest beaches, but over the years storm-driven tides sweeping along the face of sandy Hatteras Island cut ever closer to the foundation of the massive tower. Eventually the surf threatened to undermine its foundation. If nothing had been done to save the old tower, this historic national treasure would have toppled over onto the beach.

Fortunately, for those who love lighthouses and for mariners who still depend on its beacon, the Cape Hatteras Lighthouse has been saved from the hungry ocean. This was accomplished not by blocking the path of the tides, but by relocating the giant tower itself.

The idea of relocating a 193-foot-tall brick tower may have seemed fantastic, but boosted by a $12 million federal appropriation, the project was undertaken during the late spring of 1999. The International Chimney Company of Buffalo, New York, was selected to do the engineering and oversee the actual move. The technique selected by the movers called for excavating the stone foundation, raising the 3,500-ton tower with enormous house jacks, and lowering it onto steel rails not unlike those that carry heavy trains.

The actual move got under way at 3:05 p.m. on June 17, 1999, with a single forward lurch of only an inch or so. Thereafter, the tower glided along on its rails—lubricated with Ivory soap—at a painstaking rate of a few dozen feet each day. Near the end of the first week the tower passed over a dirt service road beside which some good-humored worker had put up a sign that read CAUTION! LIGHTHOUSE CROSSING.

It took more than three weeks to move the mighty structure to its new home, 2,900 feet from its original position and more than 1,600 feet inland from the Atlantic tides. When the tower finally reached its destination during the early afternoon of June 17, 1999, everyone who had wished the tower well breathed a sigh of relief. Among those who celebrated were schoolchildren across America who had watched the tower's progress from their classrooms.

The move had been completed in the nick of time. Only six weeks after the tower was placed on its new foundation a safe distance from Atlantic breakers, an unwelcome guest by the name of Hurricane Dennis arrived off Cape Hatteras. The big storm sent waves crashing over the Outer Banks dunes, inundating the former site of the lighthouse. Had the tower not been moved, Dennis almost certainly would have toppled it.

STONEHENGE OF THE OUTER BANKS

About a mile from the lighthouse and the handsome new National Seashore Visitor Center that stands beside it is another important monument. A broad circle of granite monoliths marks the original site of the Cape Hatteras Lighthouse, where it stood for 137 years before taking its epic journey in 1999.

These stones are special in another way as well. The Outer Banks Lighthouse Society had them inscribed with the names of the several dozen keepers who served at this remote light station. These Americans surely rank among the most dedicated public servants in our nation's history. Some of them lived for decades in this isolated place enduring loneliness and privation and weathering countless storms in order to save the lives of people they were never likely to meet. Standing in the presence of these timeless stone monuments that are intended to honor them, one speaks in hushed tones as if in a church or a graveyard. Perhaps the latter description serves best, because the Cape Hatteras stone circle is frequently visited by ghosts.

The specters of past storm victims, wrecked mariners, and the lighthouse keepers who labored so long and hard to save them seem to mingle here. Visitors have reported many ghost sightings either at the circle or on nearby beaches. As is the case in most other haunted places, the ghosts come out at night at Cape Hatteras. Sometimes their figures are indistinct, as if they were partly made of fog, but at other times they appear to be made of flesh, blood, and bone, like any living person.

A few brave nighttime visitors have reported conversations with ghosts. A Texas family who visited the circle shortly after dark during the spring of 2007 said they met an old man here dressed in what they thought was a sea captain's uniform.

"The steps are gone," the man said, gesturing toward the circle. "It's time to go up and light the lamps, but I can't find the steps."

At first the Texans couldn't imagine what steps the old man meant. Then it occurred to them that he might mean the steps of the Cape Hatteras Lighthouse and they pointed to it in the distance.

"No, no," said the old man. "That can't be the tower. The tower has always been here." Then he walked away into the dark.

When the family explored the Cape Hatteras visitor center museum the next morning, they found among the displays a photograph of a man who much resembled the person they had met at the stone circle on the previous evening. The uniform they had thought was that of a sea captain was actually that of a Lighthouse Service keeper. Apparently their nocturnal acquaintance had been a keeper here during the 1880s.

THEODOSIA REVISITED

Probably the ghost most commonly sighted on the dunes and beaches near the lighthouse appears to be a handsome young woman all dressed in white. Many think she is Theodosia Burr Alston. Perhaps, just as the old keeper was searching for the lighthouse steps, Theodosia is searching for the beacon that failed to save her and her companions aboard the *Patriot* two centuries ago.

However, there may be another reason Theodosia walks these dunes. Perhaps she is lost. It may be that, caught between two realities, she's not exactly sure of her identity. You see, there are other versions of the Theodosia story— several of them, in fact. One of them suggests that Theodosia may not have died as the confessed pirates described.

One element of the story that is often omitted is that Theodosia was never a particularly happy or stable woman. The death of her mother in 1794 while she was still a young teenager cut her loose in an often unfriendly world without the guiding hand of a close female relative. As a result, the pressures placed on her by her father's hard-driving ambitions proved too much for her, especially after his political career foundered following his duel with Alexander Hamilton. Her marriage to Governor Alston and her new life as First Lady of South Carolina provided her with a distraction, but only for a time. When young Aaron Burr Alston, her first and only son, developed a high fever and died late in 1812, Theodosia snapped.

Unable to console his wife or even to reach her through the fog of what increasingly appeared to be insanity, Alston suggested she visit her father in New York. Along with her he sent, as a gift for his father-in-law, a portrait of Theodosia painted in happier times. How could the governor have known that the journey he had hoped would save his wife's sanity would instead end in tragedy? Then, just off the Carolina Banks, the story took a sharp detour into the realm of legend and mystery.

Having run into a powerful gale, the captain of the *Patriot* steered west toward what he thought was calmer water. To his west he could see a ship's lantern rising and falling as if some vessel there were riding out the storm. Instead, the lantern had been tied to the neck of a mule being led along the Outer Banks dunes by pirates. These were not buccaneers who attacked their victims with an armed ship flying the Jolly Roger. No, these were landlocked pirates who lured their prey to destruction through deception. This time their trick worked perfectly, the *Patriot* ran aground, and the pirates swarmed onto her deck, slaughtering the passengers and crew with pistols and cutlasses.

One passenger was spared, however. She was a wild-eyed, crazy woman, and the superstitious pirates thought it would be bad luck to kill her. After all, who wanted to be chased around through life by a demented ghost? So she was adopted by the family of one of the pirates, and never being sure exactly who she was or where she had come from, she lived in a small cottage near Nags Head until she grew very old. Finally, on her deathbed, she gave her proudest possession, a portrait of a fine lady, to Dr. William Poole, the country physician who had attended her during her last hours. After she died, Dr. Poole took the portrait home with him. Some years later, a distant relative of the Burr family happened to visit Poole and thought the portrait looked a lot like another he had seen of Theodosia Burr Alston. Dr. Poole did not say so at the time, but years later it occurred to him that the portrait also bore more than a passing resemblance to the old woman who had given it to him.

Chapter 12

Searching for Blackbeard's Head

Ocracoke Lighthouse
Ocracoke Island, North Carolina

North Carolina's isolated Ocracoke Island can be reached from the mainland only by means of a two-hour ferry ride or by way of a shorter watery hop from nearby Cape Hatteras. In foul or foggy weather, ferry captains still rely on the powerful beacon of the historic Ocracoke Lighthouse to guide them into harbor. Although it has served mariners since 1803, the Ocracoke Light has not shined for nearly as long as the one generated by the island's most famous spook. It is said that for almost three hundred years the decapitated body of the pirate Blackbeard has walked the island's beaches at night holding a ship's lantern. What is Blackbeard searching for? Why, his head, of course.

Of all the pirates who ever plundered captive ships and butchered their helpless crews, none was more hated and feared than Edward Teach, known to most as Blackbeard. Teach made a dark science of piracy, and he practiced it without mercy and with a ferocious passion. Terrifying his victims into submission or blasting them to eternity with cannon and pistol, Teach became the scourge of the Atlantic during the early 1700s. He also became the subject of a worldwide manhunt that came to a bloody conclusion on November 18, 1718, not far from Ocracoke Island in what was then the British colony of North Carolina. On that day Teach lost his head, and apparently he has been looking for it ever since.

Born in England around 1680, Edward Teach went to sea as a teenager and turned to maritime thievery at an early age. For years he served as a privateer burning and pillaging small Spanish towns in the Caribbean, supposedly in the service of his native England, which was at war with Spain at the time. When the British made peace with Spanish, however, Teach did not. Instead he declared his own personal war against the entire world.

As captain of the forty-gun pirate ship *Queen Anne's Revenge*, Teach would attack any vulnerable vessel, regardless of the flag it flew. Ships unable to outrun or outgun him—and most could not—were forced to submit. Teach then came onboard with his heavily armed and foul-smelling companions and took whatever valuables he could find. If Teach thought any of the captured passengers or crew could be ransomed, he had them clamped into chains and thrown into his filthy hold. The rest were put to the sword or forced to walk the plank.

Those few whose vessels were attacked by the *Queen Anne's Revenge* and somehow lived to tell the tale later described their assailant as an extraordinarily tall man whose predatory eyes gleamed from above a long black beard reaching down almost to his waist. Because of the beard, which he sometimes wore in pigtails and adorned with black ribbons, Teach began to be called Blackbeard. This must have pleased the pirate, since he did whatever he could to promote his own fearsome reputation. The more frightening his aspect, the more easily he could intimidate his victims. Often when he boarded a captured ship, he stuffed burning cannon fuses into his tri-cornered cap. This wreathed his head in a hellish cloud of black smoke and gave many the impression he was the devil himself. Perhaps that was not far from the truth.

Blackbeard often carried several loaded pistols jammed into his coat and belt, and he would use them without hesitation to dispatch anyone who crossed him—friend or foe. On one occasion he pulled out a pistol and, without warning, shot his own first mate in the head. "I have to shoot one or two of you every now and then," Blackbeard told his astonished crew. "Otherwise you'll forget who I am."

For obvious reasons, Blackbeard had a lot of first mates. He also had a lot of wives—some fourteen in all. It is said that when he tired of a wife, he would pass her along to his crew for their enjoyment.

British authorities largely ignored Blackbeard so long as he preyed only upon the ships and possessions of the Spanish in the Caribbean. When he turned his guns on the lightly guarded British colonies in North America, however, they were forced to take action. In May 1718, a pirate fleet consisting of the *Queen Anne's Revenge* and three smaller ships attacked Charleston, South Carolina. Blackbeard and his men plundered several freighters anchored in Charleston's harbor and captured a number of the city's most prominent citizens. After receiving a large ransom, the pirate kept his part of the bargain by stripping his captives naked, humiliating them, and only then releasing them.

Determined to punish Blackbeard for this outrage, the British Navy launched a wide-ranging search, but they could not find the pirate. Blackbeard had located a snug hideout in North Carolina's Pamlico Sound, where the relatively shallow water made it impossible for large naval vessels to maneuver. Blackbeard was safe, but not for long. In November, less than six months after his attack on Charleston, a small fleet of armed sloops finally cornered the pirate.

Under the command of Lieutenant Robert Maynard, the sloops had been sent south from Virginia to confront Blackbeard and kill him. By this time the pirate had lost most of his fleet, including the *Queen Anne's Revenge,* to storms, wrecks, and mutinies. He had left only one ship and nineteen men, but he was still full of fight. When all but one of Maynard's vessels ran aground, Blackbeard unleashed his cannons on his remaining opponent, Maynard's flagship, the *Ranger.*

Thinking they had killed most of their enemies, Blackbeard and his men swarmed aboard the *Ranger* with cutlasses in hand, but they were in for a fatal surprise. Under the cover of the smoke produced by the cannon, Maynard and much of the *Ranger's* crew had hidden below deck. Once Blackbeard and the other pirates had been lured aboard, Maynard and his men let out a bloodcurdling cry and attacked with pistols and swords in hand. The battle went on until the deck was awash in blood. Most of it was the blood of the pirates, who could match the ferocity but not the fighting skill of the British. One by one, the pirates were worn down and slaughtered. The last of them to fall was Blackbeard himself. In all, it took five gunshots and more than twenty sword and knife wounds to subdue him.

To make sure Blackbeard was dead, Maynard chopped off his head with a cutlass. The head was tied to the *Ranger's* bowsprit, and the pirate's body was then dumped unceremoniously overboard. According to legend, when Blackbeard's still-living head saw his body hit the water, he shouted, "Come on, Edward." In response, the body swam seven times around the ship before finally sinking into the sound.

The place where Blackbeard was killed is now known as Teach's Hole, and for almost three hundred years it has been thought to be haunted by the pirate's headless ghost. It is said that his decapitated body walks nearby shores endlessly searching for his missing head, which incidentally, Maynard took home with him as evidence that he had achieved his purpose. However, the pirate's body may not be aware that his head was long ago spirited off to Virginia, since the deformed figure is often seen late at night marching along the shores of Ocracoke Island. If the wind is up, the body can be heard crying out, "Where's my head?"

Boaters and fishermen sometimes report an eerie light emanating from the shores of Ocracoke Island. Often described as a greenish phosphorescent glow, it is such a familiar sight hereabouts that it has been given a name. People who live on Ocracoke Island refer to it as Teach's Light. Indeed there may be some connection between the light and the ghost of Edward Teach, because the two are frequently seen on the same night.

More skeptical observers are of the opinion that Teach's Light is unrelated to Blackbeard and is actually a reflection of the Ocracoke Island Lighthouse beacon. The first Ocracoke Lighthouse was built in 1803 on Shell Castle Island inside the Ocracoke Inlet, not far from Blackbeard's former hide-out. However, that lighthouse was destroyed by lightning in 1818, almost exactly one hundred years from the day Blackbeard lost his life and his head.

A second lighthouse was completed some five years later, but it stood and still stands today not on Shell Castle Island, but on the banks of an inlet near Ocracoke Village. Among the oldest maritime beacons still active along the Southern coast, the Ocracoke Lighthouse is one of the many attractions of Ocracoke Island. Among the others is the ghost of Blackbeard, which somehow doesn't seem as threatening as the pirate himself. After all, he's no longer interested in plundering ships, taking captives, or hurting anybody. He just wants to find his missing head.

Chapter 13

Maryland's
Lighthouse Lady

Point Lookout Lighthouse
St. Mary's County, Maryland

Maryland is named for a lady, so perhaps it is appropriate that the state's best-remembered lighthouse keeper was also a lady. Her name was Ann Davis, and she kept the light at Point Lookout shining through storms and the chill of winter for more than thirty years. So complete was Ann's dedication to her work that she apparently refused to retire from it even in death. Generations of Point Lookout keepers felt themselves being scolded by her whenever they weren't diligent enough to meet her high standards. Some recent visitors believe she remains on duty at the lighthouse even today, more than 150 years after she died while still on the job.

Navigators have often scratched their heads when examining nautical charts of Maryland's Chesapeake Bay shoreline. Among the hundreds of peninsulas that protrude into the bay forming dangerous navigational obstructions are Point Lookout and Point Looking, not to mention Piney Point, Thomas Point, Woodland Point, Cove Point, Plum Point, Breezy Point, Sandy Point, Town Point, Rock Point, Hack Point, Concord Point, Turkey Point, and Point No Point. Even without the confusing flurry of names, it is hard enough to tell one of these long, skinny fingers of land from the others, but for mariners, knowing which point is which is extremely important. These headlands not only are hazardous to shipping, but they also mark key turning points where the captains of ships must decide which way to steer.

Most strategic of all the Maryland points is Point Lookout, for it divides the waters of the open Chesapeake from the broad reach forming the entrance to the Potomac River. Mariners have recognized the importance of Point Lookout since the first European ships entered the Chesapeake during the sixteenth century. However, no easily identifiable navigational marker was placed here until 1830, when federal maritime officials had a small lighthouse built down near the end of the point.

The Point Lookout Lighthouse was never intended to be a major maritime facility. Congress appropriated only $3,350 for the project, barely enough to purchase materials, build a modest residence for the keeper, and affix a tiny lantern onto its roof. Master stonemason John Donahue was among the few Maryland builders desperate enough to take on the project. Having already built unassuming lighthouses at Concord Point and Cove Point, Donahue moved along to Point Lookout, where he completed the job in a matter of months and pocketed a minuscule profit.

The federal government was extremely tightfisted during the early nineteenth century and was even less generous with its employees than it was with construction contractors the likes of Donahue. Often, lighthouse keepers earned only a few dollars a month in return for a laborious job that kept them up nights, provided no free weekends or other time off, and offered few if any other benefits. The job came with a house, however, and there were many who were glad enough to get a lighthouse-keeping assignment. Among them was the station's first keeper, a tough old Maryland man named James Davis. On the night of September 30, 1830, Davis climbed the tower steps to light the station's lamps, and for the first time in history, mariners moving up the Chesapeake from the sea could see a beacon shining from Point Lookout.

Low, sandy, alive with mosquitoes, and exposed to every sort of foul weather, Point Lookout was not a particularly healthy place to live. Davis proved this when, just two months into his tenure, he died of a disease of some sort, likely as not malaria. Left bereaved and penniless was Ann Davis, the lovely daughter the keeper had brought with him to Point Lookout. Fortunately for the young woman, James Davis's superiors allowed her to take over his duties and continue to live at the lighthouse, a decision that may not have been entirely due to pity. It may be that federal officials could find no one else needy enough to take the job.

Lighthouse keeping was hard, hard work, especially for a woman, but Ann Davis took to it with an eagerness and dedication that would last for the rest of her life. She kept the lens gleaming, the windows spotless, the brass railings polished, and the small station garden neat and carefully weeded. Each and every day at dusk she lit the lamps in the lantern and kept them burning throughout the night, never failing once in this essential duty for more than thirty years. Caring for the lighthouse must have taken a heavy toll on her, for in 1860, with the nation about to descend into the chaos of the Civil War, Ann Davis finally followed her father in death, leaving her work to others.

Many other keepers were destined to light the lamps at Point Lookout but none would perform this nightly ritual for longer than Ann Davis. George Willis came the closest, serving as keeper from 1917 until 1939, a stretch of twenty-two years.

But whoever was keeper and however long they remained at Point Lookout, they always felt that Ann Davis was looking over their shoulders as they worked. It was almost as if she were about to scold them. Was that window clean enough? Were the wicks in the oil lamps properly trimmed?

William Moody served as keeper from 1869 until 1871 and then again as a much older man, from 1908 until 1912, and both times he felt he shared the job—and the light-house—with some ghostly presence. Moody said he believed the presence was that of former keeper Ann Davis. Moody and other keepers not only felt Davis was near, but at times, they saw her as well. Her specter was sighted on the steps leading to the lantern, in the adjacent garden, and out along the beach. Although not often distinctly seen, the specter was said to have a kindly face and to be wearing a white blouse and blue skirt.

In 1966 the U.S. Coast Guard erected a steel skeleton tower on Point Lookout, equipping it with an automated beacon. Since the old lighthouse was no longer needed, its lamps were extinguished, the full-time keeper was removed, and the building was boarded up. Despite this, it is believed by some that Ann Davis remains at her post in the inactive lighthouse.

Today the lighthouse is part of Maryland's Point Lookout State Park. Although the building itself is rarely open to the public, park visitors are welcome to walk the grounds. Over the years visitors have had many encounters with Ann Davis, or so they claim. While they can't say for sure that the shadowy figure they've seen is in fact the lady keeper, they are quite sure she is smiling and wearing a white blouse and blue skirt.

SPIRITS IMPRISONED ON THE POINT

Ann Davis is by no means the only ghost who haunts Point Lookout. Visitors, park rangers, and docents have heard voices and seen mysterious figures here dressed in Civil War uniforms. Often the uniforms are shabby and the faces of the men wearing them tormented. All of this could possibly be explained by examining one rather dark chapter in the history of Point Lookout.

When the Civil War broke out in 1861, officials on the Union side were afraid the Confederates might attempt to attack unprotected installations such as the lighthouse at Point Lookout. To defend the point, the Union Army garrisoned a small fort here. Because of its relative isolation, Point Lookout was eventually made the site of a prison camp for captured Confederate troops. At first only a few gray-clad prisoners were kept here, but following the Battle of Gettysburg, their number swelled into the thousands.

Consisting of a fenced enclosure encompassing several acres, the prison was given the name Camp Hoffman. Designed to hold only about four thousand captive Confederates, the camp soon held more than twenty thousand. The prisoners slept in shabby tents and lived mostly in the open with little to protect them from the sun, rain, and winter cold. Thousands died from exposure, from drinking contaminated water, or from diseases that rapidly spread through the squalid camp.

More than four thousand of the prisoners who perished here are buried within a mile or so of the lighthouse grounds. A few small stones and monuments mark their graves, but for many years, their most widely recognized memorial was the beacon of the Point Lookout Lighthouse. With each flash it announced to all who knew the history of the point that thousands of lives had once burned brightly here but now had grown dark and cold.

When the lighthouse was shut down and its beacon discontinued in 1966, the dead prisoners of Camp Hoffman no longer benefited from so dramatic a symbol. If they were capable of resenting changes and events in the world of the living, then surely they took exception to this one. It may be that all victims of war die with a protest on their lips, one that can be heard long after they are gone. If this is true, then it might explain why so many people have heard strange and often anguished voices at Point Lookout.

Point Lookout park visitors say the voices seem to come from nowhere or from everywhere at once. Sometimes there are cries of pain and at other times desperate calls as if someone were trying to find a lost friend or loved one. Teams of parapsychologists have brought special equipment to Point Lookout, and they claim to have recorded on tape as many as twenty-four disembodied voices. The voices are both male and female and do not belong to any person, living or dead, who can be positively identified. Sometimes the voices sing either alone or in unison. Investigators say the faint songs are hard to identify, but they sound like what Civil War soldiers might have sung while sitting around a campfire.

Chapter 14
Phantoms of
Bloody Marsh

St. Simons Lighthouse
St. Simons, Georgia

Located not far from the site of an eighteenth-century clash of arms known as the Battle of Bloody Marsh, the St. Simons Lighthouse was the scene of a much later but no less gory fracas. During the late nineteenth century, two enraged keepers fought a battle of their own a short distance from the light tower they so carefully maintained. It ended with one of them lying on the ground in a lifeless, bloody heap. Some say that the murdered keeper's spirit still haunts the lighthouse and that at night his footsteps can be heard on the tower stairs.

First-time visitors to the Georgia coast may quickly conclude that this is a region unable to decide whether it is part of the land or of the ocean. A gap of several miles separates Georgia's nearly continuous wall of barrier islands from the dry mainland. The area in between is filled with a wriggling mass of crisscrossing inlets and seas of tall marsh grasses that often extend to the horizon. Beneath the grass is a layer of dense mud deep enough to swallow a ship or even a whole town. In fact, more than a few of the state's early coastal towns simply disappeared into the muck. One that did not was St. Simons, founded along with Savannah by General James Oglethorpe.

Oglethorpe came to America during the 1730s to establish a colony, which he named Georgia after Britain's King George I. Oglethorpe's colony might have been short-lived had it not been for a deadly confrontation in 1742 between an invading Spanish army and a relatively small band of British settlers. A few years earlier a Spanish warship had stopped the *Rebecca*, a British freighter under the command of Captain Robert Jenkins. When Jenkins refused to allow the Spanish to search his ship, a Spanish sailor cut off his ear. The incident precipitated a protracted and rather bizarre conflict between the British and Spanish known as the War of Jenkins's Ear.

By the 1740s, the Jenkins's Ear fighting had spread to the North American continent, and a large Spanish force invaded Georgia. Oglethorpe quickly raised as many troops as he could from among the small farms and plantations around Savannah, and hurried south to beat back the invasion. The decisive confrontation took place deep in the marshes near where Georgia's Altamaha River pours into the Atlantic. Under the leadership of Noble Jones, one of Oglethorpe's most trusted friends and lieutenants, the settlers defeated the Spanish, forcing them to return to their base at St. Augustine. In this way they managed to preserve the British colony of Georgia, which otherwise might have been known by its Spanish name, Guale.

In time, the small port of St. Simons grew up not far from the Bloody Marsh battlefield. Like most American ports worthy of mention, it would eventually be served by a lighthouse. The original lighthouse was built in 1810 at the southern extremity of St. Simons Island, just to the east of Brunswick, another Georgia port. The light was intended to mark an important inlet known as St. Simons

Sound. Constructed of tabby, the tower was a white, tapered octagonal structure seventy-five feet tall. It was topped by a ten-foot iron lantern lit by oil lamps suspended by chains. Serving first as a harbor light, it was raised to the status of a coastal light in 1857 when government lighthouse officials installed a third-order Fresnel lens.

However, the tower, residence, and other station buildings were destroyed by Confederate troops in 1862 as they retreated from the island. Following the war, the government let a contract to build a new station with a 106-foot tower, painted white. As was the case with the building of many Southern lighthouses, a mysterious sickness—probably malaria—plagued the construction crew. The contractor himself fell ill and died in 1870. One of the bondsmen took charge of construction in order to protect his investment, but he, too, fell victim to illness shortly after his arrival. Despite the lives lost during construction of the St. Simons Lighthouse, the tower was completed by a second bondsman, and the lamps were lit on September 1, 1872.

The St. Simons Island Lighthouse remains in service to this day, and its imported crystal Fresnel lens is still in place. The beacon flashes white once every minute and can be seen from more than twenty miles away. This historically important and well-preserved light station has been listed on the National Register of Historic Places since 1972. It might also be listed on the National Register of Haunted Places if there were such a thing.

Very few lighthouses along America's coasts and lakeshores are more widely believed to be haunted than this one, and no wonder. The tower produces strange wailing sounds, mysterious footsteps are heard on the tower stairs, and lights appear where there should be none. Island residents and visitors alike are convinced the old lighthouse is inhabited by one or more ghosts.

WHO'S THERE?

The most commonly told ghost story associated with the St. Simons Lighthouse is linked to a violent incident that took place near the lighthouse in 1880. The keeper of the light at the time was Frederick Osborne. Having gotten on in years, Osborne had hired a much younger man named John Stevens to serve as assistant keeper. Apparently the two did not much like each other. It is said that Osborne was a difficult man who forced Stevens to take on menial tasks and then was highly critical when they were not completed to his satisfaction.

One Sunday morning, after Stevens had finished washing the windows at the top of the tower, Osborne found a spot on one of the panes. Osborne angrily confronted Stevens about this, accusing him of sloppiness and general incompetence. Stevens fired back with accusations of his own. Stevens had a young wife and had grown suspicious of Osborne's apparent interest in her—all three lived in the same residence. The confrontation became deadly serious when Osborne pulled out a pistol. Seeing the weapon in Osborne's hand, Stevens fled down the tower steps, ran to the residence, and grabbed a shotgun that was housed in a gun cabinet there.

Still brandishing his pistol, Osborne found Stevens on the station grounds beside the tower. This time, however, both men were armed. When Osborne approached Stevens in a threatening manner, the assistant fired the shotgun, striking the older man in the stomach. Horrified by what he had done, Stevens hurried Osborne to a hospital in nearby

Brunswick, but the keeper soon died. Not long afterward Stevens was arrested and put on trial for murder. Convinced that Osborne had been killed in self-defense, the jury acquitted Stevens, who then returned to his duties at the lighthouse.

Eventually Stevens became the official keeper of the light, but he was never happy at St. Simons. Things never seemed to work right—oil and other supplies ran out sooner than they should have, brass rails grew tarnished just moments after he had polished them, even well-trimmed wicks refused to burn properly, and for no apparent reason, the lamps that powered the St. Simons beacon were often extinguished in the middle of the night, forcing Stevens to relight them. What's worse, Stevens was constantly bothered by strange noises, especially in and around the tower. He heard unexplained whistling and clanking and mysterious footsteps on the tower staircase. When he washed the gallery windows, he was sure he could hear a voice pointing out dirty spots and streaks he had missed. For obvious reasons, Stevens came to believe that the lighthouse and he himself were haunted—almost certainly by the ghost of Frederick Osborne.

"Who's there?" Stevens called out when he thought he heard footsteps in the tower or in the lighthouse residence. Visitors said the often agitated Stevens sometimes shouted the same question even when they themselves had heard nothing.

"Who's there?" he demanded, but there was never any reply.

Acquaintances said Stevens grew weary and old long before his time. Some said he was haunted to the end of his days by accusing specters that resided, not coincidentally, in both the lighthouse and his conscience. However, there is plenty of evidence that the sounds Stevens heard were not just figments of his imagination.

WHO'S THERE, I SAY?

In 1907 Carl Svendsen, his wife, and their dog, Jinx, moved to the then almost deserted island to tend the light. The Svendsens happily went about their professional and domestic business, unaware of the tragedy that had unfolded there twenty-seven years earlier. Mrs. Svendsen always waited for her husband to clamber down the tower stairs from the light room before she put dinner on the table. One evening, hearing a heavy tread on the steps, she set out the food as usual. But this time, when the shoes reached the bottom step, her husband did not appear. Jinx barked an alarm and then scampered off to hide in a dark corner of the room.

"Who's there?" Mrs. Svendsen called. "Who's there, I say?"

Unsure of what to think, Mrs. Svendsen climbed the lighthouse steps to look for her husband. She found him still in the lantern room at the top of the tower working with the lens. She told him what she had heard, and at first Svendsen feared that his wife had gone daft. Then, a few days later, he himself heard the phantom footsteps. They made a very distinct sound.

"Clump, clump, clump," Svendsen said when he described the noise to others. "That's the sound we hear. Clump, clump, clump."

The Svendsens lived in the St. Simons lighthouse and tended its beacon for twenty-eight years. During all of that time they never came across an adequate explanation for the footsteps, which they continued to hear for decades.

The sound of the eerie steps never failed to send Jinx into a frenzy.

Even today people still hear footsteps in the St. Simons tower when there is no one inside to produce them. Visitors have also seen apparitions both in the historic tower and around the residence, which is now open to the public as a museum. There are those who say that all this is the work of Frederick Osborne, who was never able to give up the job that was so abruptly taken from him by a shotgun blast in 1880. However, there are other theories put forward to explain the haunting. Some say the place is haunted by the ghosts of Spanish soldiers killed at the Battle of Bloody Marsh.

It has even been suggested that the ghost is that of Noble Jones, who commanded the outnumbered British forces that slugged it out with the Spanish in 1742. Incidentally, Noble Jones was not just a soldier, but also an engineer. He is credited with having designed and built the first Tybee Island Lighthouse in Savannah, another structure said to be haunted by his ghost. What's more, according to family legend at least, he may be an ancestor of the author of this book.

Chapter 15
A Girl, a Kitten, and a Cigar

St. Augustine Lighthouse
St. Augustine, Florida

One often hears the laughter of children at the St. Augustine Lighthouse and Museum, which is likely the most fascinating destination in Florida's most interesting city. It's a sunny place, the ocean is nearby, there is an enormous tower with delightful barber-pole stripes, and kids can climb way up high and see just about forever. So why shouldn't children enjoy themselves here? And with so much youthful energy and mirth around one might think that the laughter of a tiny ghost would hardly be noticed. Sometimes people do notice it, though, echoing through the hollow tower or along an empty corridor.

Parents bring their youngsters to St. Augustine because they want them to learn about a part of America's past that is sometimes overlooked in history classes. It was not just the British or the French who sent soldiers and settlers and tried to establish a permanent presence along what is now the East Coast of the United States. The Spanish, too, had colonial ambitions here and planted a settlement in Florida hoping it would grow up into a rich and populous part of Spain's far-flung empire. The capital of Spanish Florida was St. Augustine, which had a good harbor and a military garrison intended to keep the British out of the Florida Peninsula.

Near the harbor entrance the Spanish built a watchtower where keen-eyed soldiers were stationed so they could sound the alarm in the event an attacking fleet was spotted on the horizon. The tower may also have served as a lighthouse to help Spanish warships and freighters move safely in and out of the harbor. While the St. Augustine beacon may have burned brightly for a time, the light of Spanish Florida did not, and in 1821 Spain sold the colony to the United States.

Shortly after the U.S. acquisition of Florida, the Lighthouse Service replaced the old Spanish tower with a much taller structure. Reaching an elevation some seventy-three feet above sea level, the new tower was almost certainly the tallest structure in Florida, and it would remain so for a long time. While the light it produced was relatively weak and not particularly useful to ships out in the Atlantic, it served adequately as a harbor beacon for nearly half a century. The lighthouse survived the wide-ranging destruction of the American Civil War only to lose its battle against nature. Storm-driven tides were cutting away the land in front of the tower and by the 1870s they threatened to inundate the entire lighthouse. Attempts were made to hold back the Atlantic by placing barriers along the shore, but these were soon swept away

Realizing that this war with the ocean waves could not be won, lighthouse officials decided to build another lighthouse at a more secure location on nearby Anastasia Island. The structures completed there in 1874 are among the most remarkable ever built by government work crews. Counting the iron lantern at the top, the brick tower was 167 feet tall and enclosed workrooms as well as a staircase with 219 steps. The lantern was fitted with a room-sized, first-order Fresnel lens so powerful it could focus a beacon visible from up to twenty-four miles out in the Atlantic. The original lens remains in use today, and the tower still has the distinctive spiral black-and-white stripes that help mariners distinguish it from other lighthouses along the Florida coast. Adjacent to the tower is the elegant duplex residence where generations of keepers and their families once lived.

Today the old lighthouse residence is a museum, but it once percolated with the bustle of family life and the joys and tragedies that always accompany it. There were weddings held in the residence and babies born in its bedrooms. There were also deaths in the dwelling and elsewhere on the lighthouse property. According to museum records, several people died either at the current or the previous St. Augustine Lighthouse.

DEADLY OCCUPATION

The first known St. Augustine Lighthouse death came in 1853 when the keeper, John Carrera, passed away from unknown natural causes. Lighthouse keeping was hard work, and some people could not stand up to it. Carrera had spent years carrying heavy loads and climbing up and down the tower steps, and his heart may simply have given up on him.

During the nineteenth century, lighthouse towers were among the tallest buildings in existence. Keepers and their assistants were used to working at considerable heights, and no doubt they took precautions against falls. Even so, accidents did happen, and an especially tragic one befell Joseph Andreu in 1859 when he plunged to his death from near the top of the St. Augustine tower. It is not clear how or why Andreu fell, but he may have been painting or doing other types of repair work on the outer walls of the tower and slipped. Or Andreu may have been on the narrow walkway of the gallery outside the lantern room and fallen over the railing. Although the St. Augustine tower in Andreu's day was less than half the height of the current one, the keeper nonetheless fell about seven stories. He never had a chance. Some say they can still hear the scream of the falling keeper, and that is all the more interesting because the original lighthouse, including the tower from which he fell, has been gone now for more than a century.

Yet another keeper, William Harn, drew his last breath at the St. Augustine Lighthouse on April 1, 1889. Harn was afflicted by consumption, the lung disease known today as tuberculosis. Demonstrating the dedication typical of Lighthouse Service keepers, Harn had kept up with his duties even as the disease slowly overcame him, making it harder and harder for him to breathe. After his death, Harn's wife, Kate, took over his responsibilities at the lighthouse.

A BLUE DRESS

Death is never more tragic than when it comes upon children at play. When the existing St. Augustine Lighthouse was built during the 1870s, a miniature railway was constructed to bring brick, lumber, tools, and hardware to the construction site. These materials and supplies were shipped in on specially designed Lighthouse Service freighters called tenders, loaded onto small railcars, and then pulled by horses or pushed by hand over the rails to the lighthouse.

On July 10, 1873, a group of children who happened to be playing near the construction site climbed aboard one of the railcars, and it began to roll down toward the beach. No doubt it was all great fun at first, but as the car went faster and faster, the children became frightened. By that time, alas, the car was going too fast for them to jump. Probably they cried for help, but it was already too late for the workmen or other adults in the area to reach them. The car slammed into the surf, spilling the five children into the water. Workers dove in behind the car and managed to save the two youngest children, a boy and a girl. The other three drowned. Among the dead were two daughters of St. Augustine Lighthouse construction superintendent, Hezekiah Pity—Eliza, age thirteen, and Mary, age fifteen. Pity was saddened for the rest of his days by this tragic loss, but the incident would have another lasting effect. It would lead to one of America's best-known and most widely reported hauntings.

For nearly 140 years people have reported sightings of Eliza and Mary in and around the lighthouse. The girls have been seen on the steps and in the lantern room of the tower, in every room of the lighthouse residence, and down by the water's edge where the accident occurred that cost them their lives. Sometimes the Pity sisters are seen in the company of another, younger girl, apparently the third of the three children who died. However, Mary is the one seen most often. Usually she is wearing a blue velvet dress and a blue ribbon in her hair, just as she was said to have worn on the day she died.

Over the years keepers have seen the ghostly girls, as more recently have lighthouse visitors and members of the museum staff. What's more, they've heard the children's exuberant chatter and laughter. Usually ghosts frighten people, but these youthful spirits don't seem to scare anybody. Instead of haunting the place, they inhabit it. They present themselves much like dusty old family photographs, and their voices echoing from long ago serve as reminders that life can be heartbreakingly short.

SKYDIVING KITTEN

Although lighthouses can be dangerous places, they can also be delightful environments for kids. Children who visit the St. Augustine Lighthouse nowadays nearly always wear bright smiles on their faces. The same might also have been said of many of the children who grew up here and at similar light stations during the days when lighthouses served not just as navigational aids, but as homes for keepers and their families.

Cardell Daniels, who was keeper of the St. Augustine Lighthouse during the 1930s, had several children, and they roamed the property more or less at will. Of course, they sometimes got into mischief. On one occasion a couple of the Daniels kids tied a tiny parachute onto the family kitten and dropped the unfortunate creature from the top of the tower. The result was not as disastrous for the cat as one might imagine. It drifted to earth, perhaps not so gently as the Daniels children had hoped, but it hit the ground on all fours and took off running. It is said the kitten hid out in the scrub for nearly three weeks before rejoining the Daniels household, apparently none the worse for wear.

Lighthouse museum visitors sometimes say they hear a cat crying in the tower. Staff members search the premises but never find a living cat to accompany the feline calls. This may lead one to imagine that the St. Augustine tower must be counted among the many structures around the world that happen to be haunted by cats.

There are other ghosts that wander the lighthouse property, not just the Pity girls or the Daniels cat. As a matter of fact, the place is crowded with them. People hear all sorts of voices here. Some of them speak Spanish, so the haunting may date to before 1821, when Florida became a U.S. possession.

One frequently reported specter is said to be the ghost of Dr. Alan Ballard, the original owner of the property on which the lighthouse stands. Ballard was not willing to sell his property to the government, at least not for the price he was offered. Eventually the land was seized by right of eminent domain. The outraged doctor swore he would never leave the property, and apparently he has been true to his word.

Ballard may have been joined by Peter Rasmussen, an early twentieth-century St. Augustine Lighthouse keeper. Notorious for his addiction to cigars, Rasmussen was rarely seen without a fat stogie in his mouth. Smoking is not allowed at the lighthouse nowadays. Even so, the smell of cigar smoke is often evident both in the tower and the old residence. More than a few who have noticed it have drawn the conclusion that Rasmussen's spirit remains with the lighthouse and that the keeper still enjoys a puff or two.

Chapter 16
Captain Johnson's Lantern

Carysfort Reef Lighthouse
Near Key Largo, Florida

There are those who say that the Carysfort Reef Lighthouse is not haunted. The weird banging and clanging sounds heard there are caused by the tower's iron braces expanding in the hot sunshine or contracting in the cool of the night. That may be so. However, anyone who has seen this open-frame, cast-iron structure rising from the open ocean like a giant skeleton, or heard the spooky moans and groans that come from it when the wind churns up the seas, or seen the strange lights that emanate from it even when the beacon is not shining, may have other notions.

When completed in 1852, the 110-foot, iron-skeleton Carysfort Reef tower represented a completely new approach to lighthouse construction. Legendary contractor Winslow Lewis, a former sea captain who built many of the nation's early masonry light towers, submitted a bid to erect this one using familiar stone construction techniques. Lewis had invented a special lamp and lantern that was supposed to make America's lighthouses much more effective. Instead it produced a barely visible light that was more a threat than a help to mariners. Sometimes sea captains actually ran their ships aground while looking for one of Lewis's beacons. So it should have come as no surprise to Lewis when government officials rejected his bid. No doubt adding insult to injury, they ended up adopting a more radical plan put forward by the contractor's own nephew—and harshest critic—I. W. P. Lewis. The younger Lewis had described his uncle's construction techniques as "hopelessly out of date" and his lamp and lantern beacons as "less than worthless."

I. W. P. Lewis got the contract for the Carysfort Reef Lighthouse, and U.S. Army engineers built the structure he had envisioned in open water directly over the reef. The tower still stands, more than a century and a half after it was built, on eight cast-iron legs arranged in an octagon some fifty feet wide. Each leg was anchored to the sea bottom by a screw pile stabilized with massive iron discs four feet in diameter. Instead of being hammered into place like ordinary piles, the screw piles were twisted into the mud and coral underlying the reef. The heavily braced legs held aloft a twenty-four-foot-wide platform on which a two-story keeper's dwelling was built. A second platform about a hundred feet above the water held the lantern room. Keepers reached the lantern room by way of a staircase rising through a cylinder centered between the outer piles.

This structural arrangement worked well and it was adopted for use at many other offshore lighthouses built in the Florida Straits and elsewhere. The Carysfort Reef Lighthouse has proven so sturdy that it serves its purpose as well today as it did when it was completed more than 150 years ago. It has stood straight and tall through more powerful hurricanes than anyone can count, and it will very likely survive many more.

One thing has changed at Carysfort Reef, however. Although keepers and their assistants lived at this isolated offshore station for more than a century, the keeper's quarters have been empty since 1958. That's the year the U.S. Coast Guard automated the light and ordered its former keepers ashore. No one was sorry to leave. This was true, in part, because it can be rather unpleasant living in the confined quarters of an open ocean structure utterly exposed to any gale or hurricane that happens to come along. But there was another reason the Coast Guard keepers were glad to leave.

For more than a century, keepers here were troubled by a bizarre groaning and screeching heard primarily during the summer months when temperatures in the Florida Straits soared. There were those who believed the noise was the work of a ghost said to have been that of a man named Johnson who, like Winslow Lewis, was formerly a ship's captain. As the story goes, Captain Johnson had few redeeming qualities. It was said that Johnson was such a bad man that when he died in an accident during construction of the Carysfort Reef tower, his spirit was condemned by fate to roam the reef forever.

The loud noises supposedly made by Captain Johnson were first heard only a few weeks after the tower was completed and the beacon began warning mariners away from the destructive reef. Keepers assigned to the station complained about the noises, but there was very little Lighthouse Service engineers could do to help. After all, they could not change the structure itself since the tower was already built, and if the problem was a ghost, well, then, exorcising troublesome spirits was not really their line of work. So keepers had no choice but to live with the clamor, which sometimes was so loud that it jarred them awake in the middle of the night. However, relief from the racket and more restful slumber invariably came with the approach of autumn when the tower quieted down and finally fell silent.

Absent during the cool weather months, Captain Johnson began his banging again in the spring. The loud sounds were heard throughout the summer until the fall, and then quieted once again. Generations of Carysfort Reef keepers had to put up with these cyclic noisy visitations. Some believed the stories concerning Captain Johnson and others did not, but what none could deny was that the noises were very real and very loud.

During the 1920s, a young fisherman stopped off at the lighthouse, had dinner with the keeper, and spent the night. The young man had barely fallen asleep when the groaning and banging began. Frightened by the sounds, he ran for help and was calmed by an assistant keeper who told him the story of Captain Johnson, the resident ghost. As it turned out, this particular fisherman was a skeptical, hard-minded sort like I. W. P. Lewis, who had designed the tower many years earlier. He understood the basic principles of engineering and how metal responds to rapid changes in temperature. Later he informed his hosts that the noises were caused by the stretching and contracting of the tower's metal girders and braces. The key to this explanation lay in the fact that the sounds were heard only during warm months when metal was likely to expand.

The fisherman's scientific assurances had little impact on the keepers, who continued to believe in Captain Johnson. Keepers often kept an open Bible on the station table hoping this would keep the captain's ghost at bay. Sometimes the Bible served its purpose, and sometimes it did not—particularly during the summer.

During the more than half a century since the Carysfort Reef Lighthouse was automated, there have been many reports concerning the tower's noisy summertime symphony.

Boaters who approach the tower to take pictures say they hear the sounds, and some say they've seen a mysterious light shining from the supposedly empty keeper's quarters. What could it mean? Whether the ghost of Captain Johnson is or is not in residence, there may be other spirits who might have wanted to haunt the place. One, perhaps, was I. W. P. Lewis, who likely looked upon the giant iron tower as his crowning achievement. However, an even more likely candidate is Lewis's uncle Winslow, who was certainly angered by the government's decision to reject his design for the Carysfort Reef Lighthouse and select his nephew's plan instead. Maybe Winslow Lewis goes about in summer banging on the pipes as a form of protest and a way to say, "No, you've got this all wrong!" And the mysterious lights seen in the keeper's dwelling? Surely those are produced by one of Winslow Lewis's mostly ineffectual lamps.

Chapter 17
Captain Appleby's Island

Sand Island Lighthouse
Near Key West, Florida

Unfairly accused of being a pirate, Captain Joshua Appleby proved his honesty by guiding countless ships to safety with the bright beacon he kept on Sand Key, a few miles from Key West, Florida. Alas, while the good captain saved the lives of many others, he could not save his own or those of the loved ones who happened to be visiting him when a prodigious hurricane struck Sand Key. The big storm smashed the lighthouse and washed away the island on which it stood. Vanishing along with Sand Key were Appleby and his visitors, but their spirits have returned. Nowadays they haunt the open-water lighthouse built to replace what was once the captain's home.

In 1820 Joshua Appleby, an out-of-work New England sea captain, migrated from his native Rhode Island to the Florida Keys in search of a new life. There he became what at the time was commonly known as a "wrecker," one of the freebooting opportunists who salvaged foundered ships and cargoes and sold them for a profit. In the treacherous Keys, where sea traffic was on the increase and unmarked reefs and shoals ripped apart the hulls of ships almost daily, the wrecking business was booming. Although it was mostly legal, many considered wrecking a highly questionable enterprise. Seamen often looked upon the wreckers as little better than pirates, and some were, in fact, former buccaneers.

Appleby was no pirate. Instead he was a hardworking pioneer, who established a thriving settlement on Key Vaca, where he fished, hunted for turtles, and, when the opportunity came his way, salvaged shipwrecked vessels. The laws about what could be taken and what could not were notoriously vague, and Appleby may have stretched a legal point or two during an 1823 salvage operation that got him thrown into prison. The evidence was thin, though, and Appleby was soon released.

By 1837 the incident had been forgotten. That year Appleby was appointed keeper of the Sand Key Lighthouse, replacing Rebecca Flaherty, who had served as the station's keeper since it was established in 1827. A low, almost invisible islet about seven miles to the southwest of Key West, Sand Key had long been a boon to wreckers such as Appleby. Ships regularly ran aground on the island, where they were battered to bits by the waves. Ironically, keeper Appleby now undertook the prevention of just the sort of incidents that had once brought him fat profits. Every night he faithfully lit the fourteen whale-oil lamps in the Sand Key tower and made certain they burned throughout the night to give ships ample warning.

A widower, Appleby lived alone on the island except for occasional visits from friends or family. His wrecking career now far in the past, his life was mostly devoid of excitement, except when major squalls or hurricanes struck Sand Key, as they did almost every summer. Appleby and his lighthouse weathered powerful hurricanes in 1841 and again in 1842. Then came several relatively quiet years.

The summer of 1846 had also been a quiet one, so much so that, when October arrived, the keeper was sure the hurricane season had ended. He felt it safe to invite his daughter Eliza and three-year-old grandson Thomas to the island. With them came Eliza's friend Mary Ann Harris and her adopted daughter. No doubt, at first the visit was a joyous one for Captain Appleby, but it would end tragically.

On October 9, 1846, Havana was hit by a hurricane so powerful that it left the city in ruins. On the following day that same storm struck the Florida Keys. Appleby and his visitors had no way of knowing what had happened in Cuba or that death was on its way. Likely it would not have helped if they had known. There was nowhere to run. It is easy to imagine the old seaman checking his barometer every few minutes. The mercury would have dropped so low that he likely thought it was broken. Then the winds and tides came up. By the time they had settled down again on the following day, the light tower and keeper's dwelling were gone. So, too, were Appleby and his visitors—their bodies were never recovered. Even Sand Key itself had sunk beneath the waves.

The Sand Key Lighthouse was not rebuilt and returned to service until 1853. Designed and constructed under the direction of U.S. Army engineer George Meade, the same man who years later led the Union Army to victory at the Battle of Gettysburg, the new lighthouse was built in what was now open water. Perhaps with the 1846 disaster in mind, Meade gave the tower a solid foundation of twelve hefty iron pilings. Once complete, the tower stood on heavily braced legs, forming a square with sides sloping inward toward the lantern and gallery at the top. Fitted with a first-order Fresnel lens, it displayed a flashing light capable of warning mariners up to twenty miles away.

The keepers of the new Sand Key Lighthouse lived in a rectangular structure nestled between the spidery legs that held it thirty feet or more above the surface of the ocean. This arrangement kept the building safe from storm-driven waves and made it possible for Sand Key keepers to ride out major hurricanes. Had such a structure existed in 1846, Captain Appleby and his loved ones might have survived.

Some keepers thought they had reason to believe that, having been released from his body upon the open ocean, Appleby's ghost eventually migrated to the new lighthouse. Keepers were sure that at night they could hear the captain's voice and also the voices of women and children. Sometimes these voices were happy and at other times agitated. Perhaps the Sand Key ghosts wished to explain how their lives had ended on that day of stormy violence in 1846.

Just before the United States entered World War II in 1941, Sand Key's grand old Fresnel lens was removed and the beacon automated. Some time afterward the last official Sand Key keepers packed up their belongings and departed. For the past seventy years the lighthouse has continued its job of guiding mariners without the assistance of living human hands. It is difficult to say whether ghostly hands have now taken over the task of keeping Sand Key's vital navigational light burning.

Chapter 18
Guardians of the
Hurricane Coast

Pensacola Lighthouse
Pensacola, Florida

When hurricanes rolled in off the Gulf of Mexico, coastal residents could flee inland and ships could make a run for the open sea, but lighthouse keepers had nowhere to hide. Many drowned when tidal surges inundated their homes or were crushed when the fierce winds bowled over their light towers. The spirits of these brave men and women may still inhabit their former light stations, or they may have found new homes in more durable lighthouses, such as the fortresslike brick giant at Pensacola.

Covering 582,100 square miles in a warm blanket of tropical water averaging a mile in depth, the Gulf of Mexico is enclosed on three sides by land. Often, however, the shores of the Gulf are not dry land in the usual sense. The swamps, marshes, and barrier islands that line the coasts of Florida, Alabama, Mississippi, Louisiana, and Texas seem undecided as to whether they belong to the sea or the shore. In fact, they may change their status each time a major hurricane passes through to inundate islands and wash away long stretches of coast. This never-never quality of the Gulf coast makes it an extraordinarily dangerous place for mariners and lighthouse keepers. So, too, do the mighty storms that roll in off the Gulf nearly every hurricane season. Some major hurricanes pack winds of up to two hundred miles per hour, exerting a force equal to several nuclear blasts.

Given a choice, sailors and their ships will run for open water and ride out the storm at sea—better that than be caught in the shoal-strewn, hull-grinding narrows near the land. On the other hand, people onshore may not be able to get out of the way when a big storm approaches. Because they lived in exposed places only a short distance from the onrushing waves, lighthouse keepers and their families were especially vulnerable. More than a few keepers paid with their lives—and all too often the lives of their loved ones—for their dedication to duty. At one time or another, lighthouses all along the Gulf coast have been irreparably damaged or swept away altogether by hurricanes. In more than a few such cases, the keepers, their assistants, and families vanished along with the towers and residences.

Just such a calamity befell several Gulf lighthouses on September 27, 1906, when one of the most powerful and deadly hurricanes in history came racing out of the Caribbean. At Round Island Lighthouse near Pascagoula, Mississippi, this tropical behemoth sent waves crashing to the top of the fifty-foot tower. Driven up the tower steps to escape the rising waters, the keeper managed to save himself by taking refuge in his final redoubt—the lantern room at the very top. The keeper of the nearby Horn Island Lighthouse was not so fortunate. When a rescue party finally made it to the island after the storm, they found no trace of the tower, the residence, keeper Charles Johnson, or his family. Six feet of water now covered much of the island, including the site of the former lighthouse.

The great storm was most powerfully felt near the entrance to Mobile Bay, which is likely where its enormous eye first touched land. Standing guard at the entrance was the 132-foot brick tower of the Sand Island Lighthouse. Keeper Andrew Hansen and his wife might have seen the storm coming, but by that time it was far too late for them to escape. Anyway, Hansen had to try to keep the light burning in hopes of assisting mariners attempting to flee the storm. Unable to flee, the Hansens had no choice but to hunker down as best they could and endure their fate.

When the storm had finally passed by and winds subsided, the big Sand Island tower was still standing, but the raging flood tides had washed away the residence, storage buildings, and even the four hundred–acre island that had once surrounded the lighthouse. Unfortunately, the Hansens were swept away along with the island, and their bodies were never recovered. A lighthouse inspector who visited the area soon after the storm sadly noted in his report: "Sand Island Light out. Island washed away. Dwelling gone. Keepers not to be found."

Although the Sand Island tower had been severely damaged, it was soon repaired and returned to service. In place of the island that had once provided its base, the tower was protected by an artificial island of broken stone. Since there was no room for a residence, keepers went back and forth to the tower by boat from a house on nearby Dauphin Island.

Dauphin Islanders believed the Hansens' spirit surely must have remained behind to haunt the old, storm-battered tower. However, Sand Island keepers never mentioned in their official reports so much as an unexplained chill or spooky feeling, let alone a bona fide ghost sighting. It may very well be that the Hansens, so suddenly removed from the world of the living, lingered in this realm, but if so, where did they go? Ghosts do not always stay put, and it is easy to understand why the Hansens wouldn't want to remain on Sand Island, which, after all, no longer existed. Might they have sought out the comforting surroundings of another lighthouse? And wouldn't it likely be a sturdier structure, one far less vulnerable to gales and hurricanes?

HAUNTED GIANT

About fifty miles to the east of the former Sand Island stands one of the strongest and most impressive buildings on the entire Gulf coast—the 171-foot brick tower of the Pensacola Lighthouse. Located on a marshy island at the entrance to strategic Pensacola Bay, this seventeen-story monolith has stood tall in the face of more furious storms than anyone can count. Built in 1858 with a federal appropriation of $55,000—an unthinkably large sum at the time—it was intended to guide U.S. Navy warships to their base at Pensacola. Naval commanders wanted a dependable beacon, one they could be sure would be there regardless of the weather. Consequently, the Pensacola tower was given fortresslike walls several feet thick at the base.

Even so, the lighthouse had been in operation for only a few years when it was nearly destroyed, not by a hurricane, but by a storm of human making—the Civil War. The tower was cannonaded first by invading Union troops and later by the Confederates when they tried to destroy the lighthouse to prevent their enemies from making use of its beacon. Despite the pounding it took from shot and shell, the tower survived the war.

The Pensacola Lighthouse has also withstood bombardment by nature. Not only has it successfully resisted the hurricanes that descend on this stretch of coast every few years, but it has also survived countless lightning strikes.

In 1875 a pair of lightning bolts seared the lantern, melting and fusing the metal gears that turned the lens and caused the light to flash. Ten years later an earthquake shook the structure so hard that the keeper imagined "people were ascending the steps, making as much noise as possible." But while many nearby structures were leveled by the temblor, the Pensacola Lighthouse remained standing. It is easy to understand, therefore, why lighthouse keepers both living and deceased might find it a comforting place to inhabit.

Keepers and their families who lived at the lighthouse right up until the light was automated in 1965 never felt they were entirely alone here. There always seemed to be some unseen presence. They heard footsteps on the tower stairs when they were supposedly alone in the building. They heard voices calling to them, apparently from nowhere, and at times the very walls seemed to be speaking.

Emmitt Hatten, who as a child lived with his parents in the station residence when his father was keeper here during the 1930s and 1940s, said he often heard the sound of breathing in the lantern room. "When I went up there to work, I could hear human breathing," said Hatten. "I listened carefully, and I was sure it wasn't the wind."

Hatten also occasionally heard footsteps on the stairs leading to the lantern room. He would call out, "Who's there?" He never received a reply.

Hatten came to believe that the unusual phenomena he experienced at the lighthouse might be linked to a murder said to have occurred there during the early twentieth century. The killing took place in the residence when the keeper's wife became enraged during an argument and plunged a knife blade deep into her husband's chest. The incident supposedly left a bloodstain on the pine floors of the kitchen.

Others thought, and continue to think to this day, that the lighthouse would have been haunted anyway, even without the murder. The Pensacola Lighthouse was, they believed, a sort of vortex or doorway, a link between the world of our daily experience and another place altogether—the realm of light and legend. It is within this realm that the Hansens and other brave lighthouse-keeping families who lost their lives to storms now dwell.

Chapter 19

1900 Hurricane Victims Still Cry for Help

Bolivar Point Lighthouse
Galveston, Texas

On September 7, 1900, one of the most destructive hurricanes in history drove thirty-foot tides over the low barrier islands and sandy peninsulas south of Houston, Texas, drowning thousands in Galveston and other hard-hit coastal communities. A few dozen lucky refugees managed to save themselves from the merciless flood by climbing the steps of the Bolivar Point Lighthouse. However, many others reached the big iron tower too late, arriving only after the fast-rising waters had blocked the entrance. Some say that when the wind blows in from the Gulf of Mexico, the desperate cries of these unfortunate storm victims can still be heard.

Texas Highway 87 does a very odd thing in Galveston. Motorists following this scenic old coastal byway may be surprised—shocked even—when it runs up against a waterside barrier down near the northeastern tip of Galveston Island. That's not the end of the road, however. A quick glance at any foldout road map reveals that Route 87 continues along the sandy spine of the Bolivar Peninsula, which is separated from Galveston Island by two miles of water. In between the island and the peninsula is the deepwater inlet that links Galveston Bay to the open waters of the Gulf of Mexico. The road actually continues out across the inlet, but the crossing is not made on a bridge or causeway. Instead, it is made by way of a ferry that departs Galveston every half hour or so and arrives at Bolivar Point about fifteen minutes later.

Operated by the Texas Department of Highways, the Bolivar Point Ferry is a rather modest little ship. One would not make any sort of extended journey on such a vessel. It is more or less a floating strip of Highway 87 asphalt, and as if to emphasize this point, a yellow no-passing line is painted right down the middle of the deck. Despite its rather utilitarian appearance, though, the ferry has its charms. Chief among them is a terrific view of Galveston, the inlet, the Bolivar Peninsula, and best of all, the Bolivar Point Lighthouse.

When seen from the water, the Bolivar Point Light Station lends the impression that it must still be a going concern. It's not. Although the dwellings and other buildings on the property appear to be well maintained, the one hundred–foot black iron tower is showing distinct signs of aging. The tower's metal shell is streaked with rust and there is no lens at the top. The lantern room makes one think of an empty cage from which the birds have long since escaped and flown away.

Having served mariners faithfully for more than ninety years, the Bolivar Point beacon was snuffed out in 1933 and the lighthouse property sold into private hands. It remains on private property to this day and is off limits to the public. Even so, the tower can be seen and appreciated from both water and land, and on Highway 87 it is possible to get close enough to the tower to hear its sad and eerie song. The tower makes strange whistling noises when Gulf breezes blow across Bolivar Point, but some people say these are not caused by the wind. They say the tower is haunted by the souls of the men, women, and children who died here more than a century ago during the deadliest hurricane in American history.

CANNONBALL LIGHTHOUSE

Bolivar Point's first lighthouse was completed in 1852. It had an iron tower much like the one that can still be seen here today, but it survived for only about a decade. Shortly after the Civil War broke out in 1861, the Confederates pulled down the tower and used the iron to make weapons. In essence, the Union's own lighthouse was melted down and forged into shot and shell to fire at blue-clad Union troops.

Following the war, construction of a replacement was delayed for several years by lack of funding and a yellow fever epidemic that caused much of the Texas coast to be placed under quarantine. Erected at a cost of $50,000 by work crews brought in from New Orleans, the new Bolivar Point Lighthouse was finally completed in 1872.

Like its predecessor, the 117-foot tower had an iron, cocoon-like shell designed to protect it from wind, rain, and storm. The tower's sturdy construction enabled it to survive gale-force winds, and its considerable height lifted most of the structure well above the tidal surges that often accompanied major storms. All of this made the old tower one of the few secure places of refuge when hurricanes bore down on Galveston and the Texas barrier islands. The most ferocious of those hurricanes—at least, the worst such storm to date—struck during the late afternoon of September 8, 1900. The following is the story of that catastrophe and the role played in it by the Bolivar Point Lighthouse and its heroic keeper.

BEACON IN AN HOUR OF DARKNESS

Standing in the gallery of the Bolivar Point Lighthouse, keeper Harry Claiborne could see clear signs that trouble was on the way. From his high perch above the entrance of Galveston Bay, Claiborne looked down on the pristine Texas beaches, where on most days the blue-green Gulf of Mexico wallowed lazily in the sand. But now the mood of the Gulf had changed drastically. Its waters had turned gray and angry, and it pounded the dunes with enormous waves.

Earlier in the week, when Claiborne had gone into the nearby resort town of Galveston to buy a month's supply of groceries, there was already a hint of uneasiness in people's faces. All summer long the hot, humid air of Galveston Island had buzzed with mosquitoes, but now it vibrated with tension. The weather station on the island had received a distressing cable. Trinidad, on the far side of the Caribbean, had been devastated by a hurricane so powerful that few structures were left standing. It was impossible to say where this deadly storm was now, but sailors arriving at Galveston's bustling wharves brought still more troubling news. They told dock workers, saloon keepers, ladies of the night, and anyone who would listen that they had come through "hell" out in the Gulf. Somewhere out there lurked a killer hurricane.

At the turn of the century, meteorologists had no radar or computer-enhanced satellite photos to help them track weather systems; there was no telling where a big storm like this would strike next. It might drift to the east and vent its fury in the empty Atlantic. More likely, however, it would rush northward out of the Caribbean and into the Gulf of Mexico, following a well-traveled path known to sailors as "hurricane alley." In that case, it would threaten all the Gulf shore states, from Florida to Texas.

Chances were slim that the storm would hit any one stretch of coastline, so the people of Galveston had no immediate cause for alarm. But then the wind picked up, and high, wispy clouds shaped like fish scales were seen racing westward over the island. The atmospheric pressure started dropping so fast that the barometer at the Galveston Weather Station seemed to have sprung a leak. Seeing these rapid changes, the Weather Bureau put out an emergency forecast—just one word—and editors of the local paper set that word in very large type for their morning editions: **HURRICANE.** Strangely, most people ignored the warning. Some even rode out to the island on excursion trains from Houston to witness the natural spectacle firsthand. Throughout the morning of September 8, larger and larger crowds gathered to watch the huge waves slamming into the Galveston beaches. Children squealed with delight and clapped their hands as the big waves crashed down, throwing frothy spray into their faces. It was a tremendous show.

Seeing the big crowd of spectators gathered on the shore, Weather Bureau meteorologist Isaac Cline could not believe his eyes. Was it possible that these fools were ignorant of the imminent danger they faced? Cline knew hurricanes often generated tides of a dozen feet or more; the town was only eight feet above sea level. It required very little mathematical skill to deduce that a really powerful storm could wash right over Galveston Island and drown everyone on it.

Cline drove up and down the beach in a horse-drawn buggy, shouting at people to go home or, if they could, to get to the mainland. Few listened to him. The twentieth century had arrived, bringing with it trains, steamships, electric lights, and bottled soda. Why should anyone fear a summer storm? Desperately, Cline pointed to the hurricane flags cracking like whips in the wind. But few noticed the flags, even when the gale started ripping them to tatters.

The revelers at the beach would not listen to the plea of a weatherman, but the weather itself soon confronted them with a more forceful argument. A wooden pagoda-like structure stretched several hundred feet along a two-block stretch of the Galveston beach. It was used on holidays and weekends as a dance floor and as a boardwalk for strolling lovers. But now the surf was using it as a punching bag. The pagoda began to sag, and within minutes the waves turned it into a surging mass of driftwood. This calamity finally convinced people that the approaching storm meant business. Much to Cline's relief, the crowd of wave-watchers began to disperse. Those who lived nearby hurried home and nailed up their shutters. Others began to look for ways to get off the island. But for many it was already too late.

At Bolivar Point Claiborne made sure his light had plenty of oil. Its beacon would be needed by ships caught in the storm and seeking haven in the calmer waters of Galveston Bay. The keeper did not know it yet, but the lighthouse itself would soon become a haven for scores of terrified people struggling to keep their heads above a boiling flood tide.

A prosperous seaport and resort, turn-of-the-century Galveston had its share of turreted Victorian palaces. Surrounded by tall palms and oleanders, the houses lined the handsome boulevards that ran down the spine of the island. But only a few of Galveston's forty thousand residents lived in mansions. Most made do in rundown tenements and shacks clustered on the low, marshy ground near the wharves. It was the poor who first felt the murky floodwaters swirling around their ankles. Forced to abandon their meager belongings, they fled toward the center of the island, where the homes of the rich stood on slightly higher ground. The relentless tide followed, however, and soon there was no longer any spot on the island that could rightly be described as dry land. Dozens drowned, then hundreds, then thousands.

The high water was not the only danger. The wind hurled boards, beach chairs, and massive tree limbs through the air. It turned pebbles into bullets and shards of broken glass into daggers. It ripped the redbrick tiles from the roofs of public buildings and sent them spinning through the streets to decapitate or crush the skulls of hapless victims. To be out in the open meant death.

Driven from his house by the rising water, Claiborne sought safety within the strong brick walls of his lighthouse. But he had barely closed the heavy metal door behind him when people started pounding on it, begging him to let them in. Despite the gale and the fast-rising water now covering the floor of the lighthouse, Claiborne shoved open the door. After all, he was in the business of saving lives.

Before long the tower was crammed all the way to the top with frightened men, women, and children, who clung desperately to the steps and rails of its spiral staircase. More than one hundred people, many of them from a train that had been stranded by the flood, found sanctuary in the lighthouse; Claiborne must have wondered how he could fit in any more refugees. After a while, though, no one else came. In fact, the big door was soon hidden under as much as thirty feet of water.

To save themselves from drowning, people on the lower steps had to clamber over the heads and shoulders of those above. Terror-filled voices cried out in the near-total darkness. Some called the names of loved ones, hoping that they, too, were safe somewhere above or below on the steps of the tower.

As the hours passed and the storm continued to rage, the air inside the lighthouse grew stifling and fetid. Muscles and limbs became so cramped that people screamed with pain. Some grew ill and threw up on the heads of those below. But no matter how miserable they were, no matter how awful conditions inside became, no one doubted that things were much worse outside. The wind howled and whistled, blasting the tower at speeds of up to 150 miles per hour. Swept along by the flood, the trunks of fallen trees slammed like battering rams into the walls. The tower shook and the staircase quivered, but the old walls, built more than three decades earlier, held fast.

People outside the tower snatched safety wherever they could find it, often in the unlikeliest of places. Some climbed palms and clung to the fronds while the wind clawed at them hour after hour. Others grasped the girders of bridges that had been only partially demolished and pulled themselves up out of the flood. Still others hung onto floating boxes and timbers.

A few of the city's solidly built stone mansions stood up to the storm. Pressed together in the upper rooms of these fine old homes were bank presidents and black gardeners, wealthy matrons and Chinese sailors, debutantes and muscular Latin stevedores. The hurricane had blown away all traces of social distinction.

In the heart of the city, a "lighthouse" very different from the one at Bolivar Point also became a refuge from the storm. A high brick wall surrounding Galveston's Ursuline Convent served as a kind of dike to hold back the flood. Nuns pulled scores of helpless storm victims out of the torrent and over the wall to safety. Among those rescued by the nuns was a pregnant woman who had survived by using an empty steamer trunk as a boat. That night in the convent, the woman gave birth to a baby boy who, though he would remember nothing of it, had just lived through the greatest adventure of his life.

PALE FACE OF DAWN

Sometime during the early morning hours of September 9, the hurricane passed inland toward the dry plains of west Texas, where it dumped the last of its prodigious rains. Having dwindled to little more than an ordinary thunderstorm, it wreaked no further havoc other than to flood a few gullies and teach a number of lizards and horned toads to swim. But the storm had already done far more than its share of damage at Galveston.

When the waters receded sufficiently that the refugees at Bolivar Point could escape their lighthouse prison, they pushed through the tower door into the sunlight. At last they could breathe and stretch their tortured limbs. But they took no joy in freedom. Confronted by a scene of utter desolation, they huddled together in horrified silence. Buildings had been knocked down, homes flattened, bridges smashed, ships capsized, trains swept off their tracks, entire communities obliterated. But the most shocking sight of all was right there beside them, just outside the door. Piled up around the base of the lighthouse lay dozens of bodies, many of them stripped naked by the flood. It was as if the tower had been a huge tree, and all these unfortunate people had tried desperately to climb it and keep their heads above the flood. They had failed.

Similar piles of bodies could be seen everywhere throughout the ruins of what once had been the bustling city of Galveston. At least eight thousand people were killed by the storm and the flood tide that accompanied it, but many more may have died. The exact number of dead will never be known.

Even after the storm had passed, the survivors still faced much suffering and hardship. The hurricane had knocked down the bridges and washed away the causeways linking Galveston to the mainland. There were no boats. Every vessel in the harbor, from the largest freighter to the smallest dinghy, had been wrecked or sunk. Cut off from the outside world, the city was without fuel, sanitation, or medical facilities of any sort. People could find no food, no shelter, and no unpolluted water to drink. And worst of all, something had to be done with all those bodies.

At Bolivar Point Claiborne fed and sheltered as best he could the people who had weathered the storm with him in the lighthouse. He quickly exhausted the month's allotment of groceries he had purchased only a few days earlier. He figured he would get by somehow.

On the evening after the hurricane, Claiborne trudged up the steps of the tower. By this time he was no doubt approaching total exhaustion, but duty required him to start up his light and make sure it had plenty of oil. For crews on the battered ships that had ridden out the storm in the Gulf, the Bolivar Point Light was a welcome sight. It was also a comfort to the citizens of Galveston, who had endured so much during the previous forty-eight hours. Each time the beacon flashed, they were reminded that some things, at least, still worked and that even in the darkest hours, a few safe havens remained.

HAUNTING REMINDERS

Today there is no one left alive who remembers Galveston's night of utter, devastating darkness. Nowadays, Galveston is a bright, happy-go-lucky beach town. Sunbathers parade along the beaches and around the city dressed in or out of whatever they have decided to wear or not wear. Surfboards shade the windshields of small cars, mountainous scoops of ice cream threaten to shatter flimsy cones, and gentle breezes support a rainbow of fancy kites. People come to Galveston to have fun, eat fried fish, and get a suntan. Nobody wants to be reminded that for a few horrible days at the turn of the twentieth century, Galveston was a giant, watery coffin.

Even so, there are reminders of the great calamity everywhere. In more than a hundred years, the beach has never returned to the graceful crescent shape and golden color it had before the storm. Although likely left by more recent gales or by careless construction workers, bits of debris found in vacant lots here and there are highly suggestive. It is hard not to see them as the shattered pieces of an earlier Galveston, the one that vanished on the night of September 8, 1900.

Then, of course, there are the voices. If one stands still and listens carefully—at Bolivar Point or anywhere along the coast near Galveston—it is possible to hear whispers. These are not quiet remarks shared by intimate passersby who want to keep their conversations private. This is Texas, after all, and people here are not shy about speaking up. No, these faint sounds are more like the waves one hears when holding a seashell against an ear. They may be nothing more than an illusion, but impressionable listeners could certainly imagine them to be an attempt at communication—an effort to reach across the seemingly impenetrable barriers of time and death.

If these sounds are voices, then what are they trying to tell us? Are they hopeless cries for help? Are they protests from thousands of storm victims whose lives were cut brutally short? Or do they constitute a warning? Might they be trying to tell us that the exuberant Galveston beach resort we see today is itself an illusion and a highly tenuous one at that? Their message and the meaning of the great black monument of the Bolivar Point Lighthouse may be that a mighty storm is brewing out there somewhere in the Gulf of Mexico, and it is headed our way—if not today or this summer, then next year or some year soon after.

Part Three

GREAT LAKES

Chapter 20

Ghost Light of Presque Isle

Old Presque Isle Lighthouse
Presque Isle, Michigan

When a lighthouse beacon turns on and off all by itself, people are likely to take notice. This is especially true if the lighthouse has been out of service for more than century, and truer still if there is no lamp to light the lens and no electric power to light the lamp, even if there was one. Who or what lights up the long-dark Old Presque Isle beacon on warm summer nights? No one is quite sure, but curious tourists and ghost hunters now frequent the old sentinel hoping to solve the mystery.

The eastern extremity of Lake Superior and the northern extremities of Lakes Michigan and Huron form a watery vortex. It is here that the three mightiest of the Great Lakes come together, Lakes Michigan and Huron by way of the narrow Straits of Mackinac and Lake Superior with the rest of the Great Lakes via the St. Marys River and the Soo Locks. Some of the heaviest shipping traffic on the planet once passed through these bottlenecks, which still carry far more than their share of maritime commerce.

It is also here that some of the most powerful Midwestern storms strike, often during the month of November, and their effect on ships and lives can be devastating. In 1975 a November storm claimed the famed *Edmund Fitzgerald* along with twenty-nine seamen in eastern Lake Superior, only a few dozen miles from the locks at Sault Ste. Marie. A November blizzard in 1958 took the *Carl C. Bradley* and drowned thirty-three seamen in northern Lake Michigan not many miles west of the straits. And in November 1913 one of the most powerful Midwestern storms in history destroyed dozens of ships and hundreds of lives on Lake Huron, many of them in the upper reaches of the lake.

Maritime officials were long ago aware that this region was strategic and that it was a dangerous place for ships and their crews. For this reason some of the oldest lighthouses on the western Great Lakes were built here, often to mark bays and harbors thought to offer safety during a storm. One such lighthouse was the thirty-foot rubble stone tower built on Presque Isle in 1840. Its relatively crude and not particularly bright beacon was intended to guide mariners into the harbor on the south side of Presque Isle, where they sometimes sought shelter from storms or anchored while their crews gathered cordwood to stoke their boilers.

The name Presque Isle was given to this place by French trappers during the eighteenth century. It means "almost an island" or, more loosely translated, "not an island" and, indeed, Presque Isle is no island. A narrow neck of land links it to the Michigan mainland, forming what is in effect a T-shaped peninsula. The trappers who named Presque Isle may themselves have thought the area was haunted. There is little evidence that they tarried here for long, even though the harbor was good and food and beaver were plentiful in local forests.

Despite its advantages, Presque Isle was not destined to attract a large population. With the assistance of lighthouses established and run by the federal government, many harbors along the shores of the Great Lakes became thriving ports, but that didn't happen at Presque Isle. Perhaps, in part, it was frustration over this fact that led to construction of a new and more impressive Presque Isle lighthouse following the Civil War. Navigators had complained that the original lighthouse was woefully inadequate. The tower was too short and its light too weak for the beacon to be seen from any significant distance out on Lake Huron. What was needed was a lighthouse with a much taller tower and a more powerful lens. Funded by a substantial appropriation from Congress, just such a structure was completed in 1871 on a site a mile or so north of the existing lighthouse.

OLD PRESQUE ISLE LIGHT SNUFFED OUT

Once the New Presque Isle beacon began to shine, the original lighthouse was no longer needed. The keeper's residence was boarded up and the lantern room was removed from the tower along with the lamp, lens, and other critical lighting equipment. Afterward the historic lighthouse was allowed to slowly deteriorate, and by the turn of the twentieth century it had mostly fallen into ruin. By that time the crumbling residence and tower probably looked more spooky and haunted than they do today. The decaying structures might have collapsed and vanished altogether if not for a prominent Lansing, Michigan, family who happened to be fascinated by lighthouses.

In 1900 the lighthouse was purchased for $70 at a tax sale by Bliss Stebbins, owner of the nearby Grand Lake Hotel. Stebbins intended the historic buildings to serve as the centerpiece of a picnic ground enjoyed by guests of his hotel, and the structures were used in this way for many years. Eventually the property was taken over by other members of the wealthy Stebbins family who had made considerable fortunes with their car manufacturing, farm equipment, and millinery businesses in Lansing. They rebuilt the keeper's dwelling for use as a summer retreat and also restored the crumbling thirty-foot tower. To make it look like a real lighthouse again, they replaced the tower's missing top portion with a lantern room salvaged from another abandoned lighthouse. They even managed to obtain a surplus Fresnel lens and installed it in the tower. An ordinary lightbulb was placed inside the lens and from time to time it was switched on at night to delight local children and romantic summertime visitors.

By the 1950s the old lighthouse had become something of a tourist attraction. Each summer visitors flocked to Presque Isle and many knocked on the door of the restored residence asking for a tour and, perhaps, a chance to climb the steps of the tower. Usually these requests were granted, but the constant comings and goings of visitors made it difficult for the owners to enjoy their retreat. Always business minded, the Stebbins family finally gave in to the inevitable and turned the property into a profitable living history museum. Caretakers were hired to serve as live-in "keepers" of the Old Presque Isle Lighthouse and Museum.

In 1977 George and Lorraine Parris took over as keepers of the facility. A retired electrician, George Parris was a people-loving extrovert, and he put on quite a show for museum visitors. Sporting a Lighthouse Service uniform and an old-fashioned beard, Parris took them up the hand-hewn stone tower steps, telling jokes and stories as he went. In the lantern room he explained how the Fresnel lens worked, how it guided freighters, and how it saved the lives of sailors who might never have seen the lighthouse in the daytime or shaken the hand of its keeper.

Tourists often begged Parris to turn on the Old Presque Isle beacon and let it shine once more over Lake Huron, but this he could not do. The Coast Guard had ordered the Stebbins family and their museum caretakers not to light the beacon since it did not appear on nautical charts and might confuse navigators. To make sure this order was not and could not be violated, Parris had disconnected the electric lines that supplied power to the lantern room.

For most visitors the absence of an active beacon did not detract from their museum experience. The ebullient personality of George Parris was all the light they needed, and he brightened the day of nearly everyone who walked through the museum door. Parris loved his work and kept at it right up until he died of a heart attack on the day after New Year's in 1992. It was later that year that the Old Presque Isle ghost light first appeared.

Lorraine Parris was the first to see the light. Grieving for George, Lorraine had not at first wanted to return to her duties at Presque Isle, but she soon decided to resume her life as caretaker of the museum. The 1992 tourist season had begun much as it had in years past, though sadly, without George Parris. Visitors came, enjoyed the exhibits, climbed the tower, took in the spectacular views from the lantern room, and then left. Things seemed to have settled down to a routine, that is, until one evening in early May when Lorraine was driving back to the museum from a trip into town to pick up supplies. She happened to glance up at the tower and what she saw there took her breath away. The light was shining! How could that be?

Lorraine was deeply concerned, and all sorts of troubling possibilities came to mind. Had some mistake been made? During those confused months after her husband's death, had someone restored electricity to the lantern room and placed a fresh bulb inside the lens? Or had someone broken into the tower during her brief absence? Lorraine didn't know what to think, but when she arrived at the lighthouse, she found no one in the tower, no light in the lantern room, and the power supply disconnected just as it had been for more than a decade.

Surely she had just been imagining things, or so Lorraine thought. She continued to think that until the light appeared again about a week later, and this time Lorraine wasn't the only one to see the ghostly beacon. Other Presque Isle residents and summer visitors reported that they had seen it too. Some observers noticed that the beacon they saw wasn't glaring and white like the light produced by an incandescent bulb. Instead it was a soft, pale yellow glow like the light generated by an old-fashioned oil lamp. Someone said they had trained a set of binoculars on the tower at night and seen an indistinct figure moving about the lantern room.

WELL, SURE IT'S GEORGE

Inevitably, news of the ghost light's appearance attracted attention and by midsummer crowds had begun to gather along the shore at night hoping to see it. Usually they were not disappointed. As if it were being turned on and off by a keeper with a pocket watch in his hand, the light came to life shortly after sunset and disappeared again at dawn. The crowd murmured, "Who could it be up there turning on the light?" Nearly everyone agreed that "it must be old George."

"Well, sure it's George," said Lorraine. "George was an electrician, and who else would know how to turn on the light except God and an electrician?"

Eventually the light attracted official notice as well. Boaters had reported seeing an uncharted beacon at the head of the Presque Isle harbor, and before long a U.S. Coast Guard officer gave Lorraine a call concerning the light. Reminding her that an uncharted navigational beacon could pose a threat to boaters and seamen, he told her the light must be kept off at all times. "I'll be very happy to turn it off," Lorraine replied. "But first you'll have to explain how it comes on."

Later, a Coast Guard technician turned up to see if he could identify the source of the light. Naturally, he focused his attention on the lantern room at the top of the tower and on the antique Fresnel lens it housed. He made absolutely certain that the wires that once supplied electricity to the bulbs inside the lens had been cut. He rotated the big lens to change the angle of its prisms. Then when night came, he made sure all the lights were off in the museum and the tower itself, but all this was to no avail. The light came on anyway.

The coastguardsman decided to try one more thing. He requested that all the lights in the area be temporarily doused. This even included the beacon of the nearby New Presque Isle Lighthouse, which remains to this day an active aid to navigation. Even when the entire area was plunged into darkness, the ghost light continued to shine. In fact, it was brighter than ever!

The inspector shrugged his shoulders, packed up his equipment, and prepared to leave. In his opinion, the ghost light wasn't powerful enough to confuse mariners and create a navigational hazard, so the U.S. Coast Guard would wash its hands of the matter. So what was producing the light? He had no idea. Maybe it was some sort of stray reflection of the moon or the stars, but whatever it was, he was unwilling to endorse the notion that the ghost of George Parris was turning on the light.

Others were not so sure. Later that summer, during a family picnic near the lighthouse, a young mother brought her little girl to the museum. They had planned to climb the tower to enjoy the view from the lantern room, but no sooner had the girl started up the steps than she turned around and ran screaming. She said she had seen a man up there, a man with a beard, and he had frightened her. Both Lorraine Parris and the girl's mother checked the tower but there was no one either on the steps or in the lantern room. They asked the girl to describe the man she had seen. He was tall, had white hair and a beard, and he was wearing glasses. It was a description that might easily have fit George Parris.

Over the years since 1992, the ghost light of Presque Isle has continued to shine. People still see it both from the shore and from boats out on the lake. More than once over the past two decades mariners have claimed the light guided them to safety during storms. When they show up at the museum to thank the keeper, they are told that there is no official light and no official keeper. The guiding light they've followed is the famed spirit light of Presque Isle, and its keeper, if there is one, is George Parris.

Chapter 21
Witch of November

New Presque Isle Lighthouse
Presque Isle, Michigan

On windy days the tall brick tower of the New Presque Isle Lighthouse in Michigan produces wild shrieks, sending shivers down the spines of local folks and visitors alike. Some say the haunting sounds they hear are the calls of a plaintive human spirit, the ghost of a former keeper's wife driven insane by loneliness. Others say they are the cries of the Witch of November, who returns each year to terrify—or drown—Great Lakes mariners.

November brings a marrow-deep chill to the bones of sailors on the Great Lakes. It's not just that the weather turns cold—temperatures can plunge precipitously in a matter of hours—but also that the lakes themselves change character. They turn tempestuous and develop sharp, unpredictable tempers. Storms can darken the ordinarily bright blue faces of these vast lakes with little or no warning and churn their waters into a confusion of towering waves capable of breaking a ship in half.

As the lakes change mood, so do the substantial commercial shipping enterprises they support. Captains and crews work overtime, hurrying to make one last trip and deliver one last cargo of corn, wheat, iron, steel, or chemicals before winter weather and ice lock up the lakes until spring. Tired seamen, pushing themselves and their vessels to the limit, make a habit of looking back over their shoulders. They are watching for November—not necessarily the month that appears on calendars between October and December, but the one that comes calling when you least expect it. Among Great Lakes mariners it is sometimes said that "Christmas comes only if you survive November." They have endless tales of tragedy to prove their point: the November that took the famed *Edmund Fitzgerald* in 1975, the November that took the mighty *Bradley* in 1958, and scores of other Novembers that sent stout ships and strong crews into the abyss of the lakes. But when lake sailors gather to tell stories of the many calamities brought on by the year's eleventh month, there is one November they rarely leave out: November 1913.

Those who were superstitious said "the 13" would be an unlucky year, but up until the fall, 1913 had proven them wrong. The spring and summer had been kind to the Great Lakes, providing bathers, lovers, and sailors with a seemingly endless string of warm, clear days and calm, starry nights. The shipping business was booming, and the large and growing fleet of long lake freighters carried record cargoes.

Then came October and, with it, high winds howling out of the west. A sudden cold snap sent temperatures plunging below zero, and a series of early snowstorms dusted the lakeshores with white. But for all its bluster and chill, October's unexpected outburst did little damage—a broken rudder here, a severed anchor chain there, and a couple of old wooden steamers run aground in gales.

The year's fourth and final quarter had gotten off to an ominous start, but with lucrative contracts in hand, freighter captains were not willing to tie up their vessels and call it quits for the season. Instead they pushed themselves, their ships, and their crews harder than ever. They were determined to finish the good work they had begun in the spring and continued so successfully throughout the summer and early fall, attempting to make 1913 the best year ever for shipping on the Great Lakes. But it was not to be.

At first, November seemed likely to reverse the unsettling trend of the previous month. For a full week gentle breezes rippled the lakes, and temperatures were downright balmy. But experienced lake sailors knew these pleasant conditions could not last for long, not at this time of year. They knew the fabled Witch of November must be out there somewhere waiting for them, and destiny was about to prove them right.

Even as lake sailors hung up their warm jackets so they could enjoy the unseasonable temperatures in shirtsleeves while their freights cut through waters as smooth and clear as a plate of glass, trouble was headed their way. Not one or even two, but three deadly storm systems were about to descend on the Midwest. One was rushing in with freezing winds from the distant Bering Sea. Another was pouring in from the Rockies, carrying an immense load of moisture from as far away as the South Pacific. A third was spinning up cyclone style from the Caribbean to throw confusion into this witch's brew of weather. The three storms would soon slam into one another, creating what was to become, in effect, a midcontinent hurricane.

Weather forecasts were primitive in those days. To get a rough idea of what they should expect, ship's masters relied on almanacs, the logbooks of former captains, or their own personal experience. But no one could have predicted what would happen during the second week of November 1913. Beginning about the middle of the day on November 7, the wind came up. It blew in from the east at first, then swung around to the west and southwest. Navigators and the captains they served didn't know what to make of these winds, but they soon realized that the conditions they were facing threatened disaster.

Temperatures were dropping so rapidly that it was literally possible to watch the mercury in onboard thermometers fall. Starting out at around seventy degrees at noon, the temperature tumbled as much as ten degrees an hour until, sometime after dark, it approached zero. By that time the screaming winds were producing waves so high that they washed the decks of large freighters from end to end. When a big wave struck a vessel amidships, it threw up a galling spray that froze in the air and rattled onto the deck in solid chunks.

On Lakes Michigan, Superior, Erie, and Ontario, wise captains turned their ships toward port or to whatever safe anchorages they could find. Captains and crews on Lake Huron sought safety, too, but here the mighty storm had struck hardest. The worst of the weather caught dozens of vessels out on Huron's vast tossing plain. The safest place to be was on the west side of the lake where the Michigan mainland would break the force of the storm's merciless winds, but very few, if any, vessels could make headway in that direction.

Desperate captains and crews could see lighthouse beacons calling to them from Fort Gratiot, Point Aux Barques, Tawas Point, Sturgeon Point, Middle Island, Presque Isle, Forty Mile Point, and all along the Michigan shore. They yearned to reach those western lights and the safety they represented, but the engines of their steamers were not strong enough to fight the powerful westerly winds. Inevitably, the helpless vessels were driven across the lake toward the shoals, shallows, and near-certain destruction that awaited them along the Canadian shore.

As the storm pushed the doomed fleet east toward Canada, the beacons in the west dimmed, then vanished altogether. The last light most navigators could see was that of the New Presque Isle Lighthouse, which beamed from the tallest tower on the lakes. Finally it, too, flickered and disappeared.

The storm raged on for a full five days. By the time the clouds broke and the winds died down on November 12, at least forty ships and smaller vessels had been wrecked or swallowed up by the waters of Lake Huron. More than 250 ship's officers, crewmen, and passengers are believed to have perished in what is still known as the worst storm ever to hit the lakes.

WITCH'S CRY

There is no official memorial to these lost mariners at Presque Isle or at any of the lighthouses along Michigan's Huron lakeshore. However, the New Presque Isle Lighthouse occasionally provides a haunting reminder of the incident. When the wind blows hard, especially in November, piercing cries can be heard in the vicinity of the tower. Some say these eerie calls are the voices of mariners lost during the great storm of 1913.

It is probably safe to say that many more lives would have been lost over the years had it not been for the New Presque Isle Lighthouse and its bright beacon. The 113-foot brick tower was completed in 1871 and equipped with a sparkling prismatic lens imported from Paris. It was a massive third-order lens almost eight feet in diameter, and on a clear night it could focus a light visible from as much as twenty miles out on Lake Huron.

The keeper and his family lived in a modest residence attached to the tower by an enclosed walkway. The walkway provided protected access to the tower during cold, windy weather and blizzards. The keeper's duties often required him to spend long nights in the tower making sure the lamps remained lit and the machinery that turned the lens and caused the light to flash was operating properly.

Presque Isle was a very isolated duty station for keepers, but at least their work kept them busy. It must have been a far lonelier place for the keepers' wives and families. There were few if any neighbors on the Presque Isle peninsula to keep them company, and the nearest towns of any size were Alpena, about thirty miles to the south, and Rogers City, about thirty miles to the northwest.

It is said that the childless wife of a late nineteenth-century keeper was literally driven out of her mind by loneliness. One night, while her husband was working in the tower, she began to scream. The keeper heard her cries and hurried to the side of her bed, where he found her moaning and writhing uncontrollably as if caught in a terrible nightmare from which she could not awake. The next day a doctor was brought in from Rogers City. Having examined the woman, he was unable to diagnose her malady but advised her husband that she might have to be committed to an asylum.

The keeper was either unable or unwilling to send his wife away. Instead he kept her with him at the lighthouse. When she suffered bouts of mental illness, he locked her in a room at the base of the tower for her own protection. There are those who believe that it is her shrieking and moaning people hear when a cold wind blows in off the lake. However, others disagree. They say those terrible sounds are produced by none other than the Witch of November, who is calling out to sailors to let them know she is coming.

Chapter 22

Lake Superior's Mighty Ghost Ship

Whitefish Point Lighthouse
Paradise, Michigan

Practically everyone has heard of the Edmund Fitzgerald, the enormous Great Lakes freighter that disappeared on a stormy November night in 1975 along with all twenty-nine members of her crew. When she vanished, the Fitzgerald had been trying to reach the calm waters of Whitefish Bay. Ironically, the Whitefish Point beacon that might have guided the ship to safety had been knocked out by gale-force winds. The Whitefish Point Lighthouse is now the proud home of the Great Lakes Shipwreck Museum, where tourists never tire of asking questions about the Fitzgerald. Some visitors think they've seen ghostly members of the crew walking the lighthouse grounds. Others think the big ship and her crew are still out there somewhere desperately searching for the Whitefish Point Light.

At the far eastern end of Lake Superior is a stretch of cold blue water that mariners have dreaded for centuries. Some call it the "Graveyard of the Great Lakes," and for good reason, for here in frigid depths hundreds, if not thousands, of ships lie entombed. The only monument that marks the final resting place of these vessels and their brave crews is the beacon of the Whitefish Point Lighthouse. Each night its light flashes out over the lake with a steady rhythm like the mournful tolling of a bell.

Among the ships lost near Whitefish Point was the well-known *Edmund Fitzgerald*, but there have been many others. The very first large vessel known to have sailed these troubled waters was a sixty-foot trading boat known as the *Invincible*. She perished along with her crew in a gale near Whitefish Point in 1816. Over the past two centuries, countless other vessels have suffered the same fate. Some were big, well-known freighters such as the *Fitzgerald*, whose loss made headlines across the country. Many others were far lesser craft, but their destruction was no less tragic.

In November 1915 the 186-foot lumber freighter *Myron* foundered in a blizzard off Whitefish Point. The weight of the ice building up on the hull and deck dragged the freighter farther and farther down into the waves until water, pouring into the holds, snuffed out the fires in the vessel's boilers. Without steam to drive her screws, the *Myron* was doomed.

The crew managed to scramble into lifeboats but found no safety there. The water around the ship was filled with tons of lumber that had washed overboard. Thrown about like battering rams by the waves, the heavy timbers crushed the lifeboats and the men in them. The lighthouse keeper and his family at Whitefish Point could hear the prayers and screams of the sailors as they died but could do absolutely nothing to help. Ironically, the captain, who in keeping with maritime tradition had elected to go down with his ship, was the only member of the *Myron* crew who survived. When the vessel broke apart, he managed to find a floating piece of the shattered wheelhouse and clung to it until it washed up onshore.

GUIDING LIGHT

When the storms of November tear across the waters of Lake Superior, the most welcome sight a sailor is likely to see is the beacon of the Whitefish Point Lighthouse. Its guiding light has shined out over the lake more or less unfailingly for more than 150 years. Mariners out on the lake watch for it anxiously because beyond the Point lie the relatively calm waters of Whitefish Bay. Even in the worst gales, if ships reach the bay, they are usually safe.

The Whitefish Point Lighthouse is a remarkable structure. A steel cylinder some eighty feet tall, it is supported by a skeletal steel framework much like those that support offshore lighthouses in the Caribbean. Its rather modern, utilitarian appearance is all the more extraordinary when one considers that it was built in 1861 during Abraham Lincoln's first year in the White House. At that time, lighthouse engineers were experimenting with skeleton-style structures made of cast iron. The design was intended to take stress off the structure in high winds. The concept has proven especially successful at Whitefish Point, where the open-wall tower has resisted storm winds since the mid-nineteenth century.

Automated by the U.S. Coast Guard in 1970, the Whitefish Point Lighthouse no longer has a resident keeper. Even so, there are always plenty of people around. The old keeper's residence and adjacent buildings now house the Great Lakes Shipwreck Museum, which contains a fascinating array of maritime artifacts and tells the stories of many a shipwrecked crew, including that of the *Edmund Fitzgerald*. It's a rather ghostly place especially in stormy weather, when visitors may be forgiven for imagining things. Or is it just their imagination? Some visitors say they've seen spectral sailors down along the shore, their clothing soaked and their faces and beards caked in ice. Is it too much to think these grim figures are *Fitzgerald* crewmen still trying to complete the fateful journey they began during the second week of November in 1975?

LAST RUN OF THE *EDMUND FITZGERALD*

Anyone in America within hearing distance of a radio during these past few decades is sure to have heard Gordon Lightfoot's "The Wreck of the *Edmund Fitzgerald.*" The song tells the story of an enormous ship that sailed into the teeth of a prodigious storm on Lake Superior and, as if passing into another dimension, simply vanished.

Most song lyrics worthy of serious attention have meanings on several levels, and this is certainly the case with Lightfoot's haunting ballad. Surely chief among its themes is the notion that nature is unconquerable. The song reminds us that even in this prideful technological age of radar, satellite communication, and other so-called electronic miracles, human beings in general and sailors in particular are still at the mercy of the elements.

The incident described in the ballad took place in very recent times. This was no treasure ship wrecked along the Spanish Main during the era of lumbering galleys and marauding buccaneers. No indeed, Lightfoot's song is about a modern ship, a giant freighter some 729 feet in length and displacing 40,000 tons of water when fully loaded with iron ore. And the *Fitzgerald* vanished not from the trackless expanses of the Pacific Ocean or the hurricane-wracked Caribbean but from an inland lake. Here is the true story of the *Edmund Fitzgerald,* or as much of it as is known.

When launched at River Rouge, Michigan, on a bright June day in 1958, she was the world's largest freshwater freighter. Named for a successful Milwaukee banker, she was as proud a ship as was ever lapped by lake water. Some called her the "Queen of the Lakes," and her long, regal lines became a fond and familiar sight to residents of port cities and towns from Toledo to Duluth. She was such a star that a Detroit newspaper ran a regular column to keep readers informed of her activities.

Indeed, the "Big Fitz," as she was affectionately known by her crew, was quite a ship. Able to carry more than 25,000 tons of iron ore, she had a muscular 7,000 horsepower steam turbine that could whisk the big ship and her hefty cargo along at better than 16 knots (about 18 mph). Year after year from 1958 onward she set records for carrying bulk freight, and usually the records she broke were her own. Her successes swelled the breasts of her captain and crew with pride and lined her owner's pockets with fat profits. By the time the *Edmund Fitzgerald* steamed out of Duluth, Minnesota, on the afternoon of Sunday, November 9, 1975, she had plied the shipping channels of the Great Lakes for more than seventeen years. She was still in her prime, by lake standards, and just as solid and capable as the day she was launched.

On this trip her holds were filled to the brim with 26,013 tons of taconite, marble-sized pellets of milled iron ore intended for the steel furnaces of the lower Midwest. Often she carried passengers as well as cargo and had two luxury staterooms and a comfortable lounge to accommodate them. But the Great Lakes are notorious for the great howling storms that churn their waters during November. For this reason, wise lake passengers are wary of this month and choose to travel shipboard earlier in the year. So the *Fitzgerald* left Duluth carrying only the taconite and a crew of highly experienced lake sailors.

Many of those onboard were Midwesterners. Most came from Ohio or Wisconsin, but a few came from as far away as

Florida or California. All were seasoned mariners, and older members of the crew had weathered many a raging Lake Superior gale. The men ranged from their mid-twenties to near retirement age. At sixty-two Captain Ernest McSorley was among the oldest.

Signing on as a deckhand aboard a seagoing freighter at the age of eighteen, McSorley had made the merchant marine his life. Transferring to the lakes, the young sailor moved steadily up the chain of command until he became master of his own ship. By 1975 McSorley had been captain of the *Fitzgerald* for many years.

According to McSorley's friends, the "Big Fitz" was, after his wife and family in Toledo, the love of his life. He rarely took time off, even when he was ill, and spent up to ten months a year aboard his ship. He knew her every quirk and idiosyncrasy—for instance, her tendency to bend and spring back like a diving board in high waves. But McSorley had complete faith in her ability to weather a storm—even a Lake Superior gale in November. Perhaps that is why when Monday, November 10, 1975, dawned, bringing with it gale warnings and fierce winds, McSorley kept the *Fitzgerald's* bow pointed down the lake toward Whitefish Point, the locks at Sault Ste. Marie, and his home in Toledo.

The *Arthur M. Anderson*, a U.S. Steel Corporation carrier under the command of Captain J. B. Cooper, had left Duluth not long after the *Fitzgerald*. When the weather turned unexpectedly sour, McSorley made radio contact with Cooper, whose ship trailed his own by only about ten miles. The two captains agreed to stay in close contact with each other and decided jointly that their ships would slip out of the traditional freighter channel along the southern shore of the lake. Instead they would steer northeastward in hopes that the leeward shore might offer some protection from the weather. They would soon discover, however, that there was no shelter from this particular storm.

By the middle of the afternoon, the *Fitzgerald* was taking a beating and she began to show it. The force of the storm snapped the heavy cable fencing around the deck and washed it away. The ship took a more threatening blow when the waves smashed through a pair of ventilator covers. At about 3:30 p.m. McSorley radioed the *Anderson* to report that he was taking on water and the ship had developed a list. Would the *Anderson* try to close the distance between the two ships? Yes, it would, came the reply.

Cooper had caught no hint of desperation in McSorley's voice. In fact, the master of the *Fitzgerald* had given no indication at all, other than the damage report and the request that the *Anderson* move in closer, that his ship was in trouble. Even so, Cooper resolved to keep a very close watch on the *Fitzgerald*.

The blasting wind and spray and the dark cloak the storm had thrown over the lake made the huge ship all but invisible to the naked eye, but its mighty hull put a substantial green blip on the *Anderson*'s radar screen. In the fury of the gale, however, even radar contact was tenuous. Occasionally an eerie thing happened. When the towering waves swelled up to block the signal, the blip representing the *Fitzgerald* would flicker and then disappear from the screen.

Despite the damage, the *Fitzgerald* plowed steadily onward through the storm. Apparently, Captain McSorley was making for Whitefish Bay, where he hoped to find calmer waters. If he could round Whitefish Point and reach the bay, he might just get his ship out of harm's way. No doubt, at some point in the late afternoon, McSorley began to scan the horizon, searching for a flash of light, any suggestion at all of the beacon at Whitefish Point.

The lighthouse at Whitefish Point was then and remains to this day a fixed feature of the Great Lakes almost as familiar to sailors as the lakes themselves. During all its more than 160 years of service, there have been only a handful of nights when mariners could not count on its powerful light for guidance. Ironically, the evening of November 10, 1975, turned out to be one of them. The early winter storm that had churned the waters of Lake Superior into such a frenzy had also vented its rage on land. It ripped down road signs, uprooted trees, and even bowled over a heavily loaded tractor-trailer rig on the Mackinac Bridge. Among the many utility poles snapped in two by the high winds was one supplying electric power to the lighthouse. When the backup generators failed as well, the Whitefish Point lantern room was plunged into darkness. So when McSorley peered into the night, he saw only a black curtain.

McSorley put out a call to all ships in the vicinity. Could anyone see the light at Whitefish Point? The worried captain was rewarded with an immediate response. The pilot of the Swedish freighter *Avafors* in Whitefish Bay reported that neither the light nor the radio beacon at Whitefish Point could be detected. The pilot of the *Avafors* had a question of his own: What were things like out there on the lake?

"Big seas," McSorley replied. "I've never seen anything like it in my life."

Still in the relative calm and safety of the bay, the westbound *Avafors* had not yet borne the full brunt of the storm, but that was about to change. When the Swedish vessel ventured beyond the bay, its crew experienced

McSorley's "big seas" for themselves. Mountainous waves pounded the hull of the saltwater freighter, and winds approaching hurricane force tore at her decks. Eventually the *Avafors* would win her battle with the stormy lake, but not so the *Fitzgerald*.

As the storm raged on into the evening, Cooper and the crew aboard the *Anderson* grew increasingly concerned about their compatriots on the *Fitzgerald*. Still, there had been no call for help from the "Big Fitz," only the damage reports. An officer on the *Anderson* raised McSorley on the radio. "How are you making out?" he asked.

"We are holding our own," said McSorley. Those words were the last anyone heard from the *Edmund Fitzgerald*.

The men on the bridge of the *Anderson* had grown used to the wavering, ghostly radar image of the *Fitzgerald*. The sea return, or radar interference caused by the tremendous waves thrown up by the storm, made radar contact spotty at best. First the ship was there, then gone, then back again. Then, at some point shortly after 7 p.m.—no one aboard the *Anderson* could ever say exactly when—the fuzzy green image representing the *Fitzgerald* disappeared from the screen. It never returned.

Minutes passed. Officers on the *Anderson* checked their equipment. There were other ships on the screen—westbound freighters struggling through the heavy weather. But there was no sign of the *Fitzgerald*. It was as if the giant ship, as long as a sixty-story building is tall, had slid down the side of a titanic wave and never come up again. Cooper ordered his men to try to make a visual sighting, but where the ship's running lights should have been there was only darkness. Frantic attempts to reach the *Fitzgerald* by radio were answered with silence.

Wasting no time, Cooper put in an urgent call to the Coast Guard. "No lights," he said. "Don't have her on radio. I know she's gone."

At first Cooper's report was met with disbelief. How could a 729-foot-long freighter sink so suddenly and simply vanish as if she had sailed through some sort of mysterious vortex? The skepticism on the part of Cooper's Coast Guard contacts must have brought a sharp response from the veteran freighter captain, who after all had just had a harrowing day. Ship's captains are legendary for their mastery of certain forms of persuasive language. No doubt Cooper said what was necessary to convince the coastguardsmen.

A massive search and rescue operation swung into action. Despite the still savage weather, ships on the eastern side of Lake Superior changed course to make for the *Fitzgerald*'s last known position. The captains and crews of these vessels were more than willing to put themselves at risk if there were any chance at all of saving fellow sailors, perhaps even then being tossed about like toys by the waves. Squadrons of aircraft, including huge C-130 transports and helicopters equipped with powerful searchlights, crisscrossed the waters off Whitefish Point, but there was no sign of the lost ship or her crew. The Whitefish Point Lighthouse, which by then was back in operation, flung its light out over a Lake Superior seemingly empty of any trace of the *Edmund Fitzgerald*. Apparently the lake had swallowed up the ship along with its cargo and crew in a single massive giant gulp.

As the storm abated and skies began to clear, searchers found a few scattered bits of debris—a propane bottle, a wooden stool, a life vest, a lifesaving ring emblazoned with the letters **FITZGERALD**—but little else. The shattered remains of a wooden lifeboat turned up a day or so later, and with its discovery, all hope of finding any of the *Fitzgerald*'s crew alive was abandoned. Actually, there had never been much hope in these conditions. Now there was none. No bodies were ever found, and perhaps that came as no surprise to anyone familiar with the greatest of the Great Lakes. According to a legend of the Ojibwa, a people who have lived by the lakes for longer than even they can remember, the big lake we call Superior "never gives up her dead."

That the Ojibwa have such a legend is proof enough that they and other native peoples often ventured out onto the Great Lakes in their long canoes to fish, trade, and travel. Certainly they suffered calamitous wrecks of their own. The stories of those adventures, some of which no doubt ended in tragedy, are lost in the mists of time. Or like the *Fitzgerald* herself, they are locked in a coffin of ice-cold water at the bottom of a lake.

Perhaps the spirits of the *Fitzgerald* crew are restless in their lake. Maybe that is why shadowy figures are sometimes seen standing along the shore near Whitefish Point. Visitors to the Great Lakes Shipwreck Museum claim to have seen them. So do area residents. These phantoms do not respond to calls, and if anyone goes to take a closer look, they vanish. Most of the time they seem to be gazing up at the light, as if to make sure it is shining.

Chapter 23
Greeted by
the Manitou

South Manitou Island Lighthouse
South Manitou Island, Michigan

Named for a Native America god, South Manitou is a small, sparsely populated island in the middle of Lake Michigan. It is a bucolic place entirely lacking in clamor or excitement, at least among the living. However, that is not to say the island is free of crowds, for the ghosts here appear to outnumber the people.

To the Algonquin people the Manitou is a magical, godlike being who can take both human and animal form. The Manitou serves as a link between objects and people in the so-called real world and in the spiritual realm. Some believe it is the Manitou who greets the dead as they pass from one existence into the next. For reasons that are not entirely clear, a pair of prominent islands in eastern Lake Michigan were named after this important Native American religious figure. They are known as South Manitou and North Manitou.

South Manitou was once the home of one of the most important navigational stations on the Great Lakes. Among the most impressive structures anywhere on the lakes, the South Manitou Island Lighthouse tower soars 104 feet into the skies above Lake Michigan. The stark white walls of the tower stand in sharp contrast to the beautiful natural background of the island, now included in Sleeping Bear

Dunes National Lakeshore. In the eyes of some, the tower looks a little like a huge tombstone, and that may be an apt description.

The South Manitou Island beacon was established in 1839 to mark the all-important Manitou Passage, frequently trafficked by ships heading through northern Lake Michigan toward the Mackinac Straits. The original tower was replaced by the existing brick structure in 1872. Fitted with a third-order Fresnel lens, its beacon could be seen for about eighteen miles. That's far enough to have made the light useful to any vessel plying the waters on the eastern side of the lake.

This powerful beacon served until 1958, when the U.S. Coast Guard removed the South Manitou Island keeper and closed up the lighthouse. The year the Coast Guard selected to decommission the lighthouse proved a fateful one. Ironically, the lantern room of the old tower had been dark for only a few months when one of the worst shipping disasters in Great Lakes history took place not many miles from the lighthouse.

GONE IN NOVEMBER

In November 1958 the 640-foot *Carl C. Bradley* was heading home empty, making her last run of the fall shipping season. She had left behind in Buffington, Indiana, her cargo of some eighteen thousand tons of limestone, enough rock to fill three hundred railroad cars in a train perhaps three miles long. As the *Bradley* approached the top of Lake Michigan, less than a day's sail from her home port of Rogers City, Michigan, on the shores of Lake Huron, she ran straight into one of the lake's legendary November storms.

Wind whipped across the deck at upward of seventy miles per hour, and thirty-foot waves slammed into the bow.

But for the *Bradley's* thirty officers and crew, all hardened veterans of furious lake tempests, confronting such ugly weather was simply part of a day's work. Despite the pitching and rolling, no one got seasick as the men wolfed down their dinner of hamburgers, french fries, and sponge cake.

Groaning under the strain placed on them by the huge waves, some of the rivets that held together the hull plates began to shear off, shooting like bullets across the empty hold. Except for anyone unlucky enough to be caught in the line of fire, this was no particular cause for concern. It was, in fact, a common experience in a storm. But another far more alarming sound soon caught everyone's attention.

Just after 5:30 p.m. a very loud booming noise was heard aboard the *Bradley*. The first boom was followed moments later by another, then another. Captain Roland Bryan and First Mate Elmer Fleming looked back from the pilothouse and, to their horror, saw the aft section of the *Bradley* begin to sag. The ship was breaking in half!

Immediately Captain Bryan sounded a general alarm so that his crew could prepare to abandon ship. Meanwhile Fleming made an urgent call for assistance on the ship's radio phone. "Mayday!" he said to all within hearing. "Mayday!"

Ships and Coast Guard stations throughout the lakes heard Fleming's call, but at this point no one could do anything to help. For the *Carl C. Bradley* and nearly all of her crew it was already too late. Less than a quarter of an hour after the first sign of trouble, the *Bradley's* bow and stern sections parted and, within minutes, went their separate ways to the bottom. Those crewmen not carried down with the ship were left to fight for their lives on the wildly churning surface. In those brutal, 36-degree waters, it was a struggle they could not hope to win. If they could see through the storm the lighthouse beacons calling to them from nearby Beaver Island, Cat Head, or elsewhere along the Michigan coast—the South Manitou Island beacon was no longer in service—it must have been a bitter reminder that safe ground was so near and yet so far away. One after another the *Bradley's* crew froze to death or gave up and slipped into the depths.

The first would-be rescue ship to arrive over the *Bradley's* watery grave was a small German freighter, the *Christian Sartori*. No survivors could be located. The *Sartori* found only an eerie scattering of wave-tossed debris. A U-boat officer in World War II, the *Sartori's* Captain Paul Mueller had witnessed such scenes in the past. He believed that all hands had been lost, but as it turned out, he was wrong. Incredibly, some fourteen hours after the big stone carrier broke in half, a Coast Guard helicopter searching the open waters of Lake Michigan spotted an orange raft. Not long afterward the crew of the Coast Guard cutter *Sundew* pulled aboard First Mate Fleming and Frank Mays, a young deck watchman. These two alone remained alive to tell the story of the *Carl C. Bradley's* last day on the lake.

HAUNTED ISLAND

It may be that some of those who did not survive the wreck of the *Carl C. Bradley* also have stories to tell and have migrated to whatever spot of land they can find. The spirits of shipwrecked seamen are thought to haunt Michigan's islands and lakeshores, but the most haunted of all these places is probably South Manitou Island. The abandoned lighthouse on South Manitou makes strange sounds, and disembodied voices can be heard both inside and outside the tower.

A particularly spooky place is the old South Manitou Island lifesaving station. Located down by the south shore of the island, the building was once occupied by members of the U.S. Lifesaving Service, a federal agency charged with rescuing shipwrecked mariners. Lifesaving Service crewmen lived at the station and stood ready twenty-four hours a day to man surfboats and hurry off to assist sailors whose vessels were sinking or had run aground. Like the lighthouse, the lifesaving station was no longer in operation at the time of the *Carl C. Bradley* disaster. However, the building is a lively enough place nowadays since it provides housing for rangers and other employees of Sleeping Bear Dunes National Lakeshore.

Residents of the station say they often hear footsteps on the second floor. It sounds like someone is up there pacing back and forth in an extremely agitated manner, but if anyone goes to check, they find the second floor silent and empty. Doors at the lifesaving station have a will of their own, opening and closing without the assistance of the living. Perhaps most poignant, there are unexplained knocks at the station door. When the knock is answered, there is no one outside. It is almost as if the knocks are those of long-ago shipwrecked seamen desperately seeking aid from Lifesaving Service crewmen who are no longer on hand to help. That is easy to imagine because the island is ringed with the broken carcasses of wrecked vessels, making it something of a maritime graveyard. Over the past 150 years, the following ships have foundered on or near the South Manitou Island beaches:

J. Y. Scammon	June 8, 1864
Annie Vought	November 21, 1892

Adirondack	September 14, 1893
Queen of the Lakes	September 18, 1898
Maggie Avery	September 28, 1904
Congress	October 5, 1904
Margaret Dall	November 16, 1906
Robert L. Frost	November 4, 1903
H. D. Moore	September 10, 1907
Three Brothers	September 27, 1911
Lorrie Burton	November 17, 1911
P. J. Ralph	September 8, 1924
Avis	January 1, 1939
Francisco Morazan	November 29, 1960

Despite this long list and the loss in nearby shipping channels of more than a few large vessels, such as the *Carl C. Bradley*, the haunting of the lighthouse, the lifesaving station, and the island in general is likely not entirely the doing of shipwrecked mariners. There is said to be a mass grave not far from the site of a popular South Manitou Island campground. The bodies buried there are those of cholera victims who arrived on a plague-ridden passenger steamer one night during the late nineteenth century. The vessel's crewmen dug a large hole in the island dunes and buried in it the ravaged bodies of plague victims. Buried along with them were several hopelessly ill but still living passengers. It is said that on some especially dark nights one can hear the desperate protests of those who were buried alive. Perhaps their cries join those of the countless shipwrecked sailors whose remains are entombed in the cold depths of northern Lake Michigan.

Chapter 24
Light of Last Refuge

Seul Choix Lighthouse
Gulliver, Michigan

Seul Choix was once thought to be the only available shelter for vessels caught in one of northern Lake Michigan's titanic storms. Apparently it has now become a harbor of refuge for drowned sailors and deceased lighthouse keepers. Thought to be among the latter is Seul Choix Lighthouse keeper Joseph Townsend, who even decades after death has been unable to give up his smoking habit.

Early French explorers found out the hard way that there were very few places to take shelter from a storm in this part of Lake Michigan. The harbor at Seul Choix was one such welcome refuge, which is why they gave it a name meaning "only choice." Despite its inviting harbor, Seul Choix Point did not receive a lighthouse until late in the nineteenth century. Congress finally appropriated the money for the project in 1886, but partly because of its remote location, the lighthouse was not completed and fully operational until 1895.

The seventy-eight-foot conical brick tower was topped by a ten-sided, cast-iron lantern, giving its third-order Fresnel lens a focal plane just over eight feet above the lake. When the Coast Guard automated the lighthouse, the Fresnel lens was removed and replaced by an airport-style beacon, visible from about seventeen miles out on the lake.

The two-story brick keeper's dwelling still stands and is attached to the tower by an enclosed brick passageway. Although this is still an operating light station, the structures and the grounds are the property of the State of Michigan and are open to the public. The old residence contains a fascinating museum, but the visitors who come here, mostly during warm-weather months, may encounter more than lighthouse equipment and lore. Apparently the property has more than a few resident ghosts, and at least one of them has not been able to give up smoking.

GHOST WITH A SMOKING HABIT

Although it was once a bustling fishing port, the town of Seul Choix has dwindled to almost nothing. About all that is left of it are the tower and various other structures associated with the lighthouse. So, to say that Seul Choix is a ghost town is not entirely a joke. Lighthouse visitors and guides might chuckle upon hearing such a comment, but then again, they might not think it's funny. They might just think the remark is a bit too scary and too close to home since, in the tower and residence, furnishings and various other objects tend to move around without the aid of living human hands. Footsteps are heard on the spiral tower steps even when no one can be seen climbing them. Strange and unexpected odors can be detected here and there. Especially noticeable is the smell of cigar smoke. Is there a ghost at Seul Choix who has not yet learned that smoking is bad for your health? Perhaps so, and maybe there are explanations for some of the other odors as well.

Among the most widely remembered Seul Choix Lighthouse keepers was Joseph Townsend, who served here during the early twentieth century. Townsend was a hardworking man with only a few bad habits. However, his wife considered one of them to be his incessant cigar smoking. She absolutely refused to let the keeper smoke in the house, so he had to sneak a smoke outdoors whenever he could or, in inclement weather, he smoked in the tower.

In 1910 Townsend died. His body was embalmed in the basement and then put on display in the parlor until his friends and relatives could reach Seul Choix to attend his funeral. Some lived several days' journey from this remote corner of Michigan, and the body remained in the parlor for quite some time. It was summer, so no doubt there were some not particularly pleasant odors associated with his farewell.

Nowadays visitors say they can smell cigar smoke in both the Seul Choix tower and residence. That is likely a distinct improvement on the odors that likely wafted through the dwelling in 1910. The aroma of the cigar smoke is actually rather pleasant, but what is the explanation for it? The lighthouse is a public facility and no one is allowed to smoke here. Perhaps Townsend grew tired of smoking outside in the wind and the cold, and now that he is officially off duty, he can smoke whenever and wherever he likes.

Maybe Townsend also figures he can exercise his sense of humor with the occasional practical joke—another bad habit his wife tried hard to curb. Guides and docents occasionally find that when they get to work in the morning, certain museum displays have been left in disarray. They are not damaged, just moved around or changed in some way as if to attract attention and produce a chuckle. For instance, a museum mannequin dressed up like a lighthouse keeper will sometimes have his hat on backward in the morning. Occasionally cigars are found in the mannequin's pocket.

A large round mirror in an upstairs bedroom has a particularly spooky reputation. Both lighthouse visitors and museum guides have reported looking into the mirror and seeing in it something that nearly froze their blood. Instead of their own reflection, they have seen the face of a man gazing back at them. Later, when shown a picture of Townsend, most identify his face as the one they saw in the mirror.

Townsend has been seen on other parts of the property as well. One evening several years ago, a contractor sat alone in his car while writing an estimate for installation of an electronic alarm system in the Seul Choix tower. Suddenly an odd feeling came over him. The contractor felt sure someone was watching him. Looking around his car, he saw no one, but then he happened to glance up at the windows of the lantern room at the top of the tower. There was a man up there dressed in the uniform of an early twentieth-century Lighthouse Service keeper, and the man was staring straight back at him. The contractor had seen the man's faded picture in the Seul Choix Lighthouse Museum. It was Joseph Townsend. The contractor started his car, threw it into gear, and drove away as fast as he could. He never returned and never submitted his bid.

HAUNTED HARBOR OF REFUGE

As the only sheltered harbor along the northern reaches of Lake Michigan, Seul Choix is a naturally haunted place. That is because the Great Lakes themselves, and Lake Michigan especially, are haunted. Countless sailors caught in mighty gales out on the lakes have lost their lives while struggling desperately to reach a safe harbor such as the one at Seul Choix. Eventually they succumbed to winds and waves that no ship of wood or steel or man of flesh and blood could long survive. Is it too much to imagine that these valiant mariners continue to seek a harbor of refuge even in death?

Sometimes during the early evening, especially after major storms pass through, spectral seamen can be seen walking or floating along the rugged shores of Michigan's Upper Peninsula. Occasionally the police or highway patrol receive reports of such sightings, but in most cases these are not taken very seriously. That is because the patrolmen know, even though they may not be willing to talk about it, that ghosts walk the shores of Lake Michigan. More than a few have been sighted along the stretch of lakeshore near the Seul Choix Lighthouse. The beacon seems to attract them, but some of these specters may have arrived long before the lighthouse was built. Some, for instance, if they could speak at all, might speak French.

In 1679 the French explorer Sieur de La Salle and a party of fur traders built a fifty-ton sailing ship, pushing her off into Lake Erie from a rough-hewn shipyard where the city of Buffalo now stands. This was no crude, overbuilt canoe. Christened the *Griffin*, she was more than sixty feet long and had five cannons arrayed below the deck. The *Griffin* proved a worthy ship, weathering more than one fierce storm on the outbound leg of her maiden voyage to the far reaches of the Great Lakes.

By autumn the holds of the *Griffin* were bulging with muskrat and beaver pelts that had been purchased from the Indians in exchange for a few cheap trinkets. The furs could be sold for a fortune at seaports in the East, so La Salle and his men expected the *Griffin*'s cargo to make them rich. At a small fort near what is now Chicago, La Salle disembarked to continue his explorations—he would later discover the source of the Mississippi River. Then he ordered the *Griffin's* crew to set sail for the far eastern shores of the lakes.

As La Salle watched the *Griffin* disappear over the horizon, he was confident that the ship and her treasured cargo of furs would safely reach their destination. But neither the *Griffin* nor her crew was ever heard from again. Like so many other unlucky ships, she was smashed by a sudden, sharp autumn gale. No one is certain exactly where this calamity took place, but a good guess might be in northern Lake Michigan, perhaps not very far from the present-day site of the Seul Choix Lighthouse. Maybe the crew of the *Griffin* hoped to reach the calm, sheltered waters here, but likely they perished somewhere out on the lake. Perhaps their indomitable human spirits continued the effort, arriving finally at Seul Choix, this haunted region's one harbor of refuge.

Part Four

WEST

Chapter 25

Terrible Tilly

Tillamook Rock Lighthouse
Tillamook Head, Oregon

During the early 1880s, tough government construction crews completed one of the boldest building projects ever undertaken, the castle-like lighthouse that sits atop rugged Tillamook Rock just off the coast of Oregon. They succeeded despite human opposition onshore and inhuman opponents on the rock itself. However, the lighthouse they built was never a very comfortable place for the keepers who lived hard, solitary lives out on the barren one-acre rock. The lighthouse was cramped, cold, and exposed to the most terrible weather imaginable, and what was worse, it was very definitely haunted. There were strange cries in the night and visits by ghost ships and terrifying specters. Most think the rock and the now abandoned lighthouse are still haunted, and they are almost certainly correct. For decades the rock and the lighthouse have been used as a columbarium, a place to store the cremated ashes of the dead.

As an outpost of human endeavor, the Tillamook Rock Lighthouse was always as much a symbol as a navigational aid. It marked not only a dangerous maritime hazard but also the precarious and shifting border between human enterprise and the forces of nature. As we shall see, it also marked a boundary between reality and a netherworld where spirit beings both human and animal may dwell.

Located more than a mile offshore, near Oregon's magnificent Tillamook Head and about twenty miles south of the Columbia River, this storm-dashed bastion clings to a scrap of rock caught almost totally in the grip of an all too often unfriendly ocean. In a gale, mountainous waves sweep over the rock and pound the walls of the lighthouse. Few buildings anywhere in the world are so exposed to the whims and power of wind, weather, and sea. Yet the Tillamook Lighthouse has stood, more or less intact, since 1881.

Completed during the horse-and-buggy days before the era of automobiles, airplanes, helicopters, computers, electrical power tools, or diesel-powered drilling and earthmoving equipment, this amazing structure surely ranks among the foremost engineering triumphs of all time. There were many during the nineteenth century who said the lighthouse could never be built and more than a few others who said it *should* never be built. Among the latter were Native Americans who claimed the rock as sacred ground. The Indians would not speak when asked why they considered the isolated rock to be holy ground, but there were legends concerning this belief.

According to stories the Indians had long taught their children, there once existed an underwater passage leading from the mainland to Tillamook Rock, which could not be safely approached on the surface by swimmers or canoes. Whenever local tribes were faced with hunger, sickness, danger, or despair, their chiefs and holy men would follow the tunnel until they arrived at a large room hollowed from the heart of the rock. There they met with powerful spirits to hear their advice and gain their assistance. Some of the spirits were beneficent, while others were evil. If the evil spirits could be avoided or at least placated, then the friendlier ones might be persuaded to help.

Naturally enough, the government maritime officials who ordered construction of the lighthouse completely dismissed the notion that any spirits resided on Tillamook Rock, evil or otherwise. They also ignored widespread public opposition to the notion of spending large sums of tax money on what many considered a vain and foolish venture.

Well before the first stone was laid, a tragedy took place that seemed to confirm the harshest opinions of project opponents. A popular master mason from nearby Portland, John Trewavas had experience with lighthouse construction, and project engineers thought him indispensable to building this one. On a bright, clear morning in early September 1879, Trewavas was put ashore on Tillamook Rock to begin surveying the construction site. He never even got started. Although the weather was fine and the ocean relatively quiet, the sides of the rock were slick. While climbing its sheer eastern face, Trewavas slipped and plunged into the sea. The water immediately closed over him, and he was never seen again. The evil spirits of Tillamook Rock had thus made their opinion of the project all too clear.

News of the mason's death soon reached the construction crew hired to build the lighthouse. The workers were all carefully chosen men—tough veterans of other dangerous construction projects—but now even they questioned the wisdom of attempting to build a lighthouse on this sea-battered outcropping. They had seen fellow workers killed before and gone right ahead with their work, but this was different. They knew that Tillamook Rock had a dark reputation—that it was as haunted a place as any in the Northwest. Would they go to Tillamook Rock and take a chance of sharing Trewavas's unhappy fate? No, they said, but appeals to their manliness and the offer of bonus pay finally coaxed them to give the project a try.

Things got off to a very shaky start when the first two workmen put on the rock were knocked into the ocean by waves before they could scramble beyond the reach of the surf. They were rescued, however, and put ashore once again along with two other crewmen and a few provisions. Before additional supplies could be landed, a gale blew up that drove away the project tender *Corwin,* leaving the stranded workers to huddle miserably in whatever shelter they could find. Because of the terrible weather, the *Corwin* was unable to return for almost a week.

When the *Corwin* finally made it back to Tillamook Rock, construction superintendent Charles A. Ballantyne found the workers he had left there alive but not particularly comfortable or happy. Instead of rescuing them, though, Ballantyne had five more workers put on the rock along with a large quantity of construction materials. Obviously this job would require more than the usual measure of fortitude and determination.

Within a few days the crew had built themselves a crude barracks and set to work chiseling and blasting a level foundation. All through the winter and spring, the work continued. On several occasions gales with hurricane-force winds sent giant waves pounding over the rock, threatening to wash the little crew into the sea, but they gritted their teeth and held on. Then, when the winds died down again, they returned to the business of building the lighthouse.

During the summer the basalt walls began to take shape. The tower, residence, and workrooms were completed by late fall, just in time for the hardworking crew to take a brief

Christmas break. By January 1, 1881, they were back on the rock finishing the interior of the lighthouse and installing the station's enormous first-order Fresnel lens.

BARKING IN THE NIGHT

Before the first day of the year had come to an end, a tremendous gale blew in from the northwest. That very night the workers on the rock began to hear strange noises above the roar of the storm. They thought they heard the voices of men calling to them from the darkness, and they were sure they heard the sound of a dog barking. Suddenly, from out of the gloom, a large sailing ship came into view. It reeled to port and then starboard, crashing out of control through the waves. Then, as quickly as it had appeared, the ship was gone.

A day later, with the storm passed and the sun shining brightly, the fate of the mystery ship and its crew became all too apparent. Its shattered remains littered the rocks of nearby Tillamook Head. The unlucky ship had been the *Lupatia*, bound from Japan to Oregon. The *Lupatia* had arrived, but not in the manner its captain and crew had intended. None aboard the *Lupatia* survived except for the ship's dog, which later took up residence at the lighthouse.

The disaster proved a sobering reminder of just how important it was to complete their work. A beacon on Tillamook Rock might spell the difference between life and death for mariners hopelessly lost in darkness and storm. No doubt such thoughts chilled and depressed the construction crew. After their long struggle, they had missed by only a few days having the light ready and shining on the very night when it was most needed by the *Lupatia* and her doomed crew.

Although saddened, the construction crew moved ahead with their work, putting the finishing touches on the project. The oil lamp that powered the station's big Fresnel lens was fired up for the first time on the evening of January 11, 1881. The light then shined almost continuously for the next seventy-six years. It was finally extinguished in September 1957, when the lighthouse was decommissioned and replaced by a buoy.

NEVER ALONE ON THE ROCK

For more than seven decades there was always at least one keeper on duty at the Tillamook Rock Lighthouse. Keepers here lived an isolated and solitary existence even when judged by the standards of their own lonely profession. As they occasionally told their Lighthouse Service superiors or their friends onshore, however, they were never entirely alone on the rock even if sometimes they wished they were.

Often when Tillamook Rock keepers climbed the tower stairs, they heard a terrible scream. Searches of the tower, workrooms, residence, and grounds never turned up anyone who might have uttered the cry. It was hard to tell whether the scream came from within the tower or from the outside. Actually it seemed to well up from below, as if from the very bowels of Tillamook Rock. Was it caused by the wind whipping through an unnoticed crack in the tower walls? Or did it originate in the secret room the Indians said their ancestors used to visit to commune with its good and evil spirits? No one could say.

Keepers tended to believe the cry was made by Tillamook Rock itself, and they began to refer to the rock as "Terrible Tilly." The name seemed to fit since few of the Lighthouse Service and Coast Guard keepers stationed here considered it their favorite assignment. Terrible Tilly was cold, damp, lonely, and very definitely haunted.

It is said that during the early twentieth century, an aging keeper who had served at Tillamook Rock for a long time eventually went insane. When this became obvious to Lighthouse Service officials, they sent a new keeper to Tillamook to relieve him, assuming he would then go quietly into retirement. Instead the old keeper adamantly refused to leave and threatened to kill anyone who tried to force him off the rock. Retreating up the tower steps, he dared anyone to try to pull him down. Eventually his fingers were pried loose from the lantern room railing and he was taken away to an asylum in a straitjacket. Soon afterward the old man died. His last request was that he be buried on Tillamook Rock. The request was not honored. However, some later keepers believed the old keeper's ghost had returned to the rock. They were certain they could hear his footsteps in hallways or running up the tower steps.

RETURN OF THE *LUPATIA*

During the 1930s, more than half a century after the wreck of the *Lupatia*, a mysterious vessel paid a visit to Tillamook Rock. One evening at twilight the hull of a large freighter could be seen looming through the fog and mist. There were no lights on the ship and, seemingly, no people aboard. The Tillamook Rock keeper and his assistants called out, "Ahoy! Anyone onboard?" But there was no reply.

The ship had been through what the keeper could only imagine was "hell." Her paint was peeling and her sides streaked with rust. Her decks were sodden with seawater, and her rigging hung limp like a torn spiderweb. The portholes of her cabins creaked open and shut as the battered hulk rolled in the waves. It looked as if the old ship might sink at any moment, but she remained afloat, drifting relentlessly toward the rock.

The keeper radioed the Coast Guard station near the mouth of the Columbia and requested a cutter to tow the foundering ship to safety, but he had almost no hope that help would arrive in time. Indeed, a few minutes later the foundering freighter struck the rocks not so much with a crash as with a long, drawn-out groan. The hull screeched as it ground across the solid stone, cracking and splintering as it went. The rudder broke free, but the rest of the vessel continued on its way, finally disappearing into the fog.

When the Coast Guard cutter arrived, the ship had gone. A thorough search of the shoreline and ocean near Tillamook Rock turned up no trace of such a ship and no sign of wreckage. Coast Guard officials began to believe their keeper had been imagining things. Then, three days later, a rudder was seen awash in the surf below the Tillamook Rock Lighthouse. When the keeper tried to retrieve it, he fell into the water and only just saved himself by scrambling onto a bed of gravel. Although soaked to the skin he was otherwise unharmed. Meanwhile, the rudder drifted away and along with it went the only evidence that he had ever really seen the vessel that has come to be called the "Ghost Ship of Tillamook Rock."

Although the Ghost Ship had no living passengers, it is easy to imagine that the spirits of the passengers and crew of the *Lupatia* might have been onboard. Perhaps they were paying Tillamook Rock one last visit to see if its light was finally in operation. Today they would be free to haunt Tillamook Rock itself without detection by living keepers. Since 1957, no living person has inhabited the lighthouse.

However, the dead have come here in considerable numbers. During the 1980s and 1990s, the lighthouse was used as a columbarium, and urns bearing cremated remains were placed here and there within the tower and other structures, where they remain to this day. From time to time relatives of the deceased gather along the shore to gaze out toward the lighthouse and remember the lost loved ones whose ashes have been interred there. Sometimes these people swear there is also a dog out there on the rock, because they can hear above the din of the surf the distinct sound of barking.

Chapter 26

Sarah's Missing Stomach

Pigeon Point Lighthouse
Pescadero, California

When fog shrouds the central coast of California, a mysterious visitor appears beside the gallery rail at the top of the Pigeon Point Lighthouse. Some say the image is a figment of the viewer's imagination, a reflection, perhaps, in a lantern room window. Others say the figure is the ghost of Sarah Coburn, a wealthy local widow who was brutally murdered nearly a century ago. According to legend, the ghost—like the body it once occupied—is not entirely whole.

Fifty miles south of San Francisco, the light at Pigeon Point shines out over the often turbulent waters of the Pacific Ocean from an elevation of nearly 160 feet. Slightly more than 45 feet of that height is provided by the rocky cliffs of the point and the rest by the 115-foot brick tower of the Pigeon Point Lighthouse. The Pigeon Point tower is one of the tallest on the Pacific and gives the beacon such a boost that it can be seen from as many as thirty miles away.

On foggy nights, and there are many such evenings along the California coast, the Pigeon Point Light plays tricks on motorists driving the stretch of Highway 1 between Half Moon Bay near San Francisco and Santa Cruz, about twenty-five miles to the south. When the conditions are just right, the beacon fills the sky with explosive flashes. Seeing this extraordinary display, it is possible to imagine you have driven onto the runway of a major airport or that you are about to have a close encounter with visitors from beyond. It can be a very spooky experience, but seeing the lighthouse on a clear evening can be even spookier. Occasionally visitors say they can see someone up there on the walkway that surrounds the lantern room windows. They say she is wearing a long dress and staring out toward the ocean.

BRICK GIANT NAMED FOR AN EXTINCT BIRD

Pigeon Point is one of many sharp blades of rock thrusting into the sea from the rugged shores south of San Francisco. For many years mariners took care to avoid it but made no special note of it on their charts. They didn't even bother to give it a name until an incident in 1853 made this particular point of land notorious.

During the spring of that year the sleek Yankee clipper known as the *Carrier Pigeon* happened along this part of the California coast. The 175-foot boat had been launched in Bath, Maine, the previous year. She was 129 days out of Boston and bound for San Francisco when she and her crew encountered the conditions that mariners in every era have dreaded—a blanket of fog so thick they could not tell whether they were sailing north, south, east, or west. The *Carrier Pigeon*'s master, Captain Azariah Doane, soon made a navigational error that would cost him his ship, though fortunately not his life or those of his crew. Doane mistook the point for the Farallon Islands, well to the north. The Farallon Islands are due west of the Golden Gate and the calm waters of San Francisco Bay. Doane assumed that a turn toward the east would take him straight into the bay, so he ordered his helmsman to make a starboard course correction. Instead of gliding safely into the bay, however, the *Carrier Pigeon's* bow ran straight up onto the rocky shore just south of the village of Pescadero.

Before Doane and his sailors could free her, the *Carrier Pigeon* was pounded to pieces by a gale. What was left of the cargo was sold at the scene of the wreck for a fraction of its original value. Timbers from the ruined vessel are said to have been used to build local stores and houses, some of which have remained standing for more than a century and a half. The incident had an even more lasting effect on the ship-killing landfall that crushed the ship's hull, for it was known ever afterward as Pigeon Point.

The Pigeon Point Lighthouse was built in 1872. The lighthouse needed an especially tall tower so the beacon could reach ships while they were still far enough away from land to avoid a calamity like the one that befell the *Carrier Pigeon*. Since wooden walls would not have supported such a tall tower, the design called for brick. However, there was very little high-quality brick available on the West Coast. For this reason, builders imported brick from the eastern United States, shipping it in by way of Cape Horn at the southern tip of South America. The brick traveled more than twelve thousand miles before reaching California and being used to construct the thick walls of the Pigeon Point Lighthouse. Despite this, the construction effort was not a particularly expensive one. All together, the land, lighthouse, and huge first-order Fresnel lens cost the government approximately $20,000. Much of that money was spent on the lens, which was imported from faraway Paris.

Although the land was not the costliest part of the project, it may be that government officials paid a high price for it. The man who sold it to them almost certainly demanded and received a price that, if not dear, was certainly more than fair. His name was Loren Coburn, and he was not a man to be trifled with in matters of public record. Coburn knew his rights, or thought he did, and he was not about to see them violated. It is said that he would sue anyone, anytime, over anything. He sued local farmers and ranchers over water rights, builders and craftsmen over the quality of their workmanship, and county tax authorities over the assessments placed on his extensive holdings. He once sued a neighbor for allowing her children to snitch an occasional handful of strawberries from one of his fields. Coburn spent so much time in court dealing with various suits and countersuits that it is hard to see how he managed to do anything else.

Naturally enough, Coburn made very few friends with this sort of highly litigious behavior. As a result, practically no one mourned when Coburn answered a knock at the door one day and found standing there not his lawyer, but the Grim Reaper. Here was a case that would not be going to court and a judgment that would not necessarily be handed down in his favor. One of the few mourners at his funeral was Sarah, Coburn's wife of many years. Most San Mateo County residents who had known Coburn, and likely as not been sued by him, stayed away. It may be that some of them, as Mark Twain once did when he learned that a corrupt politician he knew had died, sent along a nice note saying that they wouldn't be attending Coburn's funeral but that they surely approved of it.

After Coburn's passing in 1919, Sarah Coburn did the best she could to hold together the land and business interests he had compiled through legal and other means. It may be that she, like her husband before her, made enemies in the process. Later that same year she was found beaten to death on the floor of the Coburn home near Pescadero. The walls of the room where she lay were drenched in blood, and a blood-spattered two-by-four was found beside her body.

No one would ever know who was responsible for this horrible crime or what the motive might have been, but the San Mateo sheriff vigorously pursued the case. As part of the investigation, the sheriff ordered an autopsy, which was conducted at a local doctor's office. The murdered woman's organs were preserved in formaldehyde and stored in various jars. The sheriff seemed particularly interested in the contents of Sarah Coburn's stomach. Perhaps he was anxious to learn where or with whom she had enjoyed her last meal, but he would never find out. Before the stomach could be tested, it was either lost or stolen. The rest of Sarah Coburn was eventually buried beside her husband.

Understandably, the murder produced a sensation throughout California and made headlines in San Francisco. It was a big-time news story in a state that to this day is still known for them. People still talk about the murder. Perhaps that is why whenever people see, or think they see, a mysterious figure in or around the Pigeon Point Lighthouse, they say it is the ghost of Sarah Coburn. Usually Sarah Coburn's specter is said to be standing in the gallery near the top of the tower looking out to sea. Why would she do that? California park rangers who now manage the lighthouse property think they may have the answer. "Possibly she is looking for someone to sue," they say with a wink. "Possibly she is looking for the person who murdered her. Or maybe she is just looking for her lost stomach."

Chapter 27
The Lady
of Point Vicente

Point Vicente Lighthouse
Rancho Palos Verdes, California

Point Vicente, one of the most beautiful lighthouses in the world, is haunted by an equally beautiful ladylike ghost dressed in a flowing gown. Some say she is an illusion created by stray refractions from the tower's huge crystal lens. Others say she is the spirit of a woman whose lover was tragically lost at sea.

When people dream of moving to Southern California—and many still do—they probably have in mind a place like the gorgeous Los Angeles suburb of Palos Verdes. Bathed in sunlight nearly every day of the year, Palos Verdes features lovely homes, green hills, and rocky cliffs streaked with color. The cliffs drop almost straight down into the ocean, for Palos Verdes is a peninsula. Jutting several miles out into the Pacific, it separates Santa Monica Bay, with its beaches and surfboards, from San Pedro Bay, with its port facilities and fish houses. Because of its prominence and possible threat to ships moving through the nearby San Pedro Channel, Palos Verdes is home to an important lighthouse. The tower is located atop the cliffs at Point Vicente, which is even more beautiful than other parts of scenic Palos Verdes.

Not only does the Point Vicente Lighthouse have one of the world's loveliest settings, but its handsome architecture suggests that it was designed more for looks than for utilitarian navigational purposes. It should thus come as no surprise that, located only a few miles from Hollywood, this classically styled lighthouse has been featured in dozens of movies and television serials.

Perched atop reddish-brown cliffs that drop more than one hundred feet into the azure Pacific, the white cylinder of the Point Vicente tower presents a photogenic image from almost any angle. For mariners, however, it looks best at night, when its million-candlepower beacon warns ships away from the ragged point and its deadly rocks. Among the most prominent coastal features in Southern California, Point Vicente threatens vessels swinging eastward from the open Pacific toward San Pedro Harbor at Los Angeles. An array of rocks several hundred yards offshore adds to the danger.

Despite the importance of the Point Vicente and its threat to navigation, no light was placed here until well into the twentieth century. Built in 1926, the masonry tower stands sixty-seven feet tall. Its extraordinarily powerful light can be seen from twenty miles at sea.

The lantern room is still graced by its original third-order Fresnel lens. It displays a flashing light every twenty seconds.

During World War II, the Fresnel was temporarily replaced by a small lighting apparatus that could be more easily blacked out during an air or sea raid. No such raid ever came. The lighthouse has never been assaulted except by tourists or movie cameramen, and they have been mostly well intentioned.

Equally benign has been the distinctly female Point Vicente ghost. According to keepers who first noticed her during the late 1920s, she wears a flowing white dress and seems to float above the ground in various parts of the lighthouse property. She appears only at night, when the station beacon is in operation, and is never seen inside the tower or other buildings. There seems to be nothing threatening about her, but she has sent a chill up the spine of more than one Point Vicente keeper and more than a few evening visitors as well.

As with many lighthouse ghosts, the Point Vicente lady is associated with a tragic story. According to legend, the lady's lover had drowned in a shipwreck, and she walks the grounds of the light station incessantly, waiting for him to join her.

For decades, it seemed, the faithful lady drifted over the station grounds almost every night. Keepers and visitors would look out across the station property and there she would be, an indistinct shape floating just above the ground. Unlike some other ghost stories, however, the Point Vicente apparition was not all talk and fantasy. The keepers swore they were really seeing something and were not—heaven forbid—drinking on duty. As it turns out, the keepers' eyes had not completely deceived them. The ghost stories may have been the work of their imaginations—lighthouse keeping is a lonely job—but what they were seeing was real enough.

The mystery was said to have been solved by a young assistant keeper with an exceptionally quick and skeptical turn of mind. He took careful note of the lady's habits. She appeared only at night and most often when the station's powerful rotating beacon moved in her direction. She had a particular fondness for nights when there was a light fog. A self-styled amateur detective, the assistant keeper deduced that the feminine ghost was the work of slight imperfections in the third-order Fresnel lens in the lantern room atop the tall tower. As the lens rotated, it refracted light toward the ground in a confusion of arcs. If the refractions came together in just the right way and found a patch of fog, the lady appeared.

Despite the sensibility of this explanation, many visitors prefer to believe that a ghostly lady still walks the station grounds, and perhaps she does. Sightings of Point Vicente's famous lady ghost continue to be reported, and some have occurred even on nights without fog. The lady has never spoken to anyone, but if she ever does, perhaps she will reveal her identity and the reason for her visits to Point Vicente.

Chapter 28
A Sorrowful Mother

Heceta Head Lighthouse
Florence, Oregon

One of America's most beautiful lighthouses is home to one of its most sorrowful ghosts. It is believed that a century or more ago, the young wife of a Heceta Head keeper lost her baby girl under tragic circumstances. Apparently she has been mourning the little girl ever since.

Lighthouses are known for their spectacular locations, but few can offer scenery more dramatic than the bold seascape that spreads out in front of Heceta Head. The lighthouse stands on the seaward slope of a mountain range that inclines toward the Pacific. However, the range doesn't end at the water's edge. Instead, it marches westward into the Pacific, where its peaks form rugged islands, and subsurface rocks create a navigational nightmare for mariners. More than a few vessels have been lost along with their passengers and crews in the pounding surf just off Heceta Head.

Despite the threat these rock-strewn waters represented to shipping, the Lighthouse Service made no attempt to mark Heceta Head until the 1890s. Likely this is because engineers thought it extremely difficult, if not impossible, to build a lighthouse on the precipitous cliffs here. An attempt was finally made, however, and in the spring of 1894, a fifty-six-foot white masonry tower was completed high up on the cliffs. The bright beacon shining from atop this handsome tower still warns ships to keep their distance.

During the years before the light was automated in 1963, keepers had to maintain the property and care for the all-important lens. They also had to light the station lamps each evening and extinguish them in the morning. This required keepers to live full time at remote Heceta Head, and usually their families lived here with them. Like families everywhere, they suffered occasional tragedies. During the late nineteenth century, one Heceta Head family endured an especially painful loss—the death of an infant child. The grave of a small girl was found on the station property some years ago, and this discovery has been linked in the minds of some to the lady ghost who has been said to haunt the lighthouse for more than a century.

Although nobody remembers how she got the name, the ghost is known to most as Rue. Appearing as a shimmering gray specter from time to time, Rue is a rather kindly ghost. She is not overly frightening and never plays mean-spirited tricks on the living. Her demeanor is distinctly melancholy and she has often been sighted staring out the windows of the station residence as if distracted by some great loss she suffered in life.

Rue has been a ghostly fixture of the lighthouse for as long as anyone can remember. She never speaks, although soft crying sounds are often heard in one or another room in the residence. Rue also makes her presence known by opening and closing doors and windows, and shifting tools and dishes from place to place. She seems to be concerned about tidiness, and the surest way to have an encounter with her is to abandon a cup or saucer on a side table or to leave papers and magazines lying around. The lighthouse doubles as a B&B nowadays, so Rue is likely faced with many challenges.

One of the most remarkable Rue incidents took place in 1970 when a worker was repairing some windows and fixtures in the attic of the residence. Having noticed a bizarre reflection in a window pane he was installing, the worker spun around to see what was behind him. What he saw took his breath away and chilled him to the bone. There, floating just above the floor, was a white-haired woman in a long gray dress. Terrified, he dropped the window and ran screaming out of the room and down the steps. The worker refused to return to the attic no matter how much pay he was offered. When someone finally did climb the steps to investigate, they found the shattered remains of the window swept into a neat pile.

Rue continues to be seen in unbroken windows at Heceta Head and in antique mirrors found in some of the upstairs rooms. Like ghosts everywhere, Rue is less real than she is a reflection of reality. People continue to look for her, however, and those who approach the search in the proper spirit will not be disappointed.

Appendix A
Other Haunted Lighthouses

The chilling stories you've read in the previous chapters have introduced you to twenty-eight of America's most haunted lighthouses. However, our Atlantic, Pacific, and Great Lakes shores are dotted with hundreds of historic light towers and keeper's residences, and nearly every one of them has a ghost story of some sort associated with it. That's because lighthouses are prime real estate for ghosts. After all, there are plenty of shadows in these old buildings and lots of dramatic events took place in and around them. Arranged alphabetically, this appendix provides information on a sampling of some of America's other haunted lighthouses.

Battery Point Lighthouse
Crescent City, California
Pressed by Northern California lumber interests during the 1850s, Congress designated Crescent City as a site for a lighthouse. Like many other early western light stations, this one consisted of a simple Cape Cod–style dwelling with a tower rising through the center of its roof. Beginning in 1856, the beacon focused by its fourth-order Fresnel lens guided freighters into the city's bustling harbor, then out again, bearing loads of redwood bound for San Francisco.

The thick stone walls of the lighthouse, built for a mere $15,000, outlasted several generations of keepers. Among them was Captain John Jeffrey, who came to Battery Point in 1875 along with his wife, Nellie. The Jeffreys became near-permanent fixtures of the station, raising four children and living in the lighthouse for a total of thirty-nine years.

The lighthouse still stands, and little has changed from the station's earliest days. Except for a stroke of luck, however, the station's last night might have been that of March 27, 1964. The earthquake that hit Alaska on that date sent five titanic tidal waves hurtling toward the coast of Northern California, where they stormed ashore shortly after midnight. Keepers Clarence and Peggy Coons saw them coming but could do little but say their prayers. Fortunately, the enormous waves struck at such an extreme angle that the lighthouse and its keepers were spared. Although the Coonses would not say so, there were some who believed that it was the lighthouse ghosts who saved them and their light station that day.

The Battery Point ghosts are described as a family consisting of a man, a woman, and a child. Their footsteps can be heard on the tower steps especially during storms, as if the ghosts were anxiously keeping watch for another tsunami. They have also been known to tap visitors on the shoulder or to sit in chairs and set them to rocking.

Big Bay Lighthouse
Big Bay, Michigan

Many ships have foundered in the treacherous waters just to the north of the famed Huron Mountains. To help mariners find their way safely, the government established a major light at Big Bay in 1896. It was displayed from a square brick tower attached to a two-story dwelling. The light was automated shortly before World War II, and in 1961 it was moved to a nearby steel-skeleton tower. The old lighthouse was then converted for use as a private residence and later as a bed-and-breakfast inn.

Many people prefer staying at B&Bs because they are nearly always spotless. The one at Big Bay may be even more so because the innkeepers get a lot of help from a very tidy ghost. The phantom seems to have an obsession with cleanliness, and no speck of dust or spot on the floor seems to get overlooked. Floors that needed attention are sometimes rendered spotless and shining by the time the innkeepers arrive to do the work themselves. The same often goes for windows, shelves, and woodwork.

It seems that William Prior, who kept the Big Bay Light during the late 1890s, was an extremely fastidious man and very particular about keeping the lighthouse in tiptop condition. He fired more than one of his assistants after accusing them of sloppiness. Eventually Prior's own son, William Jr., was made assistant keeper, and his work seemed to suit his father just fine. Unfortunately, the young man cut himself while on duty, developed gangrene, and died. A few days later his father disappeared from the lighthouse. Nearly a month passed before his body was found in a nearby wood. Apparently Prior had committed suicide. However, his spirit seems to have returned to the lighthouse, bringing with it his penchant for clean floors, sparkling windows, and general orderliness.

Boca Grande Lighthouse
Gasparilla Island, Florida
Built in 1890 on Gasparilla Island, Old Port Boca Grande Lighthouse lights the southern stretches of the Florida coast and, some say, marks the grave of a headless Spanish princess. The island is named for José Gaspar, a bloodthirsty

pirate with a lusty appetite for gold, silver, and beautiful women. Gaspar's raids on merchant ships netted him many female prisoners, some of whom he kept on Gasparilla, which he called Cautiva, meaning "captive woman."

According to legend, one of Gaspar's captives, a beautiful Spanish princess named Josefa, turned the tables on the pirate by imprisoning his heart. Gaspar was so smitten with the lady that he begged her to marry him. However, the proud Josefa answered his marriage plea with a curse and spat in his eye. In a fit of rage, the pirate drew his saber and beheaded her. Overwhelmed with remorse, Gaspar buried Josefa's body on the beach where he had murdered her. To remind him of his love for the princess, he kept her head in a jar on his ship. It is said that Josefa's decapitated ghost still walks the island in search of its missing head.

If Josefa's body was ever buried on Gasparilla Island, it likely washed away in the surf many years ago. The beaches here are constantly eroding, a process that threatens every structure on the island, including the Port Boca Grande Lighthouse. Completed in 1890 at a cost of $35,000, the square wooden structure was built on piles to protect it from the tides. The lighthouse held its own for nearly a century, but by 1970 seawater was washing away the sand around its supports. Construction of a 265-foot granite jetty helped saved the historic building. So, too, did the Gasparilla Island Conservation Association by raising funds to restore the lighthouse after the Coast Guard abandoned it in 1967. The station was relit and returned to service in 1986. Perhaps, in addition to guiding mariners, it occasionally illuminates the headless ghost of Josefa.

Boon Island Lighthouse
Near York, Maine

The Boon Island story reaches back at least as far as 1710, when a hapless British vessel known as the *Nottingham* wrecked on its jagged rocks. Those who survived the wreck suffered great privation, and their tale is related in the classic novel *Boon Island* by Kenneth Roberts. To save other ships from a similar fate, a beacon was established on this extraordinarily rugged and remote island in 1799, the same year George Washington died—Washington was not only the father of his country but also of the U.S. Lighthouse Service.

The original Boon Island Lighthouse consisted of a modest wooden tower and rustic dwelling. Several other light towers stood here before 1855, when the existing granite structure was completed. More than 130 feet tall, the impressive building is one of the tallest light towers in New England. The building and the small barren island on which it stands are said to be haunted by the specter of a woman. She is thought by some to be the ghost of Katherine Bright, a young woman who came here with her husband who took over keeping duties about the middle of the nineteenth century. After her husband was killed in a boating accident, she held his frozen body in her arms for days. By the time rescuers arrived, she had gone completely mad.

Execution Rocks Lighthouse
New Rochelle, New York

Located on an offshore stone pier, the lighthouse marks a jagged rock forming a small island in the western reaches of Long Island Sound. The island came to be called Execution Rock during the American Revolution when, according to legend at least, British troops chained condemned prisoners and left them to drown in the flooding tide. The rock proved no less of a threat to ships than to hapless patriots, for more than a few unfortunate mariners have lost their way in a fog and slammed into the low, almost invisible rock. Ironically, one of these was a British warship loaded with redcoats who perished when their vessel struck the rock during the latter years of the Revolutionary War.

To save other ships and their passengers and crews from a similar fate, the U.S. Lighthouse Service established a light station on Execution Rock in 1850. The granite tower and attached dwelling remain standing, though the residence is no longer in use. Automated in 1978, the light is powered by batteries recharged with solar panels.

During the years that keepers lived on the rock, they rarely complained of strange voices, footsteps, and other sorts of ghostly manifestations that plague most haunted lighthouses. Some keepers swore the structure was not haunted, but crewmen on passing ships say they've seen specters lining the shores of the island. Are they victims of shipwreck or of war? No one can say for sure.

Fairport Harbor Lighthouse
Fairport, Ohio

The Fairport Harbor Light began its long career of welcoming immigrants to the American Midwest in 1825, the same year the Erie Canal opened. Fairport served as an important refueling and supply port for westbound passenger and freight steamers from Buffalo, New York. The lighthouse remained in operation until 1925, when its duties were taken over by a simpler light positioned atop a foghorn station. The federal government planned to raze the old lighthouse, but local citizens launched a campaign to save the historic structure.

Presently the Fairport Harbor Historical Society maintains the lighthouse and keeper's dwelling as a marine museum.

According to curators at the museum, the lighthouse is haunted, but not by a ghost in human form. Instead, this ghost is a small gray cat that runs about the museum and the light tower on invisible feet. Sometimes at night its iridescent gold eyes can be seen gazing out into the museum from some dark corner or shelf. Among the families living at the lighthouse before it was decommissioned in 1925 was one that owned a small gray Persian cat. The pet was much loved by its family, but alas, it disappeared one day, never to return. In 2001 restoration workers discovered the remains of a small cat that had apparently gotten stuck in a crawlspace between the walls and died. The cat's skeleton is on display at the museum.

Hendricks Head Lighthouse
Boothbay Harbor, Maine
Established in 1829, the Hendricks Head Light has no doubt saved countless storm-bound mariners. However, some nor'easters are so severe that nothing can be done to assist the hapless vessels caught in their grip. During the 1860s, an especially powerful winter gale wrecked dozens of ships along the rocky coast near Boothbay Harbor. When the storm had passed, the Hendricks Head keeper pulled an ice-encrusted mattress from the waves. Inside, the astonished man found a crying baby and a note from a sinking schooner's desperate captain who had committed his tiny daughter "into God's hands." The keeper and his wife adopted the little girl, the lost ship's only survivor. It is said that a woman dressed in white often walks the beaches near the lighthouse. She has a sad expression on her face and never speaks to anyone who approaches her. If anyone comes too

close, she turns into a puff of fog and drifts away. Some say she is the mother of the child in the mattress.

Gibraltar Lighthouse
Toronto, Ontario, Canada
One of the earliest navigational markers on the Great Lakes, the Gibraltar Point Lighthouse on Lake Ontario near Toronto was completed and placed in service in 1806. Standing on the crook of a low, sandy island shaped like a fishhook, the brown-brick tower served mariners for more than 150 years before its beacon was replaced by a fully automated light mounted on a simple iron tower in 1958.

Gibraltar Point is said to be haunted by the ghost of the station's very first keeper, a man named Rademuller. In 1815 Rademuller vanished from the island and was never seen or heard from again. Some years later, however, his skeleton was unearthed near the tower, making it apparent that the keeper had been murdered. His ghost is said to walk the island and to climb the lighthouse steps at night. Perhaps he is joined by phantoms from the *Noronic*, a passenger vessel that caught fire near the point in 1949. The *Noronic* burned to the waterline in a calamity that claimed the lives of more than a hundred of those onboard.

Pennfield Reef Lighthouse
Near Fairfield, Connecticut
An Empire-style combination tower and dwelling, the Pennfield Reef Lighthouse sits on an offshore stone pier under siege by the waters of Long Island Sound. Established in 1871, the beacon was intended to guide ships through the sound and warn them away from a threatening shoal located immediately under the lighthouse. Known locally as "The

Cows," the shoal consists of a collection of jagged rocks capable of cutting through the hulls of even the strongest vessels like a can opener.

The lighthouse has been rather famously haunted since 1916 when its keeper, a man named Fred Jordan, was killed in a boating accident. Later keepers claim to have seen Jordan in and around the lighthouse. In 1942 two young boys approached the lighthouse hoping to catch some fish near the stone pier. Instead they capsized and would certainly have drowned if not for the strong arms of a kindly man who pulled them to safety. Afterward the helpful old man disappeared, and the boys were unable to find him. Later they saw a picture of Jordan and told their friends and family that he was the one who had rescued them. Over the years more than a few boaters who have run into trouble in this part of the sound claim to have been assisted by the spirit of the long-dead keeper.

Plymouth Lighthouse
Plymouth, Massachusetts
One of America's earliest lighthouses, the original Plymouth Light Station showed two beacons, one each from a pair of small wooden towers spaced only a few feet apart. These lights were not very effective at guiding mariners, but they did attract some unwanted attention from a British frigate that fired on the station during a Revolutionary War battle in 1778. When the lighthouse accidentally burned to the ground in 1801, its replacement, built two years later, also sported double towers. One of the Plymouth towers was dismantled in 1924, but the other still stands.

The original keepers of this historic light station were John and Hannah Thomas. When the Revolutionary War broke out, John Thomas answered the call to arms, leaving his wife to tend the light. Thomas fought for the patriot cause under the leadership of General George Washington, and he likely gave his life for it. No one was ever sure where Thomas fell or in which battle, but he never returned to Plymouth. For decades Hannah Thomas continued to keep the light, hoping against hope that someday her husband would return. She finally died, passing her lighthouse duties along to her son. However, there are those who believe that Hannah Thomas has remained the true keeper of the light for more than two centuries. At night her spirit can be seen floating around the lighthouse property, or so it is said. People who have seen her say she doesn't necessarily look old, only sad.

Point Sur Lighthouse
Big Sur, California

At Big Sur the churning Pacific makes relentless war on a chain of coastal mountains. The same natural forces—weather and geology—responsible for this scenic spectacle have also made it a very dangerous place for ships. Countless seafaring vessels and at least one dirigible—the U.S.S. *Macon*—have been lost here, and the spirits of seamen lost in these disasters may very well haunt the entire coastline.

Since 1889, the powerful beacon of the Point Sur Lighthouse has warned mariners to keep away from Big Sur's deadly rocks. But anyone who sees the tower, keeper's residence, and other station buildings today can only scratch their heads in wonder that they were ever built at all. At one time it was thought impossible to build a light station on Big Sur's precipitous cliffs, but the Lighthouse Service took up the challenge during the late 1880s. Before construction could begin, workers had to build a special railroad to carry materials and supplies to the site. The project took two years of hard work and cost more than $100,000, a bewildering sum at the time.

When it was completed, the station consisted of a forty-foot granite tower atop the cliffs and a collection of dwellings and other buildings nearer the water. Keepers found the lighthouse almost as hard to maintain as it had been to build. Every night they had to trudge up the 395 steps leading to the tower. The station was finally automated in 1972, eliminating the need for the long daily climb. At that time a rotating airport-style beacon replaced the original first-order Fresnel lens.

In 1935 an unusual sea disaster took place just west of Point Sur and within sight of the lighthouse. Caught in a squall, the 780-foot dirigible *Macon* lost buoyancy and crashed into the Pacific, causing a loss of seventy-three lives, including two seamen. Do they haunt Point Sur? Some believe so, but somehow that seems unlikely.

There is a ghost at Point Sur, however. Like the ghosts found at many lighthouses, this one appears to be a former keeper. He is often seen wearing an old-fashioned uniform that looks very much like the ones worn by Lighthouse Service keepers. No one has yet linked this ghost to any former keeper of the Point Sur Lighthouse, but no doubt there is some link between the specter and the history of this spectacular maritime facility.

Point Wilson Lighthouse
Port Townsend, Washington
Completed in 1879, the Point Wilson Lighthouse guides ships headed for Seattle or Tacoma through Washington's

Admiralty Inlet. Producing a powerful light visible from any point along a sweeping 270 degrees of horizon, the light remains in use today. The beacon is now automated, but for more than a century the station had full-time keepers.

Over the years, several Point Wilson keepers—or more often the keepers' wives—reported seeing a woman in a long, flowing gown roaming the lighthouse buildings and grounds. She had a habit of rummaging through closets and drawers when no one was in a room. Keepers or family members who happened to be nearby would hear the rummaging and hurry into the room to investigate. Usually they would arrive just in time to catch the suggestion of a white gown flying out through a window or disappearing into a wall. The apparition has been seen less often in recent years, but there is no longer anyone living at the lighthouse to take notice of her activities.

Ram Island Lighthouse
Boothbay Harbor, Maine
Located on rocky Ram Island, this light marks one of the key passages leading to Boothbay Harbor, now a popular summertime tourist destination. When the station was established in 1883, the seaside villages hereabouts were frequented mostly by fishermen. To help them avoid the ledges near the island, the government built a thirty-five-foot granite and brick tower and fitted it with a Fresnel lens. Keepers lived in an L-shaped residence some distance inland. Although the station was automated many years ago, both the dwelling and tower remain standing. The Fresnel lens has been replaced by a modern optic, but the beacon is still in operation. It warns mariners with an alternating red and white light.

Long before the Ram Island Lighthouse was built, fishermen built fires or held ship's lanterns aloft to guide their friends home to Boothbay. According to legend, when the weather was especially bad, a woman would appear down by the shore waving a torch over her head. She may once have been a living person, perhaps the wife of a Boothbay mariner who frequently got lost in the dark, but later she became a legend or, if you will, a ghost. Even today, boaters claim to have seen the lady all dressed in white waving her torch. Some even say she has saved their lives.

Split Rock Lighthouse
Two Harbors, Minnesota

An octagonal, yellow-brick structure, the Split Rock tower is only 54 feet tall, but the cliff beneath it soars more than 120 feet above the lake. This makes Split Rock, with its focal plane nearly 170 feet above the water, one of the loftiest lighthouses on the Great Lakes. It also makes this one of the most spectacular and frequently photographed lighthouses in America—or the world. Ironically, Split Rock is no longer an active aid to navigation, but rather a highly popular maritime museum.

Built in 1910, the lighthouse owes its existence to a hurricane-like blizzard that struck the Great Lakes in November 1905. This mighty storm drove more than thirty sizable ore boats and freighters onto Lake Superior's rocky shores. The calamity convinced officials that the system of navigation aids on Lake Superior must be improved. The most important improvement undertaken was construction of a lighthouse on Split Rock near where the freighter *William Edenborn* had met its end during the storm. In all, the project cost taxpayers some $72,000.

The station's flashing light, seen from up to twenty-two miles out on the lake, was produced by a Fresnel lens that looks something like a huge clamshell. It served until 1969, when the Coast Guard decommissioned the lighthouse and handed it over to the State of Minnesota for use as a park and museum.

Museum visitors often ask about the Split Rock Lighthouse ghost. Usually dressed in an old-fashioned Lighthouse Service uniform, the specter is sometimes seen in or around the tower and residence. The uniform suggests the ghost is likely that of a former keeper, perhaps Orren Young, the station's first keeper. Young was no longer young by the time he took the job in 1910 and was well past the age of seventy when he retired in 1928. Now, of course, he is ageless.

Stratford Shoal Light
Bridgeport, Connecticut

A rocky shoal lurks just beneath the surface of Long Island Sound, about halfway between Bridgeport, Connecticut, and the shores of Long Island. Over the centuries it has claimed the lives of many unwary seamen who expected to find relative safety in the sound. In 1837 the Lighthouse Service marked the shoal with a lightship, and then in the mid-1870s with a permanent lighthouse. Completed in 1877, the Stratford Shoal Lighthouse stands on a concrete-filled caisson atop a foundation of granite blocks held together with iron staples. The caisson serves as a platform for the tower and dwelling built in the Victorian style often associated with ghosts.

Most Connecticut lighthouses are not as isolated as this one, and the loneliness of this duty station proved too much for some keepers. In 1905 a young assistant keeper named

Julius Koster went raving mad. After attempting to kill another member of the lighthouse staff with an ax, Koster attempted suicide by jumping from the lighthouse platform into Long Island Sound. He was rescued and taken to a hospital onshore where he later committed suicide. After that unhappy incident, the lighthouse was never a comfortable place for keepers to live. Doors slammed unexpectedly, carefully stored pans and dishes fell off of shelves, and furniture was moved about and overturned when no one was in the room. When the lighthouse was automated in 1969, the keepers were no doubt happy to leave.

Sturgeon Point Lighthouse
Alcona, Michigan

Not far from Sturgeon Point on Lake Huron, a potentially deadly reef lies in wait for unwary vessels. Built in 1870 to warn mariners to steer clear of this dangerous obstacle, the Sturgeon Point Lighthouse has prevented countless accidents. Even so, many vessels have wrecked practically in the shadow of its sixty-eight-foot tower. On the station grounds sits a big rudder salvaged from the wooden steamer *Marine City*, which burned near here in an 1880 disaster just off Sturgeon Point. Also lost nearby were the 233-ton schooner *Venus* in 1887, the schooner *Ispeming* in 1903, the steamer *Clifton* in a 1924 gale, and many other vessels.

Today the lighthouse remains in operation but is owned by the Alcona County Historical Society, which uses the old keeper's residence as a museum. Occasionally visitors are allowed to climb the tower's eighty-five steps to the lantern room, where the station's sparkling lens sits ready to beam its warning out across the lake. No visitors have ever claimed to have met the Sturgeon Point Lighthouse ghost, but many believe that one exists. Lights inside the building go on and off all by themselves. It may be that a former keeper or the victim of a nearby shipwreck is determined to announce his presence.

Waugoshance Lighthouse
Straits of Mackinac, Michigan
The Straits of Mackinac link the often stormy and heavily trafficked waters of Lake Michigan with those of Lake Huron. To make the passage through these narrows easier and safer for shipping, the Lighthouse Service established a beacon at the Lake Michigan entrance to the straits. Built atop a cylindrical stone pier in 1851, the lighthouse was called Waugoshance, a Native American word meaning "Fox Island." However, keepers did not think the station any too foxy. They avoided it if at all possible.

Keepers came and went from the Waugoshance Lighthouse with clockwork regularity. The lighthouse was cramped and isolated and the weather often depressing, but there were other reasons the average length of service for keepers at Waugoshance was only about a year. The lighthouse was quite definitely haunted. Keepers complained that they could not sleep because of all the banging on the walls and trotting up and down the tower steps, presumably by a ghost.

John Hermann likely served the longest as keeper, devoting several years to the job during the late 1800s. Perhaps the only way Hermann could stand the place was by drinking heavily. One day in 1900 Hermann drank himself into a stupor and vanished from the lighthouse, leaving one of his assistants locked in the lantern room. The assistant believed his boss had locked him in as a practical joke, but who can say? During the years after Hermann's disappearance—likely as not he fell into the lake and drowned—the Waugoshance ghost became especially active. One of the ghost's favorite tricks was to lock doors behind keepers. The ghost came to be called Wobbleshanks, and many believed it to be the spirit of a now eternally inebriated Hermann.

The Waugoshance Lighthouse was closed down before World War II, and during the war U.S. Navy pilots used the building for bombing and strafing practice. Old Wobbleshanks must have kept his head down, since he is believed to still inhabit the building, which amazingly enough survived the punishment it took from the Navy.

White River Lighthouse
Muskegon, Michigan

During the years after the Civil War, Michigan's forest industries burgeoned and the area around Muskegon became known as the "Lumber Queen of the World." Most of the lumber produced in this part of the state was floated down rivers to small ports such as Whitehall, where it was loaded onto freighters and shipped to markets in the East.

In 1875 a lighthouse was built at Whitehall to guide the lumber freighters in and out of harbor. Known as the White River Lighthouse, it consisted of a forty-foot octagonal tower and an attached keeper's residence, both built of Michigan limestone. Captain William Robinson, the station's first keeper, served here for almost half a century. In his declining years, the good captain took to walking with a cane. Its constant tapping can still be heard occasionally in and around the lighthouse. Nearly everyone who hears this eerie but somehow comforting sound believes it is being made by the kindly ghost of Captain Robinson—or, if they don't believe it, they would never say so.

Wood Island Lighthouse
Near Biddeford, Maine

Among the oldest maritime lights in Maine, the Wood Island beacon first shined in 1808 during the presidential administration of Thomas Jefferson. The original structures have all been replaced over the years, but the existing ones are nonetheless quite old. For instance, the tower dates to 1839, while the residence was built about the time of the Civil War. These fine old buildings began to deteriorate after the light was automated in 1986. Fortunately, they have been saved and handsomely restored thanks largely to the efforts of the American Lighthouse Foundation, headquartered in nearby Wells, Maine. That may be especially good news for the Wood Island ghost, who still has a dry place to get out of the rain—or to keep his chickens.

During the 1890s, York County Sheriff Fred Milliken kept a large chicken coop on Wood Island. However, Milliken spent too much time keeping the peace and lobstering to look after his chickens, so he rented the coop to a local man named Howard Hobbs. One day during the summer of 1896, Hobbs got into a loud and prolonged argument with Milliken, presumably over the rent he paid for the coop. It ended when Hobbs drew a gun and shot Milliken. Overwhelmed with guilt, Hobbs retreated to Wood Island, where he said farewell to his chickens and then turned his gun on himself. Hobbs's ghost is now said to haunt the lighthouse, filling the tower with his sobs and moans.

Yaquina Bay Lighthouse
Newport, Oregon

Built on the crest of a hill near the entrance to Yaquina Bay, this wood-frame lighthouse is topped by lamps in a little red lantern that first burned in November 1871. Less than three years later they were permanently snuffed out. Due to an extraordinary bureaucratic bungle, a second lighthouse was mistakenly erected nearby, rendering the Yaquina Bay Light superfluous.

People might have supposed at the time that the abandoned two-story lighthouse would soon be demolished, but not so. The building was eventually put to use as a crew station for the U.S. Lifesaving Service. Later it was carefully restored and became an attractive historical museum.

The lighthouse is thought by some to be haunted by the ghost of a teenage girl named Muriel Travenard, who was supposedly killed here during the late 1800s. The young woman had explored the boarded-up lighthouse with some friends, then returned to the building alone after they had left. When her friends noticed she was missing, they went back to the old lighthouse, where they found a trail of blood, but no Muriel. Neither the girl nor her body was ever located. Over the years, many have claimed to have seen her ghost walking the lighthouse grounds.

Appendix B
Lighthouse Terms

Lighthouse keepers and other members of the U.S. Lighthouse Service used a specialized vocabulary. It enabled them to more easily discuss the important work they did and the lonely lives they and their families lived at remote light stations. This appendix includes some of the more unusual and revealing terms once used by lighthouse keepers and occasionally used today by members of the U.S. Coast Guard. Not all of these terms are directly related to the twenty-eight ghostly stories found in *Haunted Lighthouses*. Even so, you may find reading through them is both highly informative and entertaining. Particular emphasis is placed on how the people, places, or equipment these words describe may be linked to hauntings.

Attached dwelling
In some cases, the keeper's residence was attached to the tower. Often the residence was two stories tall and the tower rose from the front of the building or from one of its corners. Having the tower and residence attached enabled the keeper to conveniently service the light regardless of weather conditions. Not surprisingly, attached residences were most common in northern climes, where a winter walk to a distant light tower might give the keeper a nasty case of frostbite.

Having the tower attached to the residence put the keeper in close contact with his work. It also meant that anything going on in the tower was apparent to both the keeper and his family. For instance, if there were mysterious footsteps on the tower stairway, they would be heard day or night. In haunted lighthouses, especially those with attached towers, keepers lived in uncomfortably close proximity to the ghost.

Automated light

With the introduction of electric power and reliable timers early in the twentieth century, it became possible to operate light stations without full-time keepers. By the 1930s, the U.S. Lighthouse Service had begun to automate beacons and remove keepers from stations that were either extremely isolated or costly to maintain. Following World War II, remote control systems, light-activated switches, and fog-sensing devices made automation an increasingly cost-effective and attractive option, and by 1970, only about sixty U.S. lighthouses still had full-time keepers. Today all the keepers are gone, leaving the lighthouse ghosts, if there are any, to walk the old towers and residences alone.

Beacon

Any light or radio signal intended to guide mariners or aviators can be referred to as a beacon. Often the word is used interchangeably with "light" or lighthouse. Early beacons were often nothing more than a lantern hung from a pole, a candle kept burning in an upstairs window, or a fire banked high on a hill overlooking the sea. Eighteenth-century light towers had very dim beacons produced by tallow candles or simple oil lamps, but over the years lighthouse beacons grew increasingly sophisticated and effective. During the early nineteenth century, whale oil lamps and silvered reflectors brightened their lights considerably. The invention of polished-glass prismatic lenses by Augustin Fresnel during the 1820s enabled lighthouse beacons to reach vessels at a distance of twenty miles or more. Radio beacons, introduced in 1921, extended the effective reach of a navigational station to several hundred miles.

When seen from a distance, there is something very spiritual or even ghostly about a lighthouse beacon. It seems to reach out toward you as if it had a soul or spirit of its own. In some cases, mariners claim to have seen beacons that were no longer in operation. For obvious reasons, these are referred to as sightings of "ghost lights."

Birdcage lantern

Early lanterns in the United States and elsewhere often had dozens if not hundreds of small panes of glass held in place by a thin metal frame. Consisting of numerous metal ribs extending from the gallery deck to the roof—usually a copper dome and ventilator—the frames gave these lanterns the appearance of a birdcage.

Difficult to keep clean and often of poor quality, the small panes of glass in birdcage lanterns tended to limit the brightness and effectiveness of the station's light signal. So, too, did the metal ribs, which blocked light and dimmed the beacon. Usually too small to accommodate Fresnel lenses, birdcage lanterns were eventually phased out. However, the ruins of birdcage lanterns can be seen atop abandoned lighthouses—the very ones most likely to be inhabited by ghosts.

Boats

Not surprisingly, nearly all lighthouses keepers were familiar with the care and operation of small boats. Getting around in a harbor, on and off an open-water light station, or to and from a lighthouse tender required the deft use of small watercraft. Most early manned light stations had a boat, powered by oars or, on occasion, a modest sail. Later keepers or Coast Guard station crews had access to boats with outboard motors or small inboard engines.

Inevitably the extensive use of boats by keepers led to accidents. Of the keepers killed in the line of duty, and there have been quite a few, the majority lost their lives in boating accidents. George Worthylake, America's first lighthouse keeper, drowned in 1718 when his boat overturned while he was on his way from the mainland to Little Brewster Island, where he had tended the Boston Light for less than a year.

Lighthouse boating accidents were often mysterious. In many such cases, the keeper or one of his assistants stepped into the station boat, headed for shore, and was simply never seen again, at least not in living form. However, more than a few drowned keepers appear to have returned to their duty stations as ghosts.

Bull's-eye lens

Lighthouse lenses often have two or more convex panels or bull's-eyes that focus light and cause the beacon to flash. These radiate shafts of light that turn somewhat like the spokes of a wagon wheel as the lens rotates. Since the light focused by a bull's-eye is concentrated in a single direction, it can cause some very bizarre optical illusions. For instance, in a fog or heavy mist it can create what to an imaginative observer appears to be a lady dressed in flowing white robes.

Characteristic

The identifying feature of a lighthouse beacon is referred to as its characteristic. For example, the light may be fixed and display a white, red, or green color. It may flash at regular intervals such as every fifteen or twenty seconds. It may display a single flash or series of quick flashes. Charts and published light lists help mariners identify the characteristic of a given light.

Among the more famous lighthouse characteristics is that of the offshore Minot's Ledge Lighthouse near Scituate, Massachusetts, which displays a single flash, followed by four quick flashes, then three more. This one-four-three flashing sequence reminds some romantic observers of "I love you." On the other hand, this venerable lighthouse is unquestionably haunted, so the sequence might be interpreted as a message from beyond. Maybe the correct interpretation could be something like "I hear you" or "I know you."

Clockwork mechanism

Early rotating lighthouse lenses were often driven by a set of gears, weights, and pulleys similar to those used in large clocks. Every few hours the keeper had to "rewind" the machinery by pulling or cranking the weights to the top of the tower. Since the mechanism might need to be rewound at any time during the night, making regular sleep habits impossible, some keepers considered this an especially onerous chore. One of the early keepers at Minnesota's Split Rock Lighthouse is said to have slept on a pallet beneath the weight so that it would wake him when it reached the bottom and needed to be rewound.

These mechanisms made lots of noise, and there was always plenty of rattling and clanking going on in towers that were equipped with them. It is perhaps understandable that these noises were sometimes mistaken for the rattling of the chains said to bind dead spirits to the earth. Keepers said they could sometimes hear the jangle and clatter even when the mechanisms were not in operation.

Coast Guard

Since 1939 lighthouses and other aids to navigation in the United States have been the responsibility of the U.S. Coast Guard. As America's primary maritime agency, the Coast Guard plays a wide variety of roles, each of them vital to the security and well-being of the nation. In addition to the placement and maintenance of maritime aids, the Coast Guard also handles a vast array of assignments related to search and rescue, law enforcement, environmental protection, preventive safety, and military preparedness.

The Coast Guard is an amalgamation of five former federal agencies: the Revenue Cutter Service, the Lifesaving Service, the Steamboat Inspection Service, the Bureau of Navigation, and the Lighthouse Service. The Coast Guard was formed by executive order of President Woodrow Wilson in 1915 when the Revenue Cutter Service and Lifesaving Service were brought together under its umbrella. Later the other agencies were added to the mix, the final one being the Lighthouse Service, absorbed by order of President Franklin Roosevelt shortly before World War II. Interestingly enough, the Coast Guard traces its history not to 1915, but rather to 1789, when the Lighthouse Service came into being.

The Coast Guard maintains "aids to navigation teams" staffed by highly skilled technicians who look after navigational aids. Since all lighted maritime aids are now automated, team members need only visit them from time to time to make repairs and take care of routine maintenance. On such occasions coastguardsmen may encounter changes that are difficult to explain, such as furniture that seems to have shifted from one room to another or locked supply closets that have somehow been opened and ransacked. Most Coast Guard personnel are hard-minded observers of fact and are less likely than most to explain bizarre events in terms of the supernatural. Still, they can't help but wonder.

Daymark

Brightly painted, often in distinctive colors or patterns, light towers continue to guide mariners during daylight hours by offering them a handy point of reference. For this reason deactivated light towers were often left standing so that they could serve as daymarks. Of course, the abandoned towers made a perfect abode for bats and for any ghost that happened to be drifting about the vicinity.

Donohoo, John

A prolific early-century government contractor, John Donohoo built several lighthouses on the Chesapeake Bay during the 1820s and 1830s. Donohoo's towers were solid structures of stone or brick, and a few, such as the one he built at Cove Point, Maryland, in 1828, still stand. During his tightfisted administration of the U.S. lighthouse system, Fifth Auditor Stephen J. Pleasonton favored Donohoo largely because he was willing to work for next to nothing. Donohoo received only $3,350 for building the Point Lookout Lighthouse in Maryland. Despite its bargain price, this venerable old lighthouse remains standing.

In part, perhaps, because they have lasted so long and are so old, nearly all of Donohoo's lighthouses are said to be haunted. Some say they are haunted by the ghost of the builder himself. It seems appropriate that, having been paid so little for his work in the first place, Donohoo should be able to use the lighthouses he built as a rent-free home for his spirit.

Fixed signal

A lighthouse beacon that shines constantly during its regular hours of operation is said to display a "fixed" signal. Most beacons flash or shine intermittently to help mariners distinguish them from nearby lights. Fixed signals are more often seen near the entrances of harbors or in relatively dark areas where they are more easily spotted and identified. Although they do not flash, fixed signal lighthouse beacons such as the one at Owls Head near Rockland, Maine, are no less ghostly. The eerie glow of these beacons gives one the impression that they have an otherworldly source. It is easy to imagine that they are lit at least in part by fires of the spirit.

Flashing signal

A lighthouse beacon that turns on and off or grows much brighter at regular intervals is called a flashing signal. Beacons with a flashing characteristic are readily distinguished from other nearby lights. Nowadays the flashing characteristics of most maritime beacons are produced by switches that turn the electric lights on and off at the appropriate intervals. However, many early flashing beacons were generated by rotating Fresnel lenses. These funneled light into special panels or bull's-eyes that momentarily intensified the light and created the appearance of a flash. As explained in the section on bull's-eyes, this process could lead to bizarre optical illusions sometimes mistaken for ghosts.

Fog signal or foghorn

When thick fog or heavy weather sets in, mariners may not be able to see or distinguish a lighthouse beacon. At such times a sound signal is used to warn vessels away from prominent headlands or navigational obstacles. Many different noise-making devices have been used as fog signals. Early keepers alerted mariners by blowing trumpets, firing off cannons, or ringing heavy bells. One Lake Michigan lighthouse once used the whistle of a parked locomotive to warn mariners. It is said that more than one vessel approaching the deadly rocks off Owls Head in Maine were saved by the incessant barking of the keeper's dog. Seamen passing Owls Head still sometimes hear the barking. Are they hearing dogs that just happen to be loose somewhere around the old lighthouse, or is it possible that the ghost of the original dog just doesn't want to give up his job?

Fresnel lens

Invented in 1822 by Augustin Fresnel, a noted French physicist, Fresnel lenses concentrate light into a powerful beam that can be seen over great distances. Usually they consist of individual hand-polished glass prisms arrayed in a bronze frame. Manufactured by a number of French or British companies, these devices came in as many as eleven sizes or "orders." A massive first-order lens may be more than six feet in diameter and twelve feet tall, while a diminutive sixth-order lens is only about one foot wide and not much larger than an ordinary gallon jug. Although now thought old-fashioned, Fresnel lenses represented the finest available lighthouse technology of their day. Remarkably, they still work as well or better than most of the so-called modern optics that in many cases have replaced them.

It is important to note that Fresnel lenses are no longer being manufactured and haven't been for more than a century. Any lens that happens to still be in use is of necessity, therefore, very old. Cracks and discoloration in antique lens prisms can spray light about in odd directions and create interesting or even frightening illusions. Some ghost sightings have been explained away as optical illusions caused by damaged lenses.

Gallery

Many light towers have a circular walkway with a metal railing around the lantern. Known as a gallery, this walkway provided convenient access to the outside of the lantern for painting and repair work. Keepers could stand in the gallery while cleaning the windows of the lantern room, a vital task since even a thin film of grime on the glass would sharply reduce the beacon's effectiveness. The railing, usually of cast iron, provided an opportunity for playful decorative touches, as at the Cape Neddick Lighthouse in Maine, where miniature light towers perch on the balusters. When observers on the ground see a ghostly figure up near the top of a light tower, the phantom usually appears to be standing in the gallery, perhaps looking out to sea after a lost lover.

Keeper

The person responsible for operating a navigational beacon and maintaining the buildings, property, and equipment at a light station was known as the keeper. Early keepers often received their appointments in return for exemplary military service or as a political favor. Even so, the work was hard and the pay—often little more than $10 a month—hardly enticing. Still, keepers had a regular income and a rent-free place for themselves and their families to live.

Until 1939, U.S. lighthouse keepers were civilian employees of the Lighthouse Service, Treasury Department, or some other government agency. After 1939, most lighthouses were staffed by U.S. Coast Guard crews. Since lighthouses everywhere have now been automated, the lighthouse keeper's profession has vanished. However, the spirits of the dedicated men and women who kept the lights are still very much in evidence. If an old lighthouse happens to be haunted, the ghost is more than likely that of a former keeper or a member of the keeper's family.

Keeper's residence

The presence of a keeper's residence is what turned a coastal beacon or light station into a light "house." In many cases, lighthouses were placed on islands or other remote places that could not easily be reached from a town or even a small village. Because of the nature of their work, keepers needed to be available all night and, in foggy weather, during daylight hours as well. In the days before automation, this meant there had to be on-site residences for keepers and their families.

Keepers were never paid very well, but in most cases, their homes were provided rent-free. Most keepers' dwellings were modest but comfortable, and of course they nearly always had a great view. A typical dwelling was a one-and-a-half-story wood or stone structure built in a style similar to that of other working-class homes in the area.

Lighthouse residences are just as likely, perhaps even more likely, to be haunted than the towers. After all, this is where keepers and their loved ones lived out their lives and spent most of their time. If for some reason they could not completely abandon their former existences once they were dead, the residence is the most natural place for them to haunt.

Lamp

A lighthouse lens did not shine all by itself and required a reliable light source of some sort. During the years before lighthouses were supplied with electricity and incandescent bulbs, that light source was likely to be a whale oil or kerosene lamp. Among a keeper's most important duties were refueling these lamps and trimming their wicks. As any romantically inclined person may very well understand, lamp lights were not so cold or utilitarian as those produced by electricity. There seemed to be an emotional or spiritual force behind the lights produced by lamps. Mariners who were lost in the dark might have felt these warm, glowing lamp lights calling to them not just from shore, but from another, more friendly world.

Lantern or lantern room

The glass-enclosed space at the top of a light tower is known as the lantern or lantern room. It houses the lens or optic and protects it from the weather. Often the lantern is topped by a cone-shaped metal roof and encircled by a narrow walkway called the gallery. Many lanterns are of cast-iron construction and have a number of separate window panels. When ghosts are spotted in a lighthouse tower, they usually are standing or floating in the lantern room.

Lifesaving Service

The crews of ships that run aground on sandbars, reefs, and beaches often need help to safely reach shore. For centuries this assistance, if it arrived at all, came in the form of impromptu rescue efforts thrown together by untrained locals. Around 1850, the U.S. government began to place lifesaving stations here and there along dangerous stretches of coast, especially in the Northeast. Although well stocked with surfboats, ropes, rockets, carronades, and similar equipment, these stations had no full-time staff and were run much like volunteer fire departments.

After a deadly storm in 1870 left Eastern beaches littered with broken ships and bodies, Congress finally responded to calls for a more comprehensive and professional approach to maritime lifesaving. Funds were appropriated to employ six-man crews at existing stations and to establish many new ones. In 1878 all these stations were gathered under the wing of a new federal entity, the U.S. Lifesaving Service, which later became part of the Coast Guard. Although it existed for less than four decades, the Lifesaving Service made its mark on maritime history. Many sailors owed their lives to the quick work of service crews.

The Lifesaving Service may also have supplied more than a few of the ghosts that now haunt America's light-houses. Lifesavers were intensely dedicated men who might not have been able to abandon their calling even in death. More than one foundering seaman has credited a mysterious, unseen hand with saving him from drowning by pulling him out of the surf.

Lighthouse

The term "lighthouse" has been applied to a wide variety of buildings constructed for the purpose of guiding ships. It is often used interchangeably with similar or derivative terms, such as "light tower" or "light station," or simply "light." The traditional concept of a lighthouse is that of a residence with a light tower either attached or located a short distance away, and that is the type of lighthouse that most often gets haunted.

Lighthouse Service

Before the Coast Guard took over maintenance of American navigational lights, that job was handled by a federal agency that most referred to as the Lighthouse Service. However, that was not always the agency's official name. During the early twentieth century, for instance, it was known as the U.S. Bureau of Lighthouses. Nowadays, lighthouse lovers and ghost hunters tend to look back on the era of the civilian Lighthouse Service as a "golden age" when America's lighthouses flourished in the care of faithful resident keepers. Many of the ghosts that now haunt lighthouses are thought to have once been Lighthouse Service keepers.

Lightships

Equipped with their own beacons, usually displayed from a tall central mast, lightships were essentially floating lighthouses. They marked shoals or key navigational turning points where construction of a permanent light tower was either impossible or prohibitively expensive. Although large enough to hold foghorn equipment and support one or two light masts, often topped with a revolving optic, most lightships were quite small, usually only a few dozen tons in displacement. This meant that quarters for the crew were cramped and uncomfortable. Crewmen might serve onboard for months at a time with practically no contact with land and little to eat but salt beef and potatoes. As a result, lighthouse keepers assigned to lightships tended to get a bit stir crazy. They can be forgiven for reporting some very strange things, such as sea monsters and ghosts that walked across the water and boarded their vessels.

Lightship crewmen often faced grave danger, especially when raging storms blew in and tossed their little vessels around like corks. In 1913 *Buffalo Lightship Number 82* foundered in a mighty November gale that had swept across Lake Erie. Before his ship went down, dragging him and all hands to the bottom, the captain had just enough time to scratch a desperate message on a board. It read, "Goodbye, Nellie, ship is breaking up fast—Williams." Williams's ghost is thought to have been seen at various points along the shores of the lake.

Light station

A navigational facility with a light beacon is commonly referred to as a light station. Often the term is used interchangeably with "lighthouse," but a light station may or may not include a tower, quarters for a keeper, or a fog signal. Keeper fatalities and other dramatic events did not always happen in the tower or residence, but might occur anywhere on or near the lighthouse property. Since ghosts are often linked to such events, it is usually the entire light station that is haunted and not just the main buildings.

Light tower

Because of the curvature of the earth, objects or lights at or near sea level cannot be seen from more than a few miles away. Ancient peoples banked their signal fires on hills to make them visible over greater distances. The tower of a lighthouse is, in essence, an artificial hill, designed to raise the beacon's height.

People have been building light towers for over two thousand years. The first known to history was the Pharos, a giant 450-foot stone structure built about 2,500 years ago at the entrance of the harbor at Alexandria, Egypt. It is said that vessels were guided to the city by a fire blazing on the Pharos roof. Light towers of the modern era support a lantern, which houses a lamp, electric beacon, or some other lighting device. The height of the tower may be as little as twenty or as much as two hundred feet, and this in part determines the range of the beacon. Typically light towers are cylindrical, square, or octagonal and constructed of stone, brick, cast iron, or steel. A stairway of wood or iron—lighthouses rarely feature elevators—provides access to the lantern room.

Tower interiors can be quite dark and shadowy, and this in part may account for the large number of ghosts said to have been sighted inside them. The walls of older lighthouses tend to have cracks that may open the interior to jets of chilling air from the outside. The wind often makes whistling or moaning sounds when passing through these cracks or around the outside of the tower. Often made of cast iron, the tower steps usually spiral upward to the lantern room. Among the most common pieces of evidence put forward for lighthouse hauntings are unexplained footsteps on the tower staircase. It is worth noting that living keepers would climb those steps many thousands of times during their careers. Why then would they not continue doing so in death?

Modern optic

Nowadays, most navigational beacons are produced by so-called modern optics. The term refers to a broad array of lightweight, mostly weatherproof devices that are relatively inexpensive and easy to maintain. Removing the prismatic Fresnel lens from an old lighthouse and equipping it with a modern optic tends to reduce the number of ghost sightings, especially at night. This may be because flaws in the crystal prisms of Fresnel lenses scatter light and may create the illusion of a spirit hovering in a bank of fog or mist. Or it may be because the ghosts themselves are closely attached to antique lenses. After all, keepers spent much of their time polishing and caring for the big glass Fresnels. Once the Fresnel is gone, a ghost who was formerly a keeper may think his job is finally done.

Pleasonton, Stephen J.

A remarkable though little-known figure in American history, Stephen J. Pleasonton maintained a firm—some would say choking—grip on the U.S. lighthouse system for more than thirty years. A Treasury Department auditor and consummate bureaucrat, Pleasonton ran the Lighthouse Service on behalf of half a dozen U.S. presidents. Pleasonton was handed responsibility for the nation's lighthouses in 1820 and did not relinquish his authority over the system and its purse strings until Congress forced him to do so when it created the Lighthouse Board in 1852. Pleasonton hired cut-rate contractors even when their previous work had been shown to be of poor quality. As a result, more than a few keepers lost their lives in accidents that might never have happened if U.S. light stations had been better built and adequately equipped. It may be that some keepers who became ghosts during the Pleasonton era are hanging around in hopes that their former boss might happen by so they can throttle him.

Range lights

Displayed in pairs, range lights help mariners keep their vessels safely within the narrow navigable channels that crisscross estuaries or lead in and out of harbors. The rear light is higher and farther from the water than its partner, the front light, which is often located hard by the shore. When

viewed from mid-channel, the lights appear in perfect verti-
cal alignment. If the upper light tilts either to the right or
the left, a pilot must steer in the opposite direction to correct course. Although entirely a consequence of perspective,
this shifting of the lights produces an eerie sensation in an
observer out on the water. It is almost as if some unseen
hand is repositioning the lights to assist mariners. Perhaps,
in a sense, that is precisely what is happening.

Skeleton towers

Nothing is spookier than a skeleton, and that is true whether
it is constructed of bone or of metal. Iron or steel skeleton light towers are naked structures without any walls in
the conventional sense. They consist of four or more heavily braced metal legs topped by workrooms and a lantern.
Relatively durable and inexpensive, they were built in considerable numbers during the latter half of the nineteenth
century. Since their open walls offer little resistance to wind
and water, skeleton towers proved ideal for offshore navigational stations, such as those in the stormy Florida Keys. In
part because they have lasted so long, skeleton towers have
collected quite a few ghosts.

Tenders

Throughout its history, the U.S. Lighthouse Service maintained a fleet of small, specially outfitted tenders used to
deliver construction materials and supplies to light stations.
Throughout much of the nineteenth century, of course,
these vessels were sailing ships. Later, steam- and diesel-
powered ships were used as tenders. Like ships of any type
in any era, lighthouse tenders were vulnerable to storms
and accidents. Several were lost at sea or in collisions with

the rocks and shoals—ironically the very hazards the light-houses were meant to guard against. The captains and crew of lost tenders may haunt some lighthouses.

Twin light

A few lighthouses once displayed two or even three separate lights. This was done to help mariners distinguish their beacons from other prominent nearby lights. Usually tended by the same keeper, these double or triple beacons were usually displayed from separate towers spaced several hundred feet apart.

In 1924, government maritime officials decided to convert all U.S. multiple lights to a single-light system. This policy was enforced even at Plymouth, where one of the station's two very historic towers was torn down. The other tower remains in use to this day. Even so, mariners say they can sometimes see two lights at Plymouth. The second light is said to be a ghost beacon.

Wickie

Before electric power made lighthouse work much cleaner and simpler, nearly all navigational beacons were produced by oil or kerosene lamps. Most of these lamps had wicks that required constant care and trimming. Consequently, lighthouse keepers often referred to themselves somewhat humorously as "wickies." When speaking of a friend or associate who worked for the U.S. Bureau of Lighthouses or kept lights for the U.S. Coast Guard, a former keeper might have described him as an "old wickie." More than a few of the ghosts that haunt America's lighthouses are thought to have been wickies.

Visiting Haunted Lighthouses

Some people want to avoid ghosts at all costs. For them, an encounter with a spectral being is just too frightening, too potent a reminder of our own mortality. Many other people, while they may admit that they, too, are frightened of ghosts, think seeing one would be more than a little interesting and exciting. If you would like to meet a few lighthouse ghosts or at least visit the shadowy old towers and residences they haunt, this appendix may help. It lists in alphabetical order all of the haunted lighthouses mentioned in this book and provides simple travel directions to help you find them.

Battery Point Lighthouse
Crescent City, California
Located at the end of Front Street on the west side of the Crescent City harbor, the lighthouse is operated as a museum by the Del Norte County Historical Society.

Big Bay Lighthouse
Big Bay, Michigan
Now an attractive bed-and-breakfast inn, the Big Bay Lighthouse is located on the Upper Peninsula about twenty-six miles northwest of Marquette, Michigan. From Marquette take Highway 550 north into the town of Big Bay, then follow the signs to the lighthouse. The inn and

lighthouse are on Lighthouse Road, about three miles north of Big Bay.

Block Island Southeast Lighthouse
Block Island, Rhode Island
Block Island is a page out of America's past. To visit its quaint inns, shops, or the haunted Block Island Southeast Lighthouse, you must take a ferry from New London, Connecticut, or Point Judith, Rhode Island. It is wise to plan ahead for an overnight stay since accommodations on the island are limited.

Boca Grande Lighthouse
Gasparilla Island, Florida
From Placida, Florida, follow signs to the Boca Grande Causeway and toll bridge leading to Gasparilla Island. The lighthouse is on Gulf Boulevard at the far southern tip of the island. Meticulously restored during the 1980s, the old lighthouse was recently opened as a museum.

Bolivar Point Lighthouse
Galveston, Texas
Although the lighthouse is on private property, it can be seen from Route 87 on the Bolivar Peninsula. To reach the peninsula, take the free ferry from the north end of Galveston Island. The ferry itself provides an excellent view of the tower.

Boon Island Lighthouse
Near York, Maine
The light can be seen at a distance from Cape Neddick near York, but close-up views are available only from the air or water.

Boston Lighthouse
Boston, Massachusetts
Little Brewster Island is part of Boston Harbor Islands national park area. Commercial cruises provide excellent close-up views of the Boston Lighthouse as well as the nearby Graves Ledge Lighthouse—with a name like that, you know it's got to be haunted. Airliners landing at Boston's Logan Airport also offer thrilling views of these lighthouses.

Cape Hatteras Lighthouse
Buxton, North Carolina
The lighthouse is located just off Route 12, near the village of Buxton on North Carolina's Outer Banks. A fine visitor center stands beside the old tower and contains a wealth of artifacts and historical information. About half a mile away is the stone circle marking the original location of the tower, which was moved in 1999 to save it from the encroaching Atlantic.

Cape Henlopen Lighthouse
Lewes, Delaware
Although the Cape Henlopen Lighthouse fell into the sea many years ago, the bluffs on which it once stood can still be seen in Cape Henlopen State Park just east of Lewes.

Cape Neddick Lighthouse
York, Maine
From U.S. 1 take Route 1A into York Beach. Turn right and follow Nubble Road to Nubble Point to enjoy a breathtaking view of the lighthouse. At low tide the island is linked to the mainland by a narrow strip of gravel and sand, but do not attempt to cross it. The footing is dangerous, and tides may

strand you. While in the area, don't miss the Lighthouse Depot in Wells, several miles north of York. This extraordinary shop is a treasure house of information and keepsakes related to Cape Neddick and lighthouses throughout the United States.

Carysfort Reef Lighthouse
Key Largo, Florida
The tower is visible from CR 905 on Key Largo. To see it up close, however, you must charter a boat. Keep in mind that visitors are not allowed on the structure. The lighthouse is now part of John Pennekamp Coral Reef State Park.

Execution Rocks Lighthouse
New Rochelle, New York
Accessible only by boat, the lighthouse and its beacon are visible from a number of points in New Rochelle and along the shores of Long Island Sound.

Fairport Harbor Lighthouse
Fairport, Ohio
The lighthouse and museum, noted for its collection of artifacts from the early days of the Lighthouse Service, are at the northwest corner of Second and High Streets in the village of Fairport Harbor. From U.S. 20 at Painesville, follow either Route 283 or Route 535 to the village.

Heceta Head Lighthouse
Florence, Oregon
One of the most scenic light stations in the West, Heceta Head Lighthouse is popular with photographers. It stands on a craggy point about eleven miles north of Florence. To reach the lighthouse, turn off U.S. 101 at Devils Elbow State

Park. The station is now owned by the U.S. Forest Service and operated as a bed-and-breakfast inn and interpretive center. Guests at the inn have had personal encounters with "Rue," the Heceta Head ghost.

Hendricks Head Lighthouse
Boothbay Harbor, Maine
From U.S. 1 take Route 27 through Boothbay Harbor to Southport Island. The lighthouse can be seen from a public beach just off Beach Road.

Gibraltar Lighthouse
Toronto, Ontario, Canada
To reach Gibraltar Point Lighthouse, start at the Island Ferries Terminal, just off Queen's Quay and Young Street on the Toronto waterfront. Take the ferry to Harlan Point, and from there it is possible to bike, take a shuttle, or hike the remaining mile to the lighthouse.

Matinicus Rock Lighthouse
Near Rockland, Maine
Although it can be seen from nearby Matinicus Island, the lighthouse is not visible from the mainland. Excursion cruises from Rockland to Matinicus Island and Matinicus Rock are available during summer. The rock is a favorite destination of birdwatching cruises since it is home to puffins, petrels, and other rare seabirds.

Minot's Ledge Lighthouse
Scituate, Massachusetts
The tower can only be reached by water, but its "Lover's Light" can be seen from beaches off Atlantic Avenue in

Cohasset, Massachusetts. A few miles south of Cohasset is the Scituate Lighthouse, which dates to 1811. Although decomissioned in 1960, it is well maintained. From Route 123 follow signs to Scituate Harbor.

New London Harbor Lighthouse
New London, Connecticut
The New London Harbor Lighthouse can be seen from Pequot Avenue near Ocean Beach. The dwelling and grounds are privately owned and closed to the public.

Ocracoke Island Lighthouse
Ocracoke, North Carolina
Part of the island chain known as the North Carolina Outer Banks, Ocracoke Island is accessible only by ferry from Cedar Island, Swan Quarter, or Hatteras Island. Schedules vary. The lighthouse is located off Highway 12 on Lighthouse Road, about a mile north of the main ferry landing. A small parking area provides access to the station grounds and tower.

Owls Head Lighthouse
Rockland, Maine
From Rockland take North Shore Road and follow the signs to Owls Head State Park. From the parking area, a short drive along a highly scenic access road leads to the lighthouse. Keep in mind that this is an active Coast Guard facility. Also, be prepared to cover your ears, as the fog signal is so powerful that it can damage hearing. The lighthouse can also be seen and enjoyed from Maine's Vinalhaven Island ferry.

Pennfield Reef Lighthouse
Near Fairfield, Connecticut
The Pennfield Reef Lighthouse can be seen from Calf Pasture Park in Fairfield. Seaside Park in nearby Bridgeport also provides a view of the station as well as access to the historic, but apparently unhaunted, Black Rock Harbor Lighthouse.

Pensacola Lighthouse
Pensacola, Florida
In Pensacola, follow Navy Boulevard or Route 295 to the Pensacola Naval Air Station. The guard at the gate can provide a car pass and directions to the lighthouse. Exhibits at the nearby Naval Air Museum celebrate the history of the light station and the U.S. Navy's strong links to Pensacola.

Pigeon Point Lighthouse
Pescadero, California
Now open to the public as a hostelry, the station is located just off Route 1, about twenty miles north of Santa Cruz, California, and about one mile south of Pescadero. The grounds are open all year.

Plymouth Lighthouse
Plymouth, Massachusetts
The lighthouse is located near the end of the Gurnet, a sandy peninsula reaching several miles into Plymouth Bay. Cruises taking visitors within easy viewing distance of the lighthouse depart from piers along Water Street in Plymouth.

Point Lookout Lighthouse
Solomons, Maryland
From Solomons, Maryland, the Point Lookout Lighthouse can be reached via a half-hour drive across the Patuxent Bridge on Route 4 and then southeast along Route 235 and Route 5 to Point Lookout State Park. The lighthouse is closed to the public much of the year, but visitors are welcome to walk the grounds.

Point Sur Lighthouse
Big Sur, California
The lighthouse can be seen from Route 1 along the way from Monterey to Big Sur. Guided tours are available on weekends. The station's original first-order lens can now be seen at the Maritime Museum in Monterey.

Point Vicente Lighthouse
Los Angeles, California
The lighthouse is located south of Los Angeles off Palos Verdes Drive. A fine view of the light can be had from the grounds of the nearby Palos Verdes Interpretive Center. Exhibits recount the history of the lighthouse and provide information on the many natural wonders of the Palos Verdes Peninsula.

Point Wilson Lighthouse
Port Townsend, Washington
The lighthouse is located in Washington's Fort Warden State Park, at the far northeastern end of the Olympic Peninsula. Take Route 20 to Port Townsend and then follow signs to the park, which is open all year during daylight hours.

Presque Isle Lighthouses (Old and New)
Presque Isle, Michigan
From Presque Isle, follow Grand Lake Road past the intersection of Highway 638, or from U.S. 23 take Highway 638 to Grand Lake Road and turn left. The Old Presque Isle Lighthouse and Museum are just over half a mile to the north. A pair of interesting front and rear range light towers stands nearby. From the museum, continue north about one mile on Grand Lake Road to the New Presque Isle Lighthouse, where you'll find a second museum and gift shop.

Race Rock Lighthouse
Near Watch Hill, Rhode Island
Race Rock Lighthouse can be reached only by water, but it can be seen at a distance from Watch Hill, Rhode Island, and several points along the Connecticut coast. Ferries operating between New London, Connecticut, and Block Island or Orient Point on Long Island often pass within sight of the station.

Ram Island Lighthouse
Boothbay Harbor, Maine
The light can be seen from several parking areas along the shore road on Ocean Point at the end of Route 96 south of Boothbay Harbor. The Maine Maritime Museum in Bath operates summer cruises that pass Ram Island and other lighthouses along the state's scenic mid-coast.

St. Augustine Lighthouse
St. Augustine, Florida
In St. Augustine, follow Route A1A and Old Beach Road to Lighthouse Avenue. The beautifully restored brick keeper's

residence houses an excellent museum that celebrates the history of the lighthouse and coastal Florida. For a gull's-eye view of the Atlantic and the old Spanish town of St. Augustine, visitors may climb the 219 steps to the service gallery.

St. Simons Lighthouse
St. Simons, Georgia
Georgia's charming St. Simons Island is reached by causeway from Brunswick. On the island follow Kings Way and Beachview. Then turn right onto Twelfth Street. The fascinating Museum of Coastal History, located in the old brick keeper's residence, displays a fourth-order Fresnel lens.

Sandy Hook Lighthouse
Highlands, New Jersey
Follow New Jersey Route 36 to Highlands Beach, enter the Gateway National Recreation Area, and follow signs to Sandy Hook and its lovely and historic light station.

Seguin Island Lighthouse
Popham Beach, Maine
The lighthouse cannot be seen easily from land, but the Maine Maritime Museum on Washington Street in Bath runs regular tour boats to Seguin Island during summer. The museum is a must-see attraction for anyone interested in maritime history, shipbuilding, or lighthouses.

Seul Choix Lighthouse
Gulliver, Michigan
Turn off U.S. 2 at Gulliver and follow Port Inland Road and then CR 431 to the lighthouse. The tower and dwelling are

closed to the public, but visitors are welcome to walk the grounds. There is a small, but nonetheless fascinating, museum in the old fog-signal building.

South Manitou Island Lighthouse
South Manitou Island, Michigan
To reach the South Manitou Island Lighthouse, take the ferry from Leland, on the Michigan mainland. Passengers can get a good view of the North Manitou Island Shoal Lighthouse during the passage. Located in Sleeping Bear Dunes National Lakeshore, the South Manitou Lighthouse is a short hike from the ferry slip.

Split Rock Lighthouse
Two Harbors, Minnesota
The Split Rock Park and Lighthouse are located about twenty miles northeast of Two Harbors on Highway 61. Open year-round, the park offers an interesting history center as well as camping facilities, hiking trails, and picnicking areas. The lighthouse features a fine museum, and both are open mid-May through mid-September.

Stratford Shoal Light
Bridgeport, Connecticut
The Stratford Shoal Lighthouse cannot be seen easily from land but can be viewed from the decks of ferries that link Bridgeport to New York's Long Island.

Sturgeon Point Lighthouse
Alcona, Michigan
To reach the lighthouse, take U.S. 23 north from Harrisville, Michigan, and then follow Lakeshore Drive and Point

Road to Sturgeon Point. The parking lot is less than a mile down the road. The museum is open daily from Memorial Day to Labor Day and weekends throughout the fall color season.

Tillamook Rock Lighthouse
Near Seaside, Oregon
Tillamook Rock and its lighthouse are off limits to visitors, but they can be seen from nearby Tillamook Head. From Seaside, follow U.S. 101 to Cannon Beach and then look for signs pointing the way to Ecola State Park. The best view is from Indian Beach, located within the park.

Waugoshance Lighthouse
Straits of Mackinac, Michigan
Difficult to see from land, the lighthouse is closed to the public. It can only be approached from the water or the air.

Whitefish Point Lighthouse
Paradise, Michigan
The lighthouse and Great Lakes Shipwreck Museum, housed in the former keeper's residence, can be reached from the Mackinac Bridge by taking I-75 north to Michigan Highway 123 and the town of Paradise. From Paradise follow Whitefish Point Road to Whitefish Point.

White River Lighthouse
Muskegon, Michigan
From U.S. 31 north of Muskegon, take the White River Drive exit and proceed west to South Shore Drive. Turn left and follow the signs to the lighthouse and museum.

Wood Island Lighthouse
Near Biddeford, Maine
The lighthouse can be seen from points along the shore near Biddeford, Maine. From Route 9 follow Maine 238 or Bridge Road and park along Ocean Avenue. Walk through a closed gate and proceed about a quarter of a mile to a viewing area. A local organization called the Friends of the Wood Island Lighthouse occasionally offers tours of the property.

Yaquina Bay Lighthouse
Newport, Oregon
The Yaquina Bay Lighthouse is located near the north end of the Yaquina Bay Bridge in Yaquina Bay State Park near Newport. Filled with nineteenth-century furnishings and artifacts, the building now serves as a museum.